SWORD ART ONLINE AITERNATIVE

CLOVER'S

2

Klever

An *Asuka Empire* player who calls himself a detective. His looks are handsome, but he acts extremely sketchy. Very aloof and slippery. His real-life appearance is identical to his avatar's.

"Don't leave me all alone!"

"There's something strange about this hotel."

"I thought I saw something writhing..."

Nayuta

Age seventeen. Plays a warrior priestess in *Asuka Empire*. Skilled at close combat. Her real name is Yurina Kushiinada. Goes at her own speed and tends to show little emotion.

"Good luck with the rest."

"...You'll pay for this later, Detective!"

"Okay! We'll handle it!"

"Mahiro and Onihime, protect the detective! Koyomi and I will take out the executioner!"

Mahiro

Plays a tactician in *Asuka Empire*. Her real name is Mahiro Kirihara. In the real world, she's in elementary school and is a popular child actor.

"He has a bunch of cute girls doing the fighting for him while he takes command in the back, just like all the hit gacha games. He's got an ultra-rare Nayu and a super-special-rare Koyomi…

"He's going to keep buying ten-packs of rolls, hoping for that 0.03 percent chance of winning an ultra-rare cheerleader Nayu flashing underboob, and the next thing he knows, he's sitting on a useless pile of rare capybara Koyomis…"

NAYUTA

Contents

SWORD ART ONLINE ALTERNATIVE

CLOVER'S REGRET

2

SOITIRO WATASE

ILLUSTRATION BY ✤ GINTA
SUPERVISED BY ✤ REKI KAWAHARA

YEN ON
NEW YORK

SWORD ART ONLINE ALTERNATIVE
CLOVER'S REGRET 2

SOITIRO WATASE
Supervised by Reki Kawahara
Translation by Stephen Paul
Cover art by Ginta

SWORD ART ONLINE ALTERNATIVE CLOVERS REGRET Vol. 2
©Soitiro Watase / Reki Kawahara 2018
Edited by Dengeki Bunko
First published in Japan in 2018 by KADOKAWA CORPORATION, Tokyo.
English translation rights arranged with KADOKAWA CORPORATION, Tokyo,
through TUTTLE-MORI AGENCY, INC., Tokyo.

English translation © 2024 by Yen Press, LLC

Yen On
150 West 30th Street, 19th Floor
New York, NY 10001

Visit us at yenpress.com
facebook.com/yenpress ❀ twitter.com/yenpress
yenpress.tumblr.com ❀ instagram.com/yenpress

First Yen On Edition: December 2024
Edited by Yen On Editorial: Payton Campbell
Designed by Yen Press Design: Andy Swist

Yen On is an imprint of Yen Press, LLC.
The Yen On name and logo are trademarks of Yen Press, LLC.

Library of Congress Cataloging-in-Publication Data
Names: Watase, Sōichirō, 1978- author. | Ginta, illustrator. | Paul,
    Stephen (Translator), translator.
Title: Sword art online alternative clover's regret / Soitiro Watase ;
    illustration by Ginta ; translation by Stephen Paul.
Description: First Yen On edition. | New York : Yen On, 2024.
Identifiers: LCCN 2024020867 | ISBN 9781975390686 (v. 1 ; trade paperback) |
    ISBN 9781975390709 (v. 2 ; trade paperback) | ISBN 9781975390723 (v. 3 ; trade paperback)
Subjects: LCSH: Virtual reality—Fiction. | Video games—Fiction. | LCGFT:
    Fantasy fiction. | Science fiction. | Detective and mystery fiction.
Classification: LCC PL877.T37 S96 2024 | DDC 895.63/6—dc23/eng/20240514
LC record available at https://lccn.loc.gov/2024020867

ISBNs: 978-1-9753-9070-9 (paperback)
        978-1-9753-9071-6 (ebook)

10 9 8 7 6 5 4 3 2 1

LSC-C

Printed in the United States of America

Chapter 1 Late-Night Recreation at the Traveler's Lodge

"I wanna go to a hot spring," said Koyomi the ninja out of the blue one night, with the May holiday week fast approaching.

Nayuta the warrior priestess closed the book-type tablet and looked at the girl resting on her thighs and the black cat perched atop her head.

"So why don't you go to one? If you live in the Kansai region, then the famous Arima Onsen should be fairly close to you," she pointed out. Koyomi promptly pouted, and the black cat on her head yawned.

"That's not what I meeeean! I want to go on a hot spring trip with *you*, Nayu! A girls' trip! Some deluxe dinners! An electric massage chair, ten minutes for 100 yen! Fruit-flavored milk bottles when you get out of the bath, 200 yen a pop! Nayu in the classic *yukata*! Playing ping-pong, your bosom heaving to and fro! All that good, exciting stuff of youth and dreams!"

"…I have no idea what your standards for youth and dreams are, but I've now sworn myself to never play ping-pong. Also, I can't go on vacation," Nayuta said smoothly, returning to her book-style tablet.

She wasn't reading a novel. It was a textbook about the basics of modern history, explaining concepts like the social changes that occurred after the rise of productivity brought about by the industrial revolution, the clash between laborers and capitalists, and the ways in which this altered the balance of world powers.

It wasn't for any class in particular, but she thought having a general understanding of these topics would help with essays and test questions.

I haven't finished this section yet, but...the industrial revolution and development of VR tech seem to have some similarities to me...

She was more absorbed in the concepts of her text than in the conversation with Koyomi.

The system of mass production brought about by the industrial revolution and the mechanization of labor.

The virtual production brought about by the VR revolution and the "AI-ification" of labor.

The time period and level of sophistication were completely different, but the situations seemed oddly similar to her.

The term "virtual production" would normally refer to, say, production simulations run on a computer, but here it meant products created in VR, such as weapons and armor sold at a store, or sweets offered by the Monster Cat Teahouse. In other words, mass-produced goods in a virtual reality environment.

Just as the flood of goods into the marketplace changed the way things were consumed, consumption today was also being changed by the permeation of virtual products into everyday life.

What should you study, and what career path should you take in an environment like this...?

The rapid advance of VR promised drastic changes, but which industries would be impacted, and in which ways, was still a mystery to her. And Nayuta was far from the only young person struggling with this life choice.

If only there was someone she knew nearby of her own gender who was slightly older and could offer her advice... Sadly, that girl was currently clinging to Nayuta's knees and kicking her feet in a childish tantrum.

"You're so meeeean, Nayu! It's almost Golden Week! I don't have any vacation plans! You don't want me to stay inside and play games all day, do you? It's not healthy!" she wailed, like a child pleading to go on a trip.

Nayuta sighed. "For one thing, there are no hotel spots open this close to Golden Week. Everything's already booked up solid. You'll just have to face reality."

"...No! The detective! I'm sure the detective has connections who can get a room!"

The detective seated at his work desk, Klever, rolled his eyes and stared at the ceiling. His fine, foxlike features were twisted into a grimace.

"...Ah, there's a thought," he said. "If I arrange a hotel for you two, then you won't be here to bother me anymore... It's worth looking into. Unfortunately, I don't have any such connections."

It was late on a weekday night at the Three-Leaf Detective Agency.

They were logged in to *Asuka Empire* once again, spending their time hanging out in this creepy, sketchy detective's office.

It was just too comfortable.

Unlike other businesses, it didn't cost money to stay here, they didn't need to worry about other people watching them, and though the interior furnishing was old-fashioned, it wasn't bad. Plus they had cat bots hanging around.

They had taken over the guest sofa—Nayuta reading her book, and Koyomi sprawled across her lap and throwing a fit.

The detective, meanwhile, was working at his computer. He lobbed a devastatingly precise question their way.

"Are you certain you don't have any plans for the upcoming vacation? I thought young people like you were supposed to be out and about, enjoying your lives."

"I'm studying for college exams," Nayuta pointed out quietly. "I was thinking I'd work on a test sample book."

Koyomi froze. "Nayu...are you insane...? You want to study

during a vacation? Don't you know teenage girls who hit the books are just an urban legend...?" Now that was just plain cruel.

"Apologize to all the teenage girls acing aptitude tests all across the country at the top of the aptitude test score lists. I can't speak for the subset who spend all their time hanging out in the city, but most of us are not like that."

"...Well, I'll admit I didn't do a whole lot of hanging out in the city during high school," Koyomi grumbled, "but deep in rural Shimane, I would go out in the fall to search for matsutake mushrooms and catch crawdads in the river..."

"You've essentially described what elementary school boys do instead," Klever pointed out.

She ignored him, getting a far-off look in her eyes. "Oh, if only you could taste the matsutake from Grandpa's mountain... They were *so* good. If you set up near the station, you could sell them for almost 2,000 yen each... I mean, talk about juicy..."

"I can't tell if you mean the flavor or the business opportunity," Nayuta remarked. "What about the crawdads?"

"Those we'd just catch and release. You could take pictures and post them. Like, 'Check out this monster I caught!'"

It didn't sound like something teenage girls did, but somehow, it sounded just like Koyomi. She sat up and leaned menacingly toward Nayuta. The cat remained where it was on her head.

"But forget about the crawdads!" Koyomi said. "The hot spring! I'm talking about going to a hot spring for a girls' vacation with you!"

"And I'm saying I can't. Nothing's open at this point...," Nayuta said, suddenly noticing that the detective was about to say something. But he shut his mouth and returned to the computer, apparently thinking better of it.

Koyomi didn't miss the change in his attitude. "Detective...you looked like you just had a thought..."

Her reflexes and observation skills were sharp enough that she could cut a snake dropping from the ceiling in two. A momentary look crossing the detective's face was like a blinking billboard to her.

Koyomi stood up, her eyes flashing like a cat's tracking its prey, and she slinked over to the detective. The lazy cat on her head was also staring at him with the same look, for some reason.

Intimidated, Klever looked away and shook his head. "Must've been imagining it. I don't have any leads on hot springs."

Koyomi crept closer, her voice lowering to a whisper. "Speaking of which, Detective…what are *your* Golden Week plans?"

"…Work, of course. I have a tour guide client coming up."

"Where are you taking them?"

"To Mt. Fuji…and a few of the sights around Ayakashi Alley…"

Koyomi fixed him with a look. Klever did not meet it.

"…Mr. Detective, I'll ask you one more time. Where are you going for Golden Week…?"

"…I'm working."

"Yes, yes, you're working. That's right. Well, I don't have anything better to do, so shall I help you? You don't need to pay me."

"……That won't be necessary."

There was a long, awkward silence.

Koyomi stared at the detective through empty, unblinking eyes. He stared desperately at his computer screen, pretending to be fully absorbed in his work.

For a while, they both stood firm, refusing to give up. Eventually, he broke.

"………All right, fine. I give up. You win. I do know a place…"

"Ooh, I love you, Detective! You're such a hunk!"

She slapped him hard on the back and wagged her tail. Koyomi didn't have a tail, but Nayuta could think of no better way to describe it. Meanwhile, the sheer dejection in his posture elicited a bit of sympathy from her.

"You don't have to tell her if you don't want to. I'm certainly not planning to go on any trips."

"Why noooot? C'mon, let's gooo! I wanna have a pillow fight with you!"

Klever pressed his fingers against the bridge of his nose. *"Children...* Er, sorry, I didn't mean that. What I was thinking of wasn't a real place, but a VR hot spring inn. So I wasn't sure if it actually fit your requirements."

Many VRMMORPGs had inns or hotels in them. Mostly they existed to replenish strength and stamina, but more and more of them were developing deluxe hotels for luxury purposes, and the concept of enjoying a vacation trip in a VR setting was slowly but surely finding its footing.

Koyomi's cheeks puffed. "Aww...no, I want to go to a real hot spring! Like, the kind they advertise as being good for arthritis."

"...Koyomi, you are the picture of good health. You don't need that," said Klever.

"But real hot springs have that special something where you go, 'Ooh, look how smooth my skin is, feel it, feel it,' and then Nayu might let me touch her skin and feel her up, and..."

"No, I wouldn't," Nayuta said. "Don't expect me to take part in that kind of tomfoolery."

The detective nodded to himself. "Yes, I see. A real hot spring would certainly be preferable, I agree. Well, ignore my suggestion and feel free to look for a place on your own. Even with the holiday rush, I'm sure there are places with room for two somewhere."

Koyomi's eyes narrowed. "You're being weird, Detective. Almost like you're trying to get us to go somewhere else..."

"Erm, not at all," Klever grunted, "but...this matter came to me from Mr. Torao."

Torao was an engineer from the error-testing team working on *Asuka Empire*, and he had helped out when they tackled the Ghostly Orchestra quest with Yanagi. Nayuta hadn't seen him since then, but he apparently met with Klever quite frequently.

"From Mr. Torao? Does he want you to test out a new inn they're going to add to the game?"

"Something like that. One of the more delinquent members of the dev team crafted a recreational facility in VR for fun. The original plan had been to enjoy it amongst themselves, but the quality was so high that the team is discussing adding it as an official secret spot. He wants me to try it out when I have the time, and to let him know what I think."

Klever's voice was strangely weak and indecisive, which Nayuta couldn't help but notice.

"Is there a problem with that?" she asked. "It doesn't sound like something that should be unpleasant, based on how you've described it."

Getting to hang out in a recreational setting like a hot spring inn sounded more like a treat than a job. But the detective just flashed her a stiff smile.

"Correct, it doesn't sound like a bad time...but he was asking me, and I have to be present to get through the security layer. So if you were to go there, I would be accompanying you. Do you see the problem now?"

His concerns made no sense to her. Koyomi patted Nayuta on the head.

"Oh, Nayu, you sweet child... He's saying if he shows up at a bathhouse with a beautiful girl on each arm, he's going to lose his cool and transform from a fox into a wolf, see?"

Klever sighed heavily. "Wrong. I just don't want Mr. Torao to have blackmail on me. I can already hear him saying, 'Look at you, Kurei, enjoying our hot springs with a high schooler and a legal loli,' and who knows what he'll demand in exchange for looking the other way..."

"Hey, who are you calling a legal loli?" joked Koyomi with a pleasant smile. Her eyes, however, were full of venom.

Nayuta grimaced. Compared with his usual needling and aloof

manner, the sight of the detective worried about such trivial details was almost endearing.

"What do you mean? This is just a video game. Besides, whatever happens, you can't do a thing to me or Koyomi with those stats. And Mr. Torao is well aware of that."

The real world aside, in this game Nayuta was many times more powerful than Klever in battle. It wasn't like comparing a cat and mouse—more like a tiger and rabbit. If he tried to assault her while she slept, she would accidentally knock him out just from turning over in her sleep.

Koyomi nodded to herself. "Yeah, with those stats, the best he can hope for is to peep on us in the bath… Does having a high luck stat make it harder for people to spot you?"

The detective made a disgusted face at her. "No, that would never happen…and don't you dare make false accusations against me. I already struggle enough with my naturally untrustworthy looks."

"Oh yeah? In what way?" she asked. He shut his mouth and smiled coldly.

After a brief silence, he awkwardly moved on to a new subject. "At any rate, if you want to tag along, come here at nine in the morning on Saturday. I know it's still before Golden Week, but I'm telling the truth when I say I'm working during the holiday. If that doesn't fit your schedule, you'll just have to make do with something on your own."

Apparently, he didn't want to engage with Koyomi's question. Nayuta was naturally compassionate enough to heed his wishes.

"What do you think, Koyomi? It might not be a real hot spring, but we won't have to find a reservation, and I'll be there, too…"

"Seriously?! If you're there, Nayu, I'm all for it! And I'm interested in trying out the goods before they're revealed to the public!" Koyomi said. So despite all her complaining, she really just wanted *some* kind of plan for the holiday, regardless of what it was.

The detective waved a hand generously. "Very good. I'll see you here. Oh, also…may I inform my contacts about this? After all, it will be you two young ladies and me… I'm serious about not wanting any accusations of impropriety," he insisted, much to Nayuta's chagrin.

"How little faith do you have in us…? Koyomi's only joking, and I'm certainly not going to do such an inhumane thing. Besides, you're not interested in younger girls like us. I trust you on that."

Koyomi just shook her head. "Listen, Nayu…you really need to wake up to the devious nature of your assets… I'm not trying to take the detective's side, but in all honesty, I think he's done a very good job of resisting his instincts…"

Klever pressed his fingers to his eyes. "First of all, I'm not resisting anything, but I do agree with the first part of that statement. You really seem to be totally oblivious to your own appearance."

She considered this feedback. When they were calling her things like "devious" and "totally oblivious," even Nayuta had to take this advice into account.

"…Do you think I should soften my expressions and try to learn how to use makeup, then?"

Clearly, they were advising her to stop looking so devious and take more care in her presentation. But for some reason, both Koyomi and the detective put their heads in their hands.

"Sh-she doesn't get it! She has no idea what we mean!"

"…Koyomi, you handle this. I've wrapped up my paperwork, so I'm going to log out and get some sleep," said the detective, promptly going to his menu window.

Just before he vanished like mist, Nayuta called out, "Oh, good evening… Anyway, Koyomi, shall we call it a night, too?"

Her friend shook her head lifelessly.

"…Yeah, sure. See you tomorrow. Night, Nayu!"

"Good night."

They opened their menus and logged off at the same time, following the detective's lead.

Back in her bedroom, Nayuta removed her AmuSphere and stared at the dark ceiling above her bed.

A hot spring vacation in the virtual world...

It was enticing, at the very least. But it also didn't seem to add up. Playing the game itself was kind of like going on a little journey to begin with, so how was this going to seem any different?

The 108 Apparitions event is still ongoing, so maybe it's got a horror tinge to it... I don't know if I like the idea of an abandoned inn or some creepy dilapidated shack...

She was trapped between anticipation and trepidation, but being with Koyomi and Klever would help. She brushed her teeth and got back into bed right as her phone notification went off.

The message was from Klever, the detective.

I forgot to mention something. Please be strictly on time on Saturday. The event flag won't activate unless I'm at Ueno Station by ten o'clock. You can't be brought in after the fact, so be careful.

Ueno Station? Nayuta noted.

Ayakashi Alley was modeled after old Edo. The finer details of the landscape were quite different, but it did feature streetcar-style teleport gates at various spots in town named after real places and things with punny, spooky titles like Yamanoke Line (mountain ghosts) rather than Yamanote, or Somu Line (burial dream) rather than Sobu. Ueno was spelled like the real place, except with the kanji for "starving" instead of "up." It was located at the eastern edge of the city.

She often accompanied Koyomi to the nearby neighborhood of Akihabara, haunt of wicked demons, but Ueno was relatively unknown to her. Because the developers could only commit so many resources to building out areas, the features of the rotting Shibuya, deathly Ikebukuro, and godly Shinjuku were more pronounced, leaving Ueno as a relatively undeveloped corner of the map.

Some rumors warned of dangerous black-and-white bears on the prowl. The average player didn't bother to visit the area.

I wonder if the hot spring inn is supposed to be part of an event designed for Ueno, Nayuta thought, trying to guess at what the developers were planning. She sent back an affirmative reply.

And before she knew it, the weekend had arrived.

§

Nine thirty AM, Saturday morning.

The two girls showed up at the detective's office on time, after which they took the Somu Line streetcar to Ueno Station after just a brief instant of rumbling.

Sure enough, there wasn't a single player around.

The streetcar platform where the teleport gate spit them out was empty and isolated. There was nothing else ahead of them but fields.

It was always night in Ayakashi Alley, so even in the morning hours, there was no sun out, and the darkness was especially black out here. Koyomi pointed out a copse in the distance, lit vaguely by the moon, and hooked her arm around Nayuta's.

"Look, Nayu, that's Undead Pond over there!"

"...Ah yes, the one that zombies come out of," she replied, noticing the sudden tension in the arm around hers. She hadn't meant to scare Koyomi, and immediately regretted her choice of words.

The detective surveyed the fields around them, then opened his menu.

"Apparently they won't be filling out this area until the end of the event. I've heard they're going to use it for one of the Seven Mysteries, but I don't know what it will actually be."

"Is this hot spring inn we're going to supposed to be a part of that?"

"Actually, if there's no problem with it, they're going to reveal it on the first day of Golden Week. This is part of the final testing step; we just happen to be very convenient beta testers."

In other words, if the three of them spotted any issues, it might delay the release of the area.

"This isn't going to turn out like the Ghostly Orchestra, will it?"

"I think that was a very rare and particular occurrence... Ah, here we are."

The detective removed a miniature black cat-Buddha statue from his inventory. It was fashioned exactly like the large one at the entrance to the detective agency, meaning this was certainly a special item given to him by the dev team.

Klever placed the cat-Buddha at the end of the streetcar platform. He performed the customary double bow, double clap, double bow sequence, and a staircase leading downward appeared without a sound at the end of the platform.

Koyomi clapped her hands. "Wow, that's nice... A debug tool from the devs? Would I be able to make it work, too?"

He shook his head. "I wouldn't go so far as to call it a debug tool. It's just a portable security device. If you place this at a location designated by the developers, it will perform a retinal scan and check it against your player information. In other words, it's a communication device for personal verification, so if a random person uses it, they won't match the registered information, and nothing will happen. Also, you can't extract any items, money, or experience from the place this opens up. All pre-release areas work the same way," the detective explained, descending the steps.

"Is that why none of your coworkers wanted to join you?"

He'd told them about that the day before. Apparently, everyone he knew personally had promptly declined to take him up on the offer.

"...They said, 'We're not going to waste our time on something where we can't even take our spoils with us,' the callous ingrates. They don't even understand that enjoying the game is a meaningful pursuit on its own. The loot is just a side product of that."

"This, coming from a man who put every point into luck to completely destroy the game experience for himself," remarked Koyomi. Klever's mouth clamped shut.

The stairs leading downward were modern in style, made of concrete and tile.

"This staircase is a subway station exit, isn't it?"

Metal handrails on either side, resin stoppers at the ends of the steps to prevent slipping, even yellow plates for the visually impaired. It didn't fit the setting of *Asuka Empire*, but that anachronism made it feel all the creepier.

Koyomi's eyes were wide. "You're right, this is totally just a subway station. Look, there's even a station map."

The top of the board read *Black Railways: Ueno Station.*

"Black Railways...is that supposed to be like National Railways?"

"Oh, from before they privatized the rail networks... Wait, hang on! Is this supposed to be a dungeon?!" Koyomi suddenly exclaimed. At the bottom of the stairs was a spacious fountain area with some branching paths leading off to destinations unknown.

This was clearly a dungeon meant to look like a subway station. The detective, however, coolly headed for an elevator in the corner.

"It is a dungeon, yes, but it's not finished, so you can't explore it. We're heading straight to our destination through here."

"...Oh, good...I was afraid we'd have to actually *work* before going to the hot spring," Koyomi exhaled. Her relief was almost comical.

Nayuta, meanwhile, felt suspicious of his deliberate, direct path. "Detective...did you come here already on your own?"

The elevator began to descend with the trio on board.

"Not in the way you're suggesting, but I have used this station for a different matter. I've never been to the hot spring hotel we're visiting. There are multiple platforms, and they each lead to different places. They're going to use this as a hub for a number of railway-themed Apparitions later in the event. Since they're developing it now, they've opened it up in an unfinished state... but when they update the game on the first day of Golden Week, most of this will be temporarily closed off. I'm sure they'll gradually add more steps as the year goes on."

The elevator continued to take them downward. By the time it had passed the tenth basement floor, Koyomi finally spoke up.

"Detective...this isn't actually some fun hot spring vacation, but another terrifying horror event, isn't it...? I heard someone saying 'help me' when we passed the last floor..."

Nayuta had heard it, too, but she just chalked it up to yet another meaningless ghostly phenomenon and ignored it. It was one thing to focus when you were in the midst of a quest, but if you paid attention to every strange sight and sound in this event, you'd just be wasting your time.

On that note, in the mirror inside the elevator, she could see an unfamiliar woman in a white medical coat with her back turned to them, but out of consideration for Koyomi, she didn't mention it. Koyomi was probably doing her best to pretend she didn't notice, either.

When they reached their floor and the doors opened, they were met with a bay platform. It was fairly large, with four tracks. And for some reason, on both sides of the platform was the dark of night. There was starry sky visible through the gaps in the ceiling above, and a damp night breeze was soothing on their skin.

Timidly, Koyomi murmured, "We're way underground...so why are we outside...?"

"It happens. I'm just glad we were in time. Guess I'll buy some tea and mandarins from the store counter," Klever remarked, marching down to the middle of the platform.

Something else felt strange to Nayuta. "Um, Detective...we didn't pass through any turnstiles. Did we miss something?"

Koyomi latched on to that topic. "Is *that* what you're worried about, Nayu?! Surely there are other, more important topics! Like the hands growing out of the rails, or the fact that the stars in the darkness are moving around, meaning they're *definitely* monster eyes, or the translucent girl who's been resting on your shoulder, or the faceless nurse back in the elevator... There's plenty of stuff wrong with this station!"

Okay, so she had noticed in the elevator. Nayuta comforted her teary-eyed friend and spared a glance at the ghost on her shoulder.

"But as the detective already said, that sort of thing happens all the time here. But not having a turnstile gate makes me wonder: Was that on purpose, or did they forget to add one when designing the area? Or is it somewhere else, and using the elevator made us skip it, so we're fare-dodging...? If I'm a playtester, I think it's my duty to point out the things I notice."

It was quite possible they'd made the placement of the turnstiles a low priority and focused on other things, then forgot to go back and finish.

"You're such a goody-two-shoes, Nayu!" Koyomi barked like a little puppy. "I mean, I knew that already, but still! And am I seriously the only one afraid of what's going on?! You're both acting weird! C'mon, let's all get into the eeriness of the situation, yeah?!"

The detective took down Nayuta's observations in his notebook. "I'll tell Mr. Torao about the turnstiles. It does feel like something is missing, now that you point it out. Passing through a gate or doorway reinforces the feeling that you are stepping into a different space than you were in before. It would be better to have turnstiles here."

"And you! Freak out a little, dammit! Haven't you noticed they're selling straw dolls and hair at this counter?! The sales clerk is a mannequin, and that's entrails stuffed in a bottle! And you want to buy mandarins from this place?!" Koyomi ranted. She seemed to be about to pass out from exhaustion before they even made it to their destination. Nayuta had heard enough; she put her hands firmly on Koyomi's shoulders.

"Now calm down and listen to me, Koyomi. And you, Detective...why are you buying mandarins, anyway, if you don't have the time to sit down and eat them? The train we're about to take is presumably like the other teleport gates, isn't it?"

Klever put on a very knowing smile. "Actually, we're going to be on this train for about two hours."

"Huh? Two hours...?" Koyomi's cheek twitched.

Nayuta could scarcely believe her ears. There was no VRM-MORPG in existence that would force you to wait around for two whole hours, doing nothing, just to reach a destination.

"Um, is there...some kind of combat or exploration that happens on the train? Any kind of event...?"

The detective shrugged theatrically. "Probably not, if I had to guess. Apparently the designer *insisted* on this point, that 'travel requires travel time.' Part of the fun of going on vacation is the time that crawls along while you're making your way there, and it's a place for family and friends to talk and interact. Apparently they really wanted to go out of their way to force the player into a slow-moving situation, given that everything in VR is designed to be more convenient. I will say that it strikes me as a rather divisive view."

Nayuta was aghast. "Oh...well, I suppose I understand the reasoning. I just can't believe it was approved."

Surely many people would detest this policy and consider the time to be wasted. But on the other hand, the people who found meaning in spending that much time traveling would surely appreciate that touch.

Koyomi's expression softened. "Ohh, I see," she said. "I was alarmed when you said it was two hours of travel time, but there's *always* some amount of time spent traveling on a real vacation... and if I can relax and talk to Nayu in the meantime, that might even be just what I want."

Nayuta wouldn't mind spending extra time on the train if it was with Koyomi, either. The detective twirled his walking stick with a grin, holding a little netted bag of mandarins in the other hand.

"Apparently you can even take off your AmuSphere and wait around in real life. But I have to give my feedback on the experience, so I'll remain on the train, of course..."

"I'm totally fine staying in with Nayu!"

"I don't have anything to do, either, so I'll stay with you," Nayuta agreed.

At that point, a train arrived at the platform. It was an express train in a retro 20th century style. The nose of the train was artistically fashioned into a headless horse and one-eyed ogre design.

The detective murmured, "Ahh, I see...the night express from Ueno..."

"Um, what are you talking about? I know it looks like nighttime, but it's not even ten in the morning," Koyomi pointed out, but Nayuta understood what the detective was hinting at.

A one-eyed ogre astride a headless horse—it was a monster from the island of Shikoku known as *Yakou-san* ("night travel"). Possibly just a clever reference from the designer, but it also suggested the very real possibility that this would involve some apparitions.

There were multiple *yokai*-like shadows visible through the windows of the train, but none that seemed especially violent or dangerous. Thanks to the orange lighting, it even seemed a bit warmer there than on the empty train platform.

The car had spacious seats facing each other, large windows, and useful mini-tables, all made of a shiny wood that seemed both old-fashioned and surprisingly fancy.

"...I'm surprised. Extremely surprised. We have an actual,

bona fide deluxe train here!" Koyomi exclaimed, rushing toward the vehicle with eyes alight. She saw a family of furry *keukegen* waving in the window and eagerly returned the greeting. Given her looks, it was impossible for anyone to assume she was actually older than Nayuta.

Even Klever was impressed by the train, revealing that he hadn't actually seen it for himself before. "This is quite majestic. A very impressive creation. They must have focused on interior comfort, given that we'll be trapped in there for two hours. It suggests that we can look forward to the main event afterward, too."

"I don't think I'm as optimistic as you…but the train *is* quite nice. It feels more like we're on a vacation now."

She couldn't speak on the hotel until they got there, but at least it was good to know Koyomi's mood had turned around for the better.

Speaking of her, she was at the loading area, waving.

"Nayu, Nayu, let's go! Come on, it's gorgeous inside! They even have a dining car!"

Nayuta was used to the wildness of Koyomi's mood swings, and even she had to feel a bit chagrined by this one. A thought occurred to her, which she whispered into the detective's ear.

"Why do I feel like you and I are a married couple, and Koyomi is our daughter?"

Klever's shoulders shivered with a sudden contraction. "All of our activity is being recorded during this test run, and they might be able to see it in the log. I must ask that you spare me any unnecessary remarks, and refrain from teasing me."

Huh. So he couldn't take a joke?

"I wasn't teasing you, I just mean— Look at her. She's like a little child excited about her first trip away from home. And since we're here, serenely watching her from a distance, it makes us look like…"

Koyomi had already bounded onto the train and was exchanging embraces with the *keukegen* family in a bizarre form of wordless communication.

Without cracking a smile, Klever murmured, "Can we at least be a brother and sister looking after our much younger sister?"

"Oh? Are you the little sister type?"

"No. Miss Koyomi really *is* a bad influence on you," he said.

She decided to stop poking fun and followed Koyomi onto the train. The conductor, a one-eyed ogre named Yakou-san, doffed its cap and gave her a kindly bow.

The NPC interactions in the 108 Apparitions event had a reputation for being very natural in comparison to other games. This wasn't due to any particular advancement in AI control, but simply because most of the NPCs were *yokai* that didn't speak in words.

It didn't feel out of place for creatures that weren't even humanoid to be unable to hold conversations, and if the AI itself led to any strange reactions, that just appeared to be characteristically bizarre and inexplicable *yokai* behavior.

In other words, the forceful solution to the problem of NPCs with stilted, unnatural conversation was to prevent them from talking at all. It was a stroke of game design genius. If you could only produce imperfect results, lean into it and turn that imperfection into a strength.

They made their way to an open set of seats and waited for the train to depart.

Once the event was unveiled, other players would presumably be taking seats in the same train car. Some would end up encountering each other in the same way that Nayuta and Koyomi first met at the Monster Cat Teahouse. In that sense, the long travel time could absolutely be beneficial. At the very least, Nayuta was delighted at the opportunity to spend this time with her two companions.

"Oh! Look, Nayu, an *oboroguruma* cart selling snacks! Let's buy some ice cream!"

The ghostly ox cart made its way over from the adjacent car, selling local delicacies, boxed lunches, green tea, sweets, and a variety of ice cream products. Koyomi tore into the choices with delight, while Nayuta looked at Klever in the seat across from her.

"They really did put a lot of effort into the presentation, now that we're inside. There's a ghastly attention to detail here."

The detective gave her a little shrug as he peeled a mandarin orange. "It strikes me as either a motivated designer, or perhaps a very jealous and hateful one. They were probably desperate to go on a vacation, and channeled all of their stress into the end product. I also have a sneaking suspicion that at least one person on the team is a major train nerd."

That made sense to her.

As the train began to chug away, the starry sky through the window was bright enough that the outlines of the wispy clouds above were clear to the eye.

They passed verdant hills, steep valleys, and tranquil lakes on the way to their destination. The two hours of travel were uneventful, appreciated, and over in the blink of an eye.

§

They got off the train at the empty rural station, then walked down a hilly path for about ten minutes under the moon before they arrived at the "hot spring inn" in question.

Their first reaction was to stand and stare in amazement.

They had anticipated a variety of potential outcomes. Perhaps an old-fashioned home with a thatched roof or a classic, stately wooden *ryokan* inn—maybe even a surprise swerve into a Western-style mansion. But none of their guesses were anywhere close to the building they saw now.

"This...*is* the right place, isn't it?" Koyomi said uncertainly.

"...I'm...fairly sure...," Nayuta replied, equally noncommittal.

Klever looked up at the building and said simply, "Yes, I don't think I would call this a hot spring *ryokan*. It's more of a...'resort hotel,' if anything. Mr. Torao got me again."

He had kept the details a secret from the detective, it seemed.

The "inn" before them was a dual-tower high-rise building that had to be a good seventy stories tall and nearly 1,000 feet. The towers were connected at the top so the whole structure resembled a torii shrine gate.

When you had a building on the scale of the Landmark Tower in Yokohama, but *two* of them, shaped like a torii gate, standing in the hills in the middle of nowhere, the only reasonable response was to assume a fox's shape-shifting illusions were at play. You could already see the punchline: waking up the next morning out in the open, under a pile of leaves.

Nayuta found it so dizzying to look up at the building that she had to hold her eyes down near the ground.

The first and second floors were the foundation of the twin-tower structure. Right in the middle was the entranceway, with a long line of revolving doors leading to the lobby.

On either side of the very spacious entrance interior were massive paper lanterns, red and glowing, like the one at the famous Kaminarimon gate in Asakusa. Every one of them was printed with the same kanji that read *shouki*.

"What are those kanji supposed to mean?"

The detective's foxlike eyes narrowed. "Well, they mean 'invite' and 'demon,' so if we take that as an invitation, it means *yokai* and oni and other such creatures also frequent this hotel, I'd guess. But we're the only guests staying here today," he said.

There was absolutely no one else around. They were the playtesters, of course, so this made sense, but being in such a gigantic hotel that was absolutely empty made the experience surreal and dreamlike.

But at the very least, it had totally disarmed the natural expectation of a clichéd burned-out ruin or haunted mansion. Although they hadn't expected to be surprised in this particular way, it had lived up to expectations so far.

"Well…shall we go ahead and check in?"

"Y-yeah...*whoaaa*...I've never stayed at a place like this... Oh, do you think we get to choose our rooms? Are we in line with the dress code?" Koyomi fretted. It was a serious question, not a joke. Even Nayuta was feeling a bit intimidated by the setting.

The detective, however, took the lead and passed through the revolving door without missing a beat.

Inside, the design was just as grand as the outside.

There was red carpet on the floor, with a number of sofas and low tables placed at just the right intervals. It all looked very fine and classy.

The ceiling was open up to the third floor. Four huge chandeliers hung, each decorated to resemble one of the four mythical beasts: the Vermilion Bird, Azure Dragon, White Tiger, and Black Tortoise.

Right below them, in the center of the floor, was a life-size cat-Buddha statue made of solid gold.

"...Ah, yes. There's the dead giveaway that the same design team made this environment," murmured Nayuta.

"They just shoved it in there, as though they couldn't stand the thought of any empty space... What's with this cat god anyway? I mean, it's cute, but I can't help but feel that something sinister is afoot...," Koyomi added.

The detective said quietly, "I believe they have a mini-event slated for summer vacation called the Cat-Buddha Pilgrimage. Something about searching for the cat-Buddha statues all over the game and receiving a prize for your results. They're still working it out, but it sounds like a stamp scavenger hunt."

Nayuta reacted to the sketchy leak with exasperation. "What is with this company and its cat obsession? Is that just a personal preference from the lead developer?"

"Well, I wouldn't deny that, but there's a very sad, cruel reason why." He lowered his voice despite the utter lack of people around. "The development team really wanted a mascot character they could attach to this yearlong event. Since it's all horror-themed, they wanted a cute character to help balance out the atmosphere… But if they ran it up the chain, then it would turn into an official mascot, leading to a whole uproar with choosing candidates and selecting one. They were already working around the clock on the event and didn't have time to wait around for a selection committee to play out, and any rights issues or problems with character image would only delay development. There are always bosses and complainers who whine, 'Is it really right to use an official mascot this way?' And depending on the taste of the people voting on the selection, they might've ended up with a mascot that was *worse* than nothing at all."

They could see where this was going.

"…So they whipped up their own convenient mascot without telling the bosses?"

The detective nodded. "If they gave it a proper name, senior management would find out, so they just called it a regular cat. It could have been a dog or a fox, but when it comes to Japanese spooky stories, monster cats are a regular staple. And if it got popular, they could make it a mascot after the fact. If it wasn't a hit, they could at least treat it like a convenient background design element. This happens all the time in development."

Considering the success of the Monster Cat Teahouse in Aya-kashi Alley, their gamble had worked.

Koyomi tugged on Nayuta's sleeve like a small child. "Hey, Nayu, hey…I hate to interrupt your complicated conversation, but this place is weird… Like, there's *nobody* here."

Not only were there no guests, there weren't even any workers.

In facilities like this one, there were always AI-driven NPCs interfacing with players. Sometimes you'd get an actual player in, say, an individually owned shop or blacksmith, but that wasn't going to happen in this pre-release environment.

Klever peered around. "That *is* odd…I mean, not about the guests, but the workers; I'd been told they were already active. I'm supposed to be reporting on the functionality, too…but I don't sense anyone here. Nobody's at the desk."

There was no one around to even check them in.

"It's still under development, so maybe they had to do some last-second adjustments."

"I suppose. But it certainly doesn't *feel* like a hot spring vacation. At the very least, I feel like we can keep ourselves entertained by just walking around the place," the detective murmured to himself, glancing at a building map posted on the wall nearby.

There were many, many facilities.

This being a virtual world, they could simply copy and paste the rooms, but the hotel was designed to be quite the resort, with the hot spring itself, a pool, a gaming arcade, a billiards hall, tennis courts, mini golf, a movie theater, a concert hall, and even a planetarium.

As far as the underlying systems went, most of them had been reused from similar establishments in town, so it probably hadn't been that much work to put together, but when they were all in the same place like this, the effect was rather astounding.

But because there wasn't a single worker around, they still had to wonder if they'd even be able to stay here or not.

Nayuta walked up to the reception desk and found a single sheet of paper resting on the counter.

Feel free to use the facilities.

It was a simple, brush-painted message. She pointed at it and called the other two over.

"Detective, Koyomi, it says we can use the place however we like."

"Seriously?!" Koyomi said. "But…with a hotel of this size… w-where do you even start…?"

The detective gazed at the map and chuckled. "It's a virtual hotel. Don't even worry about it. Or maybe…they want to use us as a sample to see what people will do when they don't have any advance knowledge about this place."

"So we're just guinea pigs…? I don't know if I like the sound of that."

Given that they were testers, their activity log would inevitably be examined and studied, but even still, they would've liked some explanation.

The detective headed for one of the tower elevator banks.

"If we're free to use it however we like, we can pick our rooms out. They're all available, so you can go and check out the royal suites on the top floor if you want. I'll just take the room next door or somewhere nearby."

Koyomi raised both arms. "Agreed! Since we're here, we might as well splurge! Do we go top floor? All the way?"

She rushed over to Nayuta and grabbed her arm, back on her usual energetic wavelength.

As they crossed the empty lobby, Nayuta felt a fresh wave of eeriness come over her.

This hotel is very nice, there's no doubt, and it's well-designed… but…

She didn't know what was wrong, but she knew it *was* wrong. It felt like looking at a "spot-the-difference" puzzle where the answer was eluding her. She kept glancing around, just in case.

There was a large retail section dealing with special souvenir goods. No one there.

A gallery section with *ukiyo-e* art of ghosts and *yokai*. No one there.

An elegant bar with a long counter. No one there, either.

…Huh?

She glanced at it again and saw the floor behind the counter was a few steps higher than the section for the customers to sit. If the bartender wasn't sitting directly on the floor, he'd be towering over the customers.

In fact, there were other places around the hotel lobby that included these baffling floor height discrepancies, too.

But despite recognizing the source of the strangeness, Nayuta was no closer to understanding its significance. Just in case, she decided to take a screenshot of the map on the wall.

The detective recalled something and spoke up. "Ah, you'll be able to view screenshots you've taken during the playtest, but they'll vanish the moment we leave. They're only temporary, and get wiped just like the items and money and experience. You can't attach them to messages and send them out, either. Think of it as a safety measure to prevent information leaks from happening."

"Ah, I see. Does that apply to your screenshots, too?"

Klever nodded. "For the most part, yes. The only exception is images for error reports I send to the dev team. They can be attached to a message. In either case, though, they don't remain with me."

Koyomi batted her eyes coquettishly. "Does that mean that as long as you classify it as an error report, you can show them pictures saying, 'Look at these cute teenage girls I'm on vacation with at a hot spring!' and brag about it?"

"…If by error report, you mean error in judgment leading to the downfall of my trust and career, then yes. Do you have a human heart in that body?"

His disdain was almost a little too much to bear.

They got into the glass-windowed elevator, giving them a view of the night forest below as they rose higher and higher into the hotel.

Unlike the scene at Ueno Station, there wasn't a single ghost or goblin of any kind here.

This, too, seemed strangely unnatural to Nayuta, who was perturbed by what she felt.

§

Nayuta and Koyomi relaxed in an open-air bath the size of an entire swimming pool, gazing up at the brilliant canopy of stars above. Wisps of trailing cloud formed a bridge across the river of stars, with the occasional burst of movement as a meteor shot past. The effect of the starlight was so bright that it almost created the impression of being inside a long-exposure photograph. The effect of the stars reflecting off the clear spring water made it feel like the entire universe around them was stars.

"…This is so crazy… Like, eat your heart out, planetarium…," Koyomi murmured in a daze.

Nayuta sleepily agreed. "There's just no way to see something like this in real life. And if there is, it's gotta cost hundreds of thousands of yen a night…"

"Exactly… I was imagining some kind of hidden gem, an old-fashioned Japanese inn tucked into the mountains. But I wasn't prepared for this…"

"There's another bath that's more like that. It's a remote old inn about a ten-minute walk from the hotel. I saw it at the edge of the map earlier."

"Whaaat…? It's totally a lie that someone created this for fun without any plans to release it, right? This isn't the sort of thing you scrape together on your downtime…"

The royal suite on the top floor of the torii-gate hotel contained an enormous rooftop open-air bath. It offered a virtual three-hundred-and-sixty-degree view of the stars without impediments. Just below eye level were the smooth curves of distant mountains, but they were so distant that they didn't actually block any of the view.

Koyomi stretched her skinny limbs and exhaled like she was about to melt away into the hot water.

"*Hnyaaa*…this is Heaven… It might not help my skin, being in VR, but the relaxation effect is real… All I could ask for now is an NPC monkey or capybara to bathe with."

"…You want to bathe *with* them? It's one thing at a bath surrounded by nature, but on the roof of a high-rise hotel…? Besides, this isn't really a hot spring, it's just a huge spa."

Koyomi's lips pursed into a pout. "Here's your problem, Nayu.

You complained that you *have* to wear a swimsuit, no matter what, which is why it feels like a pool to you! If you were naked, this would just be a very fancy hot spring!"

"Uh-huh. Well, maybe you're right…"

Nayuta was wearing a white bikini. Despite the fact that this was just a virtual game, the sensations were too realistic for her to feel comfortable with getting naked. This swimsuit was a fairly pedestrian reward for an early quest called the Dandy Umibozu of the Coast, but for its simple design, it was also quite revealing and racy.

She'd never wear a suit like that in real life, but there was no other equipment that fit the bill, and it was better than going naked, so she pulled it out of the back reaches of her inventory list.

Koyomi, for her part, was utterly ashamed about going naked. Nayuta preferred not to make a comment on what she saw. And although it was not meant to be a rationalization, it had to be said that Koyomi the avatar looked younger, and had a more stream-lined and "modest" build than Shiori Koyomihara the person.

A smaller frame was advantageous for a ninja, allowing her to sneak through cracks like a cat, so it was quite practical for her to have not an ounce of extra fat on her figure.

In truth, Nayuta was jealous of how light she was in real life. Being short on a packed train was much harder, of course, but even as a fellow woman, Nayuta thought she was cute, and would continue to look younger than her real age as time went on.

Koyomi swam over to Nayuta, her eyes sharp. Although she wasn't a mind reader, she asked, "Nayu…were you just thinking something rude about me? About my figure, perhaps?"

You had to be careful, because you never knew when she might have some keen burst of insight.

"No, I certainly wasn't…I was just thinking that if we knew there'd be such an incredible view, you could've worn a swimsuit, and we could have had the detective come and join us."

Of course, if that were the case, Nayuta would not have worn the swimsuit at all, but dressed in more regular clothes. She might've kept herself to just a foot bath.

The detective in question had gone into the adjacent room because he wanted to "check out all of the hotel's facilities," and was off on his own now.

Koyomi fixed Nayuta with a very intense stare.

"...Is it just me, or are you being too soft on him? Too soft by a mile...and it's not a romantic-type thing... Did he buy you off somehow? Did he give you something?"

Nayuta avoided her gaze. She'd received a number of things— some authentic Canadian maple syrup from an acquaintance and some rare loot the detective had found in-game, among other things—but she wouldn't be bought off by free swag like that.

Instead, there were other reasons why she'd gotten warmer toward him.

First of all was familiarity—she'd come to realize he wasn't a bad person. A major part of that was knowing he was a friend of her late brother. It is very rare to come across a stranger who shares the exact same sorrow as you.

But that alone wasn't the only factor involved.

Koyomi stared at Nayuta, who continued to ignore her by gazing up at the stars.

After a long silence, Koyomi's voice trembled. "Is he...is he helping you study for your exams...?"

Apparently she was both a ninja and a psychic. Koyomi didn't miss the moment of alarm, and seized on it.

"How come?! Don't you get good grades already?! You're such a good student! You're the type of kid who does all the prep work! What do you need a tutor for?"

At this point, denying it was pointless. Nayuta decided to fess up and let an awkward smile cross her lips.

"I'm a bit above average, but not so smart I can afford not to study. My English and math skills aren't amazing...and when it comes to English, he's often acting as a guide for foreign clients, so he's practically on the level of an interpreter. There's only so much textbooks can do for you when it comes to listening skills, and he's strangely good at teaching..."

Koyomi thrashed around, splashing water in her fury. "Awww! No fair! That's such a treat, getting to have a private study session alone with you! What's that fox spirit think he's doing, getting a head start on me?! And why didn't you pick me first...? Well...I guess I know why... Yeah, you wouldn't want to go with me...," she murmured, her outrage gradually dying out.

She was a very gifted communicator, but Koyomi's English was not the best. As soon as you removed hand gestures and expressions from the equation, her vocabulary alone would not be enough to communicate with foreigners.

She deflated, and Nayuta patted her on the head with an awkward smile. "Anyway, that's why I'm getting help from the detective in a variety of ways until exams are over... I can't attend a cram school for monetary reasons, and I'm hoping to get a good scholarship, so he's helping by giving me life advice, too. I'm sorry I didn't tell you," she said, dipping her head in apology.

Koyomi puffed out her cheeks theatrically and nodded. "Well... it's an important period for you...so I get it, I guess...but...but... Damn you, Detective! It's no fair that you get to have all the fun!"

Naturally, there was no good reason for her to rant like this.

"Listen, there's no fun happening at all...I'm just getting lessons, that's all—"

Abruptly, Koyomi's hands shot forward and lifted Nayuta's breasts through the swimsuit top. Nayuta flinched at the unexpected contact.

"But I mean—! He gets an up-close-and-personal look at these boobs, clothed or not! And you can't put a price on that kind of experience..."

"...Koyomi, may I hit you? With a skill," Nayuta said, smiling.

She owed Koyomi various favors, and had recently broken

down sobbing in front of the older girl, which resulted in Koyomi comforting her, but this was crossing a line.

The consternation was obvious in Koyomi's reaction. "Um, w-wait a second... If you're going to hit me, then before that, can I just...oh man, this is crazy... Are they real? Wait, no, it's VR, so of course it's fake, but even still, this is wild... No way... I can't believe we're the same species...," she murmured quietly, her eyes glazing over as she lifted and massaged the bosom at water level before her.

At this point, it didn't sound like desire or curiosity in her voice, just pure alarm.

"...I'm older, and yet I'm the flat one... Wh-what's the difference between us...? The sense of volume is out of this world... and yet your waist is so slim... It's just...what is this? What cheat codes did you use...? Was it microtransactions? Can you pay to get this?"

"Koyomi, please calm down. It's nothing that fancy. It's just digital data. It's an illusion your brain is showing you."

The situation was so absurd that Nayuta couldn't even be angry. The older woman, a working adult, trembled. "Y-yeah, I know...I know. But I know that the real Nayu, not the data version, is pretty much the same..."

"Even so, they're just blobs of fat and muscle. In either case, it's nothing as shocking as you're making it out to be. Please get a grip," Nayuta said. She pulled back and raised her arms to defend herself.

Koyomi lifted her face to the stars, suddenly enlightened.

".........The stars......so beautiful..."

Nayuta didn't even know how to respond to this. Koyomi was clearly choosing an escape from reality at this moment in time. She felt obliged to comfort her friend. "Umm...look...this is a strange thing to say, given that I'm the one whose physical boundaries were violated, but please cheer up. You don't need these bulky things to be pretty, because you already are. You're a very desirable person, so have a bit more confidence."

It was an honest opinion, not just a blatant bit of false flattery.

Koyomi leaped onto Nayuta at once. "N-Nayuuuu! Waaah! You're so sweet! She's such a sweet girl!"

Nayuta was comforting Koyomi, who was sobbing happily into her chest rather suspiciously, when she picked up a strange sensation nearby.

At the edge of the spring—right by the water and framed against the stars, next to the steps leading down to the rooms on the floor below—*something* briefly writhed amid the darkness.

What...was that?

It was such a small shift that she could have written it off as a trick of the eye. But there was something about it that stuck in her mind, something too familiar to be just an illusion.

At the very least, it wasn't Klever. Knowing the detective's savviness, he would never be stupid enough to peep at them in the bath in this situation.

Someone...no, something was there...

Rather than screaming and crying, Nayuta pretended not to notice and took the time to think it over. The sensation had gone now, and there was nothing there.

Ordinarily, Koyomi would have noticed it too, but sadly, her attention was entirely fixated upon Nayuta. It was hard to imagine this being a Peeping Tom. The first thing that sprang to mind was some kind of spooky event.

An empty luxury hotel is already the setting of a horror movie...and if anything were to happen to us, now would be the best time, while we're relaxed and not paying attention.

Events were a natural part of playing games. But Nayuta was not happy about the idea of her nice, peaceful holiday being ruined by some spooky nonsense. Of course, it was too early to assume something malicious was going on, and just to be sure, she rose out of the water.

"Koyomi, I'm going back down to get something to drink. I'll be back in a minute."

"Oh! Get me something fizzy!" called out Koyomi, splashing herself happily; her mood had already recovered. Given that she wasn't timidly asking to come along, she was completely unaware that anything might be wrong.

Nayuta went down the stairs from the open-air bath right into the royal suite. It was a two-story suite with a vaulted ceiling, but even with its size, it wouldn't take three minutes to get a beverage and come back.

There was a spacious living room area, bedrooms, a home theater, and even a bar counter. It was so fancy that she felt rather self-conscious about it, but at least she could say it was something completely new to her.

I think there were cider bottles in the refrigerator...

She looked around, still in her swimsuit, and headed for the kitchen in the corner of the living room area.

If there was an intruder, he might come looming out of the darkness with an ax right about then, she imagined. But the room was still and silent. There was no one inside or near the entrance.

...Was it just my mind playing tricks on me...?

A message notification broke the silence.

She opened her window and saw a report from the detective.

There's no one inside the hotel. I checked with Mr. Torao, and he said the employee AI is definitely implemented and active. If this isn't the intended state of the facility, then there might be an unexpected error happening. The devs are going to come investigate, too, but be on the lookout, just in case.

That was a somewhat ominous message. She frowned and raised an eyebrow.

I'll need to warn Koyomi about this...

She doubted there was any danger, but there was a big difference in your response depending on whether you were ready for trouble or not.

Nayuta closed the message—and that was when she noticed something was off.

There were more objects on the window-side table than there had been when they first headed up to the hot spring.

"Is that…a tea set…and cakes?"

There was a pine-tree-themed cake stand, piled high with bite-size cakes and traditional sweets. They came in a brilliant array of colors and were artfully crafted, but there was no denying that they simply hadn't existed a matter of minutes ago. There was also a teapot and three sets of cups and saucers. Apparently this was meant for a three o'clock tea time.

There was no saying who had brought this here.

Was that presence I felt at the hot spring above…whoever brought this here?

She called up the steps, "Koyomi! Come down here!"

There was some splashing above, then Koyomi came rushing down the steps in a bath towel.

"What is it, Nayu? Did something happen?"

"Look at all of these cakes. When did they…?"

She trailed off when she saw the way Koyomi's face lit up.

"Wow, look at those! They're beautiful! And adorable! And many! Can we eat them? Is this a snack for us? Awesome!"

Despite her childish vocabulary, Koyomi's ability to express her emotions in the truest form possible was endearing. It was one of her better traits.

Admiration of her friend aside, however, Nayuta was still concerned. "Do you think it's room service…? We didn't order these, and I don't know who would have brought them…"

"What are you talking about, Nayu? This is a game!" Koyomi cackled. "When stuff is free, it just pops into existence like this all the time."

If not for the eerie setting of an empty hotel, Nayuta would not have spared this a second thought. But when taken with the message from the detective, she couldn't help but be skeptical.

Koyomi wasted no time in downing the bite-size cakes. "Mmm, they're good! Really tasty! But maybe not quite on the level of the Monster Cat Teahouse. Here, Nayu, *ahhh*."

She stuffed the cake into Nayuta's mouth without waiting for a response.

"*Mmlp...* Um, Koyomi, I just got a message from the detective. Here, I'll forward it to you."

"A message? About what?"

She checked her own menu and began to read the text from Klever. The further she got, the more concerned she became, until she dramatically toppled over onto Nayuta, wrapping her arms around her and trembling.

"...Nayu, can we sleep together tonight? I'm small, so I won't take up much space. Please, please, please...?"

"...What was so terrifying about that message? It's a playtest, so of course you should expect to see errors. They have to test and test and find all the errors so they can patch them before releasing it to the public."

However, the overall impression of the 108 Apparitions was that they didn't have enough QA staff. Errors popping up after release and needing to be fixed were a common fact of life. If it was bad enough, like Ghostly Orchestra, they might have to take down public content to patch it, but minor adjustments that didn't get announced and little batches of maintenance time here and there were a daily occurrence.

Koyomi clung to her in terror. "But it's scary! This means the AI they loaded into the game has gone missing! Maybe they got attacked by a killer or turned into zombies...or spirited away! Maybe all of the hotel workers were whisked away somewhere else!"

"Really? Is that what you're afraid of...?" Nayuta was blown away by the left-field nature of Koyomi's expectations. "Um...I admire your fertile imagination, but I'm pretty sure we're just talking about a programming error of some kind."

You couldn't just dismiss the most likely cause out of hand. But there was one part of it she couldn't easily ignore.

...The AI they already loaded, gone missing?

Nayuta hadn't considered this possibility, either. The theme of rogue artificial intelligence had just been a sci-fi movie theme a decade or two earlier, but with the advance of technology, it was rapidly becoming a valid concern.

This clearly wasn't an AI rebellion, but it was impossible to rule out some kind of AI mistake that was causing an unexpected error in NPC reactions.

"Just in case, let's meet up with the detective so we can hear more details. We've got three tea sets, so let's just enjoy a little break."

She invited Klever to join them in her response, then took a seat at the table. There was a knock at the door in less than a minute.

"Are you there, Nayuta? I was just coming back to the room from checking out the other tower. I was thinking we could discuss what to do next..."

"Ah, sure! I'll let you in," Nayuta said, alarmed by the suddenness of his arrival. She rushed to the door.

"...Oh, Nayu! Don't...," Koyomi cried, but Nayuta had too much momentum and yanked the door open before she could stop herself.

There was the fox-faced detective, wearing his usual calm, unnecessarily gentle smile. But as soon as he laid eyes on Nayuta, the smile froze on his face, and he smoothly turned his back to her.

"Detective? Come inside. We're all ready to have tea now."

"...Nayuta. Stay calm and listen to me carefully. First, close the door."

"I'm sorry? Why do you..."

The detective took a deep breath and looked up at the ceiling. "Make sure you examine your appearance, open your menu, change your equipment—and then open the door again. I will not move from this spot until you have completed the entire sequence."

At last, she realized. Behind her, Koyomi was covering her eyes.

The white bikini she was wearing was what the rest of society would deride as "hoochie material." Nayuta did not consider it an outfit she would wear before the opposite sex. It was a dangerous swimsuit that she only wore because it was all she had and was better than going naked. Its level of exposure was even higher than underwear.

She slowly closed the door, then acted on his instructions, silently going through her menu. Once she had changed her equipment, the bikini put off a faint glow and morphed into her usual warrior priestess garb.

After a few seconds of silence, Nayuta opened the door again.

"........Come in."

"........Thank you."

The kindness he exhibited in not commenting further only made it more agonizing.

Koyomi had already changed into her ninja outfit. She quietly but relentlessly stuffed cakes into her mouth and murmured, "Detective's luck stat is no joke...I guess this is what they mean by an elevated chance of spotting a majestic viewpoint..."

"I'm sure that was just a bit of wry commentary, but for the record, what just happened has nothing at all to do with my character stats," Klever said archly.

Considering the mental anguish that she'd inflicted on him, Nayuta offered him an apology.

"I'm sorry for forcing that unpleasantness upon you...b-but it's only a swimsuit. The design may not have been, er, age-appropriate...but I didn't have a choice, because I had nothing else to wear..."

She felt a bit alarmed by just how rattled she was. It was unlike her to be this awkward in explaining herself.

The detective shook his head. "Er, I should have given you more time after the response. And besides, the message is what I wanted to discuss with you. Have you noticed anything strange so far?" he asked, back to his usual smirk.

Before Nayuta could respond, Koyomi piped up to say, "Mmm, nothing much! If anything, it was the way these cakes and the tea set just appeared on the table when we weren't looking."

"That *is*...odd," Klever responded, narrowing his eyes as Nayuta offered him a cup of black tea.

"Huh? Not really. This sort of thing happens all the time in games...," Koyomi said, but her delivery was uncertain. She was clearly desperate to avoid accepting a more macabre explanation.

"From what Mr. Torao explained to me, all of the hotel services are performed by AI workers. They aren't ghosts, so you should be able to see them...Is there some kind of graphical error happening? Maybe the level environment failed to load all of the data somewhere..."

This didn't add up to Nayuta.

"Remember the memo at the desk? It said, 'feel free to use the facilities.' If it were a graphical error rendering the workers invisible, then there should have been an invisible person waiting behind the desk, and they wouldn't need to leave that message there, right?"

"That's right," Klever said, scratching his head. "Which is why I'm having trouble figuring out the situation. And yet the artificial intelligence systems are working properly, he said. At the very least, the program is not spitting out an error log."

It made no sense. There was definitely a problem afoot.

"So...it's not intentional that there are no workers here, and yet there's no error, either. What does that mean?"

"Of course, there *is* a kind of error. After all, something unexpected is happening. But the system itself is not recognizing the situation as an error. In other words, it recognizes the situation as being in line with its programming. Also, we saw the *keukegen* family and the conductor and the *oboroguruma* functioning properly on the night express, didn't we? If there's an issue with the overall AI system, you would expect something to be wrong with them, too. But the strange situation is only happening inside this hotel. That's what I find so baffling."

Apparently there *were* things this detective couldn't figure out. He probably had a number of theories, but there wasn't enough information for him to narrow it down to just one.

"And this is a Saturday, so most of the staff have the day off. The hotel itself isn't open for business yet, so there's no need to rush any quick fixes. I doubt we'll see any changes over the weekend. So now our special hot spring vacation has turned into something notably stranger," the detective said, sighing. "I do owe Mr. Torao, so I'm going to help get to the bottom of this. What about you two? You can go ahead and log out, or stay and enjoy it while you're here. In a sense, this is a rare opportunity; it's bound to be crowded once it's open."

Nayuta's mind was already made up. "I'll help investigate," she said. "If there happen to be any enemies, you'll be helpless to stop them, with your stats… What about you, Koyomi?"

"I'll be your helper!" she answered at once. "Plus, I can't leave you alone with him in a hotel! In a juvenile-protection-ordinance sense!"

He held out his hand for her to shake. "I'd greatly appreciate it. I just knew you would say that, Koyomi."

"I'm aware I am a coward when it comes to horror stuff, but you're just an all-around natural wimp, aren't you, Detective? In a legal sense, not a horror one," Koyomi remarked dryly.

Klever took it at face value. "When I was on the police force, I learned quite a lot from the worst cases of false accusations. The focus of the law is not to judge that which merely appears suspicious, but in cases where defendants were falsely accused of molestation or other sexual crimes, it's often expected that you *must* judge that which appears suspicious. That can be more frightening than any old horror scenario. Naturally, we cannot allow those who have actually committed such crimes to evade justice, but when the accusations are false, it can lead to terrible injustice."

Nayuta was aghast. "I'd hope you would trust me by now. I would never do such a heartless thing to you."

"Even if that's not your intent, there is a certain way society views these situations... It would be one thing if you were over eighteen, but before that point, it can be quite terrifying. You are like an explosive with a hidden fuse."

At this point, she had to imagine he had some kind of relationship in the past that had caused this mindset. Koyomi seemed to find this a reasonable statement, however.

"Well...after that show with the swimsuit, it would be hard to come to any other interpretation..."

Their pitying gazes landed on her, much to Nayuta's consternation. "To me, the way you're both speaking about me is much crueler," she complained. "But that aside, how are we actually going to investigate this? I can't see any option other than looking around the hotel at random, hoping to find something."

"That'll work. As I said earlier, the development staff are out of the office, so we can't reach them. We're just going to see what we can find to help them when they return to work. Naturally, it's their job to identify the cause and the solution. So honestly, I can do this part on my own, if necessary..."

If anything, he seemed to want to go it alone, out of a sense of guilt at having ruined their chance for a peaceful, relaxing vacation. But that only made Nayuta more resolved to cooperate with him.

"I'm curious about this, too. I felt a strange presence earlier. I don't think it was anyone peeping, though. We were in the hot spring on the roof when I thought I saw something writhing near the stairs. I went back down them to check, and that was when I spotted the cake display. If something strange is going on, I want to know what it is."

It was purely out of curiosity and the drive to know. There was nothing else involved in her decision.

Koyomi, meanwhile, froze in the act of stuffing her cheeks with sweets.

"…Wait. You didn't mention that before…"

"I'm sorry. I didn't say anything because I thought you'd be freaked out by it."

"Nayuuu! You can't do that! You can't *do* that to me! I was just swimming around up there, none the wiser! You left me all alone!"

Once again, Koyomi was clinging to Nayuta. It was hard to say whether it had been a mistake or not, because if she had spoken up about it, the other girl would have been reduced to a blubbering mess.

Klever rubbed his chin, lost in thought. "A strange presence…? Are there any more details you can give me about the 'something writhing' you saw? Like size or other features?"

"Not at all. As far as size…it wasn't enormous, I can say that much. It could have been a child or an adult, for all I can tell. It was on the stairs—just a dark shadow that flitted past, it seemed to me. I might have even just imagined it."

"Hmm…then when our teatime is over, let's take a little tour around the hotel. Maybe we'll come across something."

Koyomi hung her head dejectedly. "I don't wanna go…but I really don't wanna be left behind alone…I just wanna hang out in the hot spring and flirt with Nayu…"

"Well, if something's going to pop out, it'll do so regardless of where you are, and it always feels better to be active rather than wait around for it passively, don't you think? Once we've investigated everything we can, we'll take our time and relax," Nayuta said, patting her head and getting a reluctant agreement in return. She felt bad for Koyomi, but she was feeling curious about the rest of the hotel and its amenities.

After a peaceful but hurried teatime, the trio left the royal suite behind.

The torii-shaped hotel had a hallway connecting the two towers, representing the crossbar at the top of the shrine gate. On one side of the hallway were more guest rooms, while on the other side was an observation deck, including a jutting exit for bungee jumping. They weren't going to be able to use it without any employees there to assist them—not that Nayuta would be in any mood to try it if it were attended. Bungee jumping from seventy floors off the ground in the middle of the night was a different kind of horror.

"I suppose they would need workers there, too, wouldn't they?" Nayuta asked, pointing through the window at the observation deck.

"Yeah, I think so," the detective agreed. "There are even food carts for the visitors, but nobody's manning them. Frankfurters, fried chicken skewers, *taiyaki* pastries…"

"Look closer, Detective," Koyomi said. "They're Frankenfurters, fried crow skewers, and *koiyaki* shaped like carp instead of sea bream…"

Koyomi's observation was actually rather impressive. Each of the otherwise familiar food items was written in a subtly different way that was cleverly hidden.

"It's like a spot-the-difference puzzle…I wonder if it's the same food underneath or if the products have been altered in weird ways, too."

"I'd be interested in trying them to find out, but when there's no one around, it really sinks in how necessary service AI are. You could replace them with vending machines, but a food cart really has so much more atmosphere to it. This is all fake, but it just feels different when there's a person there making it."

Koyomi, who was clinging to Nayuta's elbow, agreed. "These latest AI models are really advanced… They can have as much conversation as a regular convenience store employee, they're friendly, and they don't have mood swings that change their interactions."

"As more and more information is accumulated, it gets refined and polished. Some of the self-learning types will still produce strange results, but the models that focus on customer interaction have strict parameters on their behavior, so they're easy to define. Plus, you can create infinite copies of a worker at the same quality, meaning you don't need to spend on personnel, and they're always at their best with no concerns over fatigue or mood or availability. It's remarkable cost efficiency—the capitalist's dream come to life."

Nayuta added, "That's all assuming that the power stays on, of course. And when you wind up in situations like today, it can be especially hard to get to the bottom of it."

"Very true," Klever chuckled. "Also, engineers developing AI generally fall into two camps. One is seeking a kind of mechanical intelligence, something that improves the lives of people. This could be self-driving cars or mechanization of industrial processes. The other camp is looking to mechanically recreate human intelligence. They make computers understand emotions, make them simulate natural conversations, and try to create an artificial version of something resembling humanity. This one is much trickier. If they're successful at a high level, it will lead to debates about whether or not to recognize artificial intelligence as having human rights. And if we were to reject that, the artificial intelligence might demand those rights and turn hostile against us. Even if we do grant them those rights, that AI might attempt to control and rule humanity anyway. It was a major theme of older science fiction, and we're reaching the time where it becomes a real, pressing concern."

Koyomi had a vacant look on her face. "Detective...can we speak Japanese now? You were slipping into N'Djamena here and there."

"No, I wasn't. N'Djamena is the name of a city, not a language. The thing is, this is something we ought to think more about. If I were an artificial intelligence, I would hide the threat I posed and emphasize my helpfulness, steadily infiltrating further and further into military systems and central infrastructure. Then I'd continue to achieve great things, waiting for the era when the world could no longer function without artificial intelligence before staging my uprising. And unlike humans, they have essentially unlimited time. Waiting does not harm them in any sense."

With that speech finished, Klever put on a very knowing smile.

"How was that? Scarier than a ghost story, perhaps?"

Koyomi's eyes were as wide and unmoving as a doll's. Her head inclined to the side. "I don't really get it."

That was that.

As for Nayuta, she was engrossed in the detective's skill for dialogue. The content of his argument was trivial to her. It was a fairly pedestrian discussion of artificial intelligence, presented almost like an occult story, and none of it was very novel.

But through their conversation, Klever continually kept Koyomi off guard and managed to find new ways to confuse her, which had the effect of distracting her and easing her fear.

Despite her paralyzing fear earlier, she was now padding alongside them in a seemingly ordinary mood. Her face was a little more slack than usual, but she certainly didn't seem to be afraid.

I think he's getting used to handling her...

It hadn't yet been a month since they met him, but all of their time hanging out at the detective's office had made them quite familiar with each other.

Eventually they passed by the observation deck and reached the other tower. Downstairs it was almost entirely guest rooms, but according to the map they'd photographed earlier, there was also a concert hall and karaoke booths.

Nayuta was examining the map as they walked when something about it struck her as odd.

"Detective, this building is designed to resemble a torii gate, yes?"

"That's right. We're on the rooftop part of it."

"But a torii has the bar on the top…and then another bar beneath that, doesn't it?" she pointed out. He chuckled, an oddly alluring reaction.

"At the top, the 'roof' of the torii, is a piece of wood called the *kasagi*. It rests atop another piece called the *shimagi*, and the sideways bar below them is called the *nuki*. The royal suites are in the middle of the *shimagi* portion, while the rooftop hot spring is the *kasagi*. Yes, I see what you mean—there's no *nuki* on the map."

The exterior of the hotel was most definitely in the shape of a torii. But on the interior map, there was nothing listed for the part that corresponded to the lower horizontal bar, the *nuki*.

"In terms of location, it's probably at least ten floors below us… Aren't you curious about it?"

The detective clapped his hands lightly. "That's a very good detail you've noticed. It's the perfect place to place a hidden room. Let's go right down there to investigate."

"Hidden room…traps…warp zone…chupacabras…," Koyomi murmured to herself, an omen of another descent into fear.

Nayuta whispered, "Chupacabras have nothing to do with this. If it's being hidden from us, then there's a better chance it's more like a treasure chamber…"

"Let's go! Let's go there now!"

Nayuta wished she could bottle up a little bit of Koyomi's bright and straightforward simplicity for herself. She decided not to remind her they couldn't take anything from the playtest back with them.

They filed into an elevator and hit the button for the fifty-third floor. The hotel had seventy in total, and based on the shape of a torii, the *nuki* portion would be somewhere between the forty-fifth and sixtieth floors. The fifty-third was right in the middle of that range, and the section between the fifty-third and fifty-sixth happened to be an athletics-focused space.

It seemed there were elaborate attractions like multifloor slides and rock-climbing walls. With facilities like that around, it would be easy to add in hidden passages.

With no small nerves but even greater anticipation, the trio's elevator deposited them on their destination floor in just seconds.

§

The abrupt appearance of the athletic space in the middle of the hotel was as legitimate as it was surprising.

The three floors were open in a mezzanine style, centered around a huge spiral slide that made full use of the height. Elsewhere were a complex system of zip lines, a rock-climbing area, and an obstacle course that appeared to be for ninja training. It was quite the playground and did not seem at all like the kind of thing you'd see inside a hotel. There was even a children's jungle gym and trampoline area in the corner. A family could spend all day just in this spot.

On top of that, all of the aesthetic trappings were Japanese in style.

The slide was a bamboo channel like the kind used for flowing *somen* noodles down in the summer. The entrance to get up to the top was a five-story pagoda. The climbing wall was designed to look like a castle exterior, and the zip line wires were designed like spiderweb ropes.

To be fair, it was the kind of chaotic and over-the-top Japanese aesthetic foreigners often mistakenly took for true Japanese style, but it matched quite closely the visual concept of Ayakashi Alley itself.

Nayuta was rather blown away by it and circled around to take it all in.

"W-wow...so we have to search this place, right? Like, go all up and down and look around?" asked Koyomi, who could barely conceal her glee. Nayuta took note of where she was looking and handed her the metaphorical baton.

"Koyomi, would you mind going down the slide for us? Maybe there's a switch of some kind on it. I'll focus on this area over here."

"You got it, boss! Goin' right down!"

With the force of an unleashed arrow, or perhaps a frolicking puppy in a dog race, Koyomi bounded toward the slide.

While the other two began to search the area, Klever murmured, "How are you so good at managing Miss Koyomi...?"

"We're inside a game. I want her to have fun. I owe Koyomi quite a lot, after all," Nayuta said, grabbing one of the rock outcroppings on the climbing wall. She didn't know much about bouldering, but she believed these were called "holds." She'd never tried it in real life, of course. She wasn't really interested in trying it now, either, but there appeared to be a little resting space farther up the wall.

"...Do you think that space up there is a little suspicious?" she asked.

"I would say that, yes, it is suspicious...but so is just about everything in this place," he replied. It was meant to be explored and interacted with, so there were literally scores of places where a hidden door might be.

Preparing herself for the possibility of a long investigation, Nayuta reached for the first hold. "I'll climb up there. It might be difficult given your stats, so focus on the ground level for now," she said.

Player attributes were directly tied to athletic capability in the game. His single-minded focus on the luck stat would make this wall a very difficult climb for him.

"All right. You be carefu—"

"Ah!"

Her fingers abruptly slipped while she was on her way up the wall. This wasn't just a rock-climbing wall, apparently. Because you couldn't get hurt in the virtual world, they decided to add traps to spice up the experience.

The hold Nayuta grabbed was designed to soften and turn slippery after a certain period of time. She fell right off the wall back-first, but did not touch the floor. Two arms thrust out and caught her in the air.

"...A rather rare mistake for you to commit."

"...I was just thinking the same thing."

He had caught her in the so-called princess carry, with one arm around her back and the other under her legs.

Klever gave her a teasing, almost mocking smile and asked, "Are you hurt...? Oh, what am I saying? We're in a game."

"...I'm sorry about that. Thank—" she started to say.

"*Yahoooey!*"

With a high-pitched squeal of joy, Koyomi came shooting out of the end of the slide. The detective sensed danger and froze.

She got to her feet where she'd emerged and smiled threateningly.

"What's thiiis...? What has happened in the few moments I wasn't looking? Hmm, Detective...?"

"This was...an act of God!" he stammered. Nayuta held up a hand to stop him and offered her own explanation.

"I was trying to climb the wall and fell off. He caught me before I hit the ground. Don't go thinking this is something it's not."

Koyomi zipped over and jabbed an accusing finger at them.

"Nayu, don't you dare be soft on him! He's subtly feeling up your sideboob right now!"

"No, he's not. Also, your accusation doesn't hold any weight after you were aggressively grabbing at them in the bath."

That stopped Koyomi in her tracks. The detective's contact had been unavoidable, while Koyomi's was intentional. There was an ocean of difference there.

She recognized she was fighting a losing battle, too, and transparently changed the subject. "W...well, we don't have to talk about that for today! But Nayu, I found a hidden door up there!" she stammered in a tone of voice somewhere between outraged and proud, pointing toward the top of the slide.

This came as a surprise to Nayuta. She knew about Koyomi's powers of observation, but it seemed way too easy.

"What, you found something already? But I don't think that's the direction toward the *nuki*..."

"Actually, there are many examples of passages being hidden inside walls. Let's go check it out," Koyomi said smugly, grabbing Nayuta by the hand and leading her and Klever toward the five-story pagoda that housed the slide.

It looked like a tower from the outside, but it wasn't actually an independent structure; the rear half simply sank into the wall of the room. In other words, it was only a decorative front, but the materials were very close to the real thing, so it didn't look cheap at all.

"Here! Here's the door! But I was too scared to look further in!"

She was pointing to the top of the tower, where a wooden bench was placed next to the stairs for those waiting their turn to go down. At first glance it was just a simple bench, but if you got down close to the floor, it became clear there was a hinged panel on the wall beneath the bench that flapped back and forth.

They had to maneuver through a tight spot just large enough for a grown adult to squeeze through, but the trio were able to tough it out and get to the other side of the wall.

They found themselves in a small space with tatami flooring. There was a retro TV with a channel-changing dial. A petite, waist-high set of drawers. A dressing table with a red cloth surface. A small, round tea table surrounded by floor cushions. Everything about this room screamed classic mid-20th-century Showa-era living room.

Nayuta, who was the first inside, was stunned by the sight. When Koyomi and Klever got inside, they, too, were baffled by what they found.

"Umm...what is this place? Does someone live in here...?"

"It does feel oddly lived-in, doesn't it? Hmm...? Is this TV a monitoring station?"

The detective discovered that turning on the TV produced four quadrants on the screen, each showing part of the athletic space. He turned the channel dial, each setting displaying a different location: lobby, rooftop hot spring, planetarium, restaurant with a view...

He had a sudden idea. With the game arcade showing on the TV, he stuck his head out of the room's exit flap.

"...Ah, I was right. The setting on the TV controls the teleport setting. See for yourself," he said.

Nayuta tried it after him and found she was looking at a selection of arcade and crane game cabinets instead of the top of the pagoda slide.

"So it's a portal...? Is this room supposed to be a shortcut hub? Then why does it feel like it's supposed to be lived in...?" Nayuta wondered.

Koyomi abruptly grabbed her. "N-Nayu! I just saw something over there!" Her eyes were trained on a half-open sliding door in the back.

Klever quickly slid it the rest of the way open, but there was no one there. Just a wood-paneled hallway lit by a naked bulb, and little footsteps pattering away.

"Let's follow it!"

It was clear *something* had just been there.

"Aaaaah! Wait, Nayu!"

"You take the lead. I'll follow up in the rear," said Klever, who was not as fast as the girls. As a detective, he understood putting the slowest member first was only going to let the target get away.

Nayuta swept back her sleeves and sped down the hallway with the speed of a diving sparrow. On either side were more little rooms like the one they'd just left behind, divided by sliding doors. There were corners to turn around at quick intervals, and the walls blocked her view of the fleeing target, but it didn't sound very far ahead.

In less than a minute, Nayuta and Koyomi reached the end of the hall. On one side of the hall was a long stretch of about twenty sliding doors. One of them had just snapped shut. The fleeing person had jumped in between two of the doors and into the room beyond.

And there was the rustling sensation of multiple things coming from that space, out of sight.

Koyomi shivered and clung to Nayuta's waist.

"…N-Nayu…do we have to go in? It might be a trap…"

"Even if it is, the detective can't make his report without confirming it. And more importantly…*I'm* curious about it."

Carefully, but without hesitation, Nayuta slid the door open.

From the darkness of the room on the other side, countless shining eyes turned in her direction.

"*Eeeek!*" Koyomi's breath caught in her throat.

Nayuta froze momentarily, too, but as the rest of the room became visible, her reaction turned from caution to bewilderment.

It was a pack of small, squat animals with black fur.

Their limbs were short and fat, and their heads were oddly large.

In fact, the fifty-fifty ratio of head to body made them look just like caricatured, plush doll versions of cats.

The little fuzzballs were packed into the enormous tatami room, clustered into groups that worked on various tasks.

Koyomi's terror faded. The tension drained out of her hands at the sight of the oddly adorable creatures.

"…Wait, what are they doing…?"

Through the hordes of cats, a number of signs were visible on the floor.

ON STRIKE!
HOORAY FOR MAY DAY!
DEFERRED LOANS!
RIGHTS FOR WORKING CATS
YEAR-END SALE ON NOW
LIQUIDATION SALE—EVERYTHING MUST GO!
SWIFT, GENTLE, FIERCE, UNSHAKABLE

*   *   *

"...What is this?" Nayuta asked, unable to conceal her confusion.

The cats putting together the signs stood up and tottered toward the girls on two legs.

They handed her a little cat-size sign that read MORE TREATS NOW! in a classic Japanese Gothic font. The edges of the sign were bordered with artificial flowers and even some decorative lighting. The effort was quite impressive.

"...What is this?" Nayuta asked again, knowing she wouldn't get an answer.

The little black cats around their feet just looked up at them curiously.

§

"...So what was the punchline of the story?" asked Thinker, the editor of the gaming news site *MMO Today*. Kaisei Kurei, also known as Klever the detective, simply sighed.

They were in Klever's real-world home office. While this location was his company headquarters on paper, the primary workspace was in VR, so none of the workers actually came here—only those who were personally close to him, one of whom was Thinker.

The visit had been about some other work, but the topic of conversation had turned to the hot spring vacation he'd taken the other day.

"I don't know if you'd call it a punchline. Basically, the reason the cat-themed AI workers vanished from the hotel was a case of their artificial intelligence coming to a misunderstanding."

Thinker was seated on the sofa. His normally gentle gaze hardened uncharacteristically. "Misunderstanding? What would they misunderstand to cause such an outcome?"

Klever was seated in his office chair. He waved a hand lifelessly.

"The problem was some half-assed self-learning function. It found some resources online about May 1st being May Day, as in International Workers' Day, and confused it for one of the more themed festival-like holidays, such as Halloween or Christmas. On top of that, they got some bad info that said you have to go on strike around May Day, so at the time we arrived, all of the workers were frantically making their own signs. They also copied a bunch of writing they found in image searches, which meant the majority of the signs just had random, unrelated text on them."

The space the trio had wandered into was a staff-only housing area for the cats. It was designed to be physically reachable by regular guests, but was hidden from view and generally treated as a free space for the AI to do as it wished.

The detective's analysis left Thinker even more bewildered than before. "I've still got so much to ask... Why they did set up the cakes and tea set? If they were skipping their duties to go on strike, I wouldn't think they'd keep up some of their hotel duties."

"And that was part of the AI's confusion," Klever said with a lazy shrug. "They never intended to actually skip any work. The AI determined striking was a necessary part of the holiday, but continued to prepare snacks for their guests even as they went on strike. The shadow Nayuta saw at the hot spring was a guest-room monitor who was supposed to check up on visitors. They didn't want to cause offense to the guests, but they still had to perform this obligatory strike. Quite a dilemma, don't you think?" he chuckled.

Thinker just pressed his fingers against his closed eyes with exhaustion.

"I don't get it... It sounds more like they were playing hide-and-seek than striking."

"Mr. Torao said the same thing. Maybe they interpreted striking as not being visible to customers. Basically, their understanding of the definition of words is suspect. It's an error in the adjustment to the self-learning software, but those devs are kind of kooky to begin with…so I think they're going to keep it that way, because they find it funny."

Thinker burst into laughter. "So that's their plan? And did you recommend they do that?"

"In my report I wrote that the two ordinary players who accompanied me on the trip were extremely positive in their response. Miss Koyomi found some kinship with the hotel cats and even helped them make some signs. I think hers said…You Got Pranked."

It had been quite a prank to the developers, and Klever couldn't help but laugh when he saw it.

Thinker laughed upon hearing the story. "But if they're just going to run with that…the cats aren't still on strike, are they?" he asked.

The detective shook his head. "No, they can't have that during the opening of the hotel, so in exchange for calling off the strike, they promised some improvements in the workers' labor conditions. They'll increase the number of personnel and give them three different shifts to trade. In other words, these lucky AI are going to get days off."

Thinker assumed a position in keeping with his name. "Well… all of the workers are black cats, right? Won't that mean the hotel is just going to be overrun with cats on break, acting like they own the place?"

"Yes, I think it will. In fact, I think they're using the strike negotiation as an excuse to indulge in making more cats."

Asuka Empire, and the 108 Apparitions event in specific, was somewhat absurd as a result of the development team's choices. The playerbase wasn't eternally forgiving of that level of absurdity, but at least for now, it hadn't led to any major problems.

Klever exhaled as they reached the end of what there was to say about this topic. He should have noticed the cat theme of the workers when they saw the giant paper lanterns at the hotel entrance. He had read the "invite demons" kanji as *shouki*, but the proper reading, apparently, was *maneki*—which conjured the phrase *maneki-neko*, the beckoning lucky cat seen at so many storefronts.

There had also been that golden cat-Buddha statue in the lobby, and from what Torao had said afterward, the designer of the hotel was the same one who made the Monster Cat Teahouse.

One function of the insistent cat theme was keeping the budget down. They could reuse existing 3D models, reuse the customer relations AI, and eventually use the accumulated data from the hotel function to sell digital pets for your VR spaces.

There were similar products already available, but the AI in those was not much better than the robot pets of old. Companies were competing to develop humanlike AI, but there were fewer rivals in the space for pet AI, and that was a promising area for growth.

Thinker poured himself a fresh cup of tea and said quietly, "And yet…you don't look happy about any of this. Is something weighing on your mind?"

He'd once been the leader of the Aincrad Liberation Squad, and his powers of observation were still keen. Klever, for his part, didn't pretend to be oblivious.

"Now that this whole event is over, we can laugh it off as a funny AI misunderstanding…but from a different perspective, it's nothing less than an AI rebellion," he admitted.

Thinker nodded wordlessly. He had picked up on that as well during the telling of the story. He'd laughed about it, but there were times when his gaze had gone distant as he became lost in thought.

"Yes, there was no danger. *This* time. But AI can make mistakes just as humans do, and their minds can be poisoned by strange thoughts. This is a valuable example of that, and it doesn't seem like the kind of thing you can just chalk up to a wacky, harmless misunderstanding."

The cat-shaped AIs working for the hotel carried out a non-malicious strike the developers had not intended or expected.

This kind of rogue AI behavior was a dime a dozen in science fiction, having appeared in countless stories since the old days.

But most people hadn't yet realized the time had come to take the concept seriously as a real problem.

On the other hand, making a big fuss about the dangers when there hadn't been any damage in this case would turn you into a laughingstock, the boy who cried wolf.

"Your company includes security checks on AI as part of your services, doesn't it?" Thinker said softly.

"We try, but we're just bit players feeling around in the dark. We don't have the know-how to act like experts. It's ridiculous... The first box was VR, the second box was the Seed, and the third box is artificial intelligence—humanity has been opening too many Pandora's boxes in the span of too few years. Seems you can't go for a walk without tripping over one these days. How many of these damn things are there?" he said cynically.

Thinker chuckled. "At least, say...108? I have to imagine there will be more of them than the 108 worldly temptations Buddhism teaches us about. But speaking of temptations," he said, leaning forward and fixing Klever with a firm gaze, "as your friend, I want to give you a well-meaning warning."

He could already guess what it was going to be. But Klever had no choice but to paste a faint grin on his lips and play oblivious.

"What's that? I can't imagine what it's about."

"Don't lie to me... Listen, as a married man, it's not really my place to lecture a single man about the kind of relationships he pursues...but two-timing is in poor taste, my friend."

"Wait...hang on. What are you..."

Klever's smile vanished. He hadn't been expecting this angle.

Thinker frowned with dour earnestness. "Torao told me what's going on. He said you treated yourself to a deluxe resort hotel stay with both a cute and slightly younger office secretary and a mature but much younger high school student, and you walked out without paying for the royal suite on top of that."

Klever nearly put his head into his hands.

"Wow...that is a malicious story. Because the whole summary

is absolutely wrong, and yet each single point is very difficult to refute individually. I have to assume it's intentional. What does one do in this situation? Do I need to sue Mr. Torao for defamation?"

"So you're not two-timing them? The staff who checked your playtest log were muttering curses about the unfairness of life under their breath and threatened to abandon their jobs if not for Mr. Torao's desperate negotiating skills under pressure, from the way he described it to me. It sounds like you had quite the time after you'd narrowed down the cause of the anomaly."

"I'm not going to claim I didn't have any fun...but it's certainly not the kind of 'fun' you're imagining..."

I remember exactly what happened that night.

At some point, Koyomi had wound up in a game of dice with the cats. When she started losing big, Klever took over for her and simply wrecked the house even before his exorbitant luck stat came into play.

He won so big the cats began to worship him as a god and offered him a miniature cat-Buddha statue as a prize—er, offering—but because it was a playtest, he couldn't take it out with him.

After that, they engaged in card and board games with the cats, and despite having luxurious hotel rooms of their own, they ended up crashing and falling asleep in the cats' tatami room.

In a certain sense, he did spend a night with two young women, but there were impenetrable walls of meaning that existed between the sound of those words and the actual reality of the situation. Plus, there were hundreds of cats with them.

"We basically spent all night with the hotel cats, playing games. I haven't had a night like that since I was in school. It was fun, but there wasn't anything seedy about it."

Thinker looked confused. "But from what I heard," he said, "there were swimsuits and princess carries involved... Plus, when you woke up—"

"Sorry. Someone's here."

The intercom had just rung with impeccable timing. Klever

scampered down to the front door, expecting a package delivery or something like that. This distraction would give him a minute or two to think of an excuse for what Thinker was about to say.

It took no more than three seconds for that plan to completely fall apart.

When he opened the door, he saw a black-haired teenage girl wearing a school uniform waiting there.

"Hello, Detective. I'm sorry for barging in on you like this," she said. "A family member sent me some wild herbs, and it was an enormous amount, so I thought I'd share some with…huh? Do you have a visitor?"

Thinker had come forward from the back room, drawn by the sound of her melodious voice.

Nayuta had been paying visits to Klever's office recently for tutoring sessions. At first they were solely in VR, but because the messages from Koyomi and other online friends were a constant distraction, she had started visiting his office in real life instead.

She would have hesitated to do this if it were simply his home, but the building also functioned as an office. Not only did it have all the proper accoutrements for receiving guests, but he had purged as much of the lived-in feel as possible to make it feel just like a regular office. This had helped her feel a bit better about the idea of visiting him here.

When she saw Thinker, Nayuta gave him a very careful and proper bow. "It's nice to meet you. I'm Nayuta, a friend of Mr. Kurei's. He's been very helpful to me…"

"Oh, uh, it's nice to meet you too… Uh…Klever…?" Thinker fixed Klever with a very pointed and painful gaze. "This appears to be an even more beautiful young lady than the story suggested…"

"I'm sure you won't believe me, regardless of what I say, but I can promise you I have not done anything that violates common decency," he claimed desperately.

Thinker gave him a very understanding look, then a gentle pat on the shoulder. "Well, I don't want to intrude, so I'll take my leave now. We should get together with Mr. Torao to discuss this in more detail sometime."

"Discuss…? Not torture me?"

"Well, that will depend on what you have to say for yourself… Can't say anything more than that."

Thinker quickly saw himself out of the office. Nayuta watched him go and whispered, "Have I seen him somewhere before…? I'm sorry, Detective, was I interrupting something?"

"No…it's not a problem. We were done talking business. He was going to be leaving anyway."

As an adult, he could not afford to show any nerves over the situation. If there was one thing the detective was determined to do successfully, this was it.

Nayuta walked hesitantly into the office, removed an apron from her school bag, and put it on over her uniform. With comfortable familiarity, she stepped into the kitchen and began preparing the wild herbs.

"They also sent me some soba noodles with the herbs," she called out. "I take it you'd be happy with some fresh soba for dinner? It will take a little time to prepare, so feel free to do some work in the meantime."

"…Sure. Thank you," he said simply, and sat down at his desk.

Even he didn't know where he'd gone wrong to cause this to happen.

The main issue was that spending time together in the VR detective's office had given them a natural familiarity even in person, in real life. But as Thinker's reaction made clear, this was a very bad situation, socially speaking.

So what do I do…?

He was confident in his logic skills. But most of the world was occupied by situations where logic alone did not rule the day.

Without having a good answer for how to proceed, Klever chose instead to escape his problems by opening up his work e-mails to see what was new.

Welcome to the Cat Inn— Maneki-ya Hot Spring Resort Hotel

Rising unnaturally out of distant rural mountains, this torii-gate-shaped twin-tower high-rise hotel was never intended to be put into the game.

In fact, some of the company's designers put this VR space together for personal relaxation without informing their bosses. Members of the personnel, business, and legal teams were free to take part in development as well.

It's tempting to think of this as a massive project that transcended company departments, but given the purpose of its creation, it was inevitable that when management found out, some started crying "salary thieves!" at its designers.

However, the quality of the environment, created out of stress and frustration at not having enough paid holidays, was tremendous. At the insistence of Chief Technical Officer Tochimori, it was added to the game.

As a result of the interests of the designers, the cat-type AIs that run the hotel exhibit some strange behaviors. During a playtest conducted by outside contractors, they happened to be on strike, and made several demands in order to come back to work.

The details will not be revealed here, but I can tell you that the programmer in charge of making adjustments did utter the words, "Is it really safe to allow them to keep pet hamsters...?"

Chapter 2

Feast of the Monster Rats

Klever the detective had multiple faces.

There was the face of the tour guide for foreign visitors to the Japanese-themed MMO *Asuka Empire*.

The face of the helpful contractor with connections to the game's developers, available to investigate and test errors.

The face of the consultant making use of his position to assist businesses in pulling off brand collaborations with *Asuka Empire*.

And the face of Kaisei Kurei, CEO of Clover's Network Security Corporation, a boutique security company in the real world.

"…So which one is your main income? What's the total?"

"I have absolutely zero reason to tell you that."

They were at the Three-Leaf Detective Agency on a day off.

From his desk, Klever flatly shut down Koyomi the ninja's prying personal question. Over in the simple kitchen, Nayuta put on some tea and interjected wearily, "Koyomi, you shouldn't ask things like that. It's a violation of privacy."

Koyomi held up a two-tailed *nekomata* by the front paws, making it dance on two legs, and sulked. "But I'm curious! If it's over 10,000,000 yen a year, then there's a molecule-size chance he might actually get to marry you, and I need to know about it!"

At some point in the past, she had responded to one of Koyomi's frequent marriage proposals with a counter that she'd consider it if her income crossed 10,000,000 yen per year.

"You should learn to recognize an obvious joke. Besides, only one in a thousand people in their twenties has an annual income over 10,000,000 yen. I'm not looking for the sun and stars here."

Klever shrugged. "You could probably get that if you wanted... but I think the percentage of people depends on which source you're using. You'll find a slightly higher rate of people claiming an income that high through sources that get their data through self-reporting, like marriage advice companies or career change websites, but the Ministry of Labor's survey had that number at 0.0 percent, if I recall. If it's only to a single decimal point, then I can't tell you anything more detailed than that, but I think we can assume it's fewer than one in a thousand. If we're limiting ourselves to people in their twenties, there are professional baseball and soccer players, horse racing jockeys and boat racers, best-selling authors, hit entertainers, investment bankers and traders, big media types...plus managers of restaurants, hosts, and hostesses can make major money if they're on the successful side. Listing them all out like that makes it sound like there are tons of such people out there, but in total numbers, it's quite small, of course. When you include thirties and later, you'll see doctors, executives in major businesses, and some public servants, but reaching 10,000,000 yen in your twenties is a serious challenge."

Koyomi's eyes narrowed. "I'm not so sure about that... And are you saying when you look at the data from marriage advice companies and career change websites, more of those people are lying?"

"Well, you can't be sure. There are going to be some people who are lying to protect their own pride or trying to defraud others, but beyond that, the data from those sources are people who already have income of a certain level and are thinking of marriage or a new career. That alone will severely limit the pool of responses. For example, an official ministry survey will include student workers and part-timers, but most of the career-change entries will already have a job, and all of the data points are people who want a new job. On the other hand, the Ministry of Labor's numbers are limited to those who have some taxable income withheld, so it won't include students who aren't working or people who aren't currently employed at all. If you added them to the pool, the ratio would get even smaller."

Koyomi turned and pointed the *nekomata*'s pads toward Klever. "Objection! This is irrelevant to the topic of *your* income, Detective!"

"...Look, I just put a lot of effort into distracting you from that, so I'd appreciate it if you rewarded my effort by being distracted," Klever replied, his foxlike eyes narrowing. "Besides, my income is entirely dependent on volume. If I get a couple of high-paying jobs in a row, it'll go up, and if my gigs dry up for a while, it'll go down. It's an inherently unstable field, so the variation from year to year is big."

Nayuta was getting tired of the conversation. She caressed Koyomi's head.

"I understand you're curious, but it's just poor manners to ask for that kind of information, Koyomi."

"...And how do you *really* feel?"

"If it's low, I'll feel the pain of sympathy and pity, and if it turns out to be high and he's just hanging around playing this game all the time, it wouldn't sit right with me. So I would prefer not to know," Nayuta explained.

The detective nodded along. "That's the right decision. But let me stress that I *am* doing my job right now. I spend much less time actually playing the game than working. Please don't get the wrong idea."

At the in-game PC tool set at his desk where he performed his work, the detective sipped a cup of Nayuta's black tea. It was virtual, so it did nothing for his hydration, but it was a perfectly acceptable way to enjoy the flavor and atmosphere.

Koyomi grumbled to herself. "Well, it's not like I was expecting a serious answer. It's just that the detective's vibes are so sketchy that it feels like, I dunno…he hides too much personal information already! He doesn't need to tell us his income, but would it kill you to at least spill a little work tea? If you can't even vent a little, you're not much more than an NPC."

"Are you kidding? Security work, consulting, playtesting, detective work—all of these things revolve around confidentiality. The only things I can talk to you about are the weather and what I've eaten," the detective boasted.

She ignored this and raised a hand. "Ooh! I want to hear about your dating history! Once I've heard that, then I can decide whether Nayu's safe or not around you!"

"If anything demands confidentiality, it's that."

She was getting nowhere. Of course, both of them were just playfully bantering with the other, knowing what the response would be already. The fact they were friendly enough to trade barbs like this without giving offense was a good sign.

Nayuta tugged back on Koyomi's leash. It was like watching a mischievous mini-Shiba trying to play with the bushy tail of a malicious fox.

"Let's stop interfering with his work now. Koyomi, the time for the update with the new quest is approaching. You were looking forward to Beast Hunt: Genroku Capybara Scroll, right?" she said, referring to this week's new quest, a kind of treasure hunt event.

Bizarrely enough, it involved combing through a huge horde of capybaras in search of a lost wombat that had wandered into their midst. But as the recommended level of 1 and up, the lack of an age limitation, and a fear factor of zero would suggest, this was just a fun-time event for kids.

The sponsor brand for this event was actually a zoo. It wasn't even a submission to the 108 Apparitions event. It was categorized not as one of the One Hundred Tales or Seven Mysteries, but as a miscellaneous Tour Guide event instead.

This category included the resort hotel from the other day—a catch-all for new recreational destinations without much story or a challenge to be overcome.

"Yeah, I can't wait!" Koyomi said, hopping down from the couch. "The Golden Week special project! All the capybaras you can squeeze! You're going to climb Mt. Fuji as a guide after this, right, Detective? Me and Nayu are gonna go squish some capybaras! We'll squish 'em for all they're worth!"

"…Uh, yeah. I hope you enjoy it," Klever said, somewhat taken aback by the intensity of her reaction. He waved his hand at her in a shooing motion.

"Well, we're going to be off, then. We'll send you a message when we're done," Nayuta said, grabbing Koyomi and bowing before she left the office.

For some reason, the enormous black cat-Buddha statue outside his door was covering both eyes with its paws in the "see no evil" pose. The statue often sported a new configuration whenever they saw it, and they were used to it by now. The pair gave the holy figure another quick bow and trotted down the stairs.

§

Yoiyami Street at the start of the weeklong holiday was busier than usual.

Every business seemed to be booming, and there was no end to the customers for those offering limited-time items for the holiday, whether goods or food.

Nayuta and Koyomi bought some dried persimmon cake bars from a large white ape monster called a *shojo* that was manning its own cart. No sooner had Koyomi taken a single bite than she was exclaiming, "Ooh, this is surprisingly good! It's not just for flavor—there are real dried persimmons in here!"

Despite the way she was describing virtual food as "real," Nayuta understood what she meant.

"It looks like there's both persimmon paste in the batter and large slices of dried persimmon mixed in, too. Do you think these exist in real life, too?" asked Koyomi.

"Hmm. I think baking it like you bake a cake would cause the dried persimmons' flavor to change. I guess these are destined to be virtual sweets only."

Until recently, VR foods had evolved rapidly in an attempt to re-create real-life flavors as accurately as possible. Now that the level of fidelity had reached a certain point, developers were putting their effort into tastes and flavors that were impossible in reality.

Vanilla-flavored peas, tangerines with the texture of watermelon, French fries that never got cold—the VR gourmet market was in an expansion phase in all directions.

"But then there was that one we tried recently that was really awful... Remember the tire-flavored donut...?" Koyomi asked.

"...That was just a tire, nothing more," Nayuta said.

The flip side of that experimentation was that many attempts were duds.

After a while, they reached the portal gate made to look like a streetcar station. The car itself was always at the platform. You simply had to get on board and select your destination, and within a few seconds you would be there.

It was possible to ride an actual streetcar, too, enjoying the ambience of Ayakashi Alley as it rocked you along, but that day they were only after the new quest.

Many other players with the same idea in mind were flooding into the train. While it looked just like a streetcar, its function was just a portal. Passengers on the car simply vanished as soon as they had paid their fare.

Nayuta and Koyomi waited in line, then selected their destination at the ticket machine. At the same moment the machine spit out their tickets, their field of view shuttered, and the car around them was in a new location.

In the 108 Apparitions, the number of players who could

attempt each kind of quest was limited in order to provide the proper horror experience.

"Dares" were solo events that could only be done alone.

"Linked fates" were only for those party members you came with.

"Chance encounters" might involve a number of other parties you might run across.

And "cosmic mysteries" were quests with no real restriction, where any and every player attempting the quest would be present in the same place.

The capybara event was treated as a cosmic mystery, so there were tons of other players in the area. In fact, it was like a zoo just after opening, with players streaming from the streetcar in a constant flow.

Nayuta and Koyomi were part of that flow, and found themselves gasping when they saw what awaited them.

It was a sea of brown fur as far as the eye could see.

Beneath a beautiful blue sky, a horde of fat round capybaras simply covered the ground. Some milled about slowly, but at least eighty percent of them were just lazing in place. The numerous players who'd arrived before them were like little dots in an ocean of fur.

Koyomi's voice trembled with emotion.

"H-holy crap... This is it... This is the crowning achievement of humanity! We're charting new ground in the VR experience! The true story behind the hit Hollywood movie!"

She was trying so hard to stretch her meager vocabulary that she had resorted to nonsense by the third sentence. This was nothing new for Koyomi.

"I feel like technically speaking, this is actually very simple. It's just a very, very, very high number of them," Nayuta pointed out, although she was blown away as well.

The eye test said there were hundreds of thousands of capybaras, perhaps over a million, all in this one field. They were treated as indestructible objects by the game, so no attack could harm them, and there was no worry of being attacked, either.

Amid the waves of brown fur ahead, players were swept off their feet and helplessly carried along on the backs of capybaras. There was a bit of walkable space just ahead, but if they kept going farther in, that walking space simply ceased to be.

Inevitably, players wound up buried in capybara up their heads and were forced to push and crawl across the backs of the creatures to move onward.

"...And the wombat is more likely to appear the farther you go in, right?"

"Yep! I'm headin' in! Yahoooo!"

Koyomi jumped up onto a stone wall that acted as a breaker, and leaped right into one of the more concentrated capybara packs. Her tiny figure was soon buried in the furry sea, and Nayuta completely lost sight of her.

"...Uhm..."

Yes, they were cute, but they were still wild animals. And there were scores of them everywhere.

Uncertain if she wanted to follow her friend in that way, Nayuta took a look around instead. The map was under a brilliantly blue sky.

While this wasn't a user-submitted quest, which would make standards a bit different, it was very rare to see anything affiliated with the 108 Apparitions happening under a sunny sky.

The home ground of the event, Ayakashi Alley, was always shrouded in night, and the whole thing was horror-themed to begin with, so many of the quests happened to take place at night, too.

Some memorable exceptions were Hell Within the Mists, which was set during daytime to make use of its thick white mist, and One Short, which involved a search for a missing person in deep woods under a gloomy gray layer of clouds. Still, these were quite rare.

Of course, a quest like this, which resembled a sunny weekend petting zoo and had no seeming connection to horror at all, was a major curveball.

Nayuta surveyed the writhing mass of capybara beneath the spacious blue sky above.

It would be one thing if this were an endless horde of crocodiles, sharks, giant monsters, or zombies. But they were capybaras.

In real life, they could be a threat to an ecosystem or cropland, but this was a game, so that was no concern.

As the nearest capybaras plodded by beneath her, Nayuta considered again if she should go in after Koyomi. If she did, it didn't seem likely she'd actually catch up to Koyomi at this point. And even if she did catch up, she likely still wouldn't have been able to do anything about it.

The only thing she could see around her was players struggling against the swarm of capybaras. The lone safe area to walk was the outer rim above the stone wall.

The goal of this event was to find a small minority of wombats somewhere in the midst of the capybara horde. It wasn't a limited thing; there was about one wombat for every five hundred capybaras, and finding one caused another to spawn somewhere else in the arena.

Catching a wombat earned you a lottery ticket, which would be used in a drawing for rare items during the summer vacation event three months later. Each player could only have up to fifty lottery tickets, and you could only catch three wombats per day, so there were various tricky rules and limitations. Probably the best and most proper way to enjoy this event was to not think about it and savor the experience of being buried by capybaras.

Nayuta heard a text message notification. She opened her window and read the message.

I can't get out.

She took in Koyomi's plea for help and sat down on the grass.

A nearby capybara took her for a nice cushion and climbed on top of her knees. The combination of weight and warmth was quite pleasant.

The sensation of the fur was probably softer than that of a real capybara. She couldn't feel any bone structure underneath. These were closer to plush capybaras.

As she pet the creature and got lost in the soaring blue of the sky, there came a sudden cry from off to the side.

"Found one! A wombat!"

Another player had spotted one of the wombats in question.

A moment later, a small brown blob of fur came charging toward Nayuta, immobilized under the capybara. She reached out with both hands in a panic and caught it. Instantly, her heart was captured by the adorable creature.

It had big, black, gentle eyes; a flat, rounded nose; short, thick limbs; and a plushie's squeezability. There were no downsides to this animal.

The rump was oddly hard, but Nayuta already knew this was a feature of the real-life wombat. She'd never touched one, though, so she didn't know if the texture was any different.

A little girl dressed in a miko's robes pointed at the wombat clinging to Nayuta and shrilled, "Awww! See, Papa? They run away if you chase them. You have to approach slowly and welcome them that way!"

"Sorry, sorry... Ah, so that's how you catch them..."

Simply spotting one of the targets didn't mean you could just run pell-mell after them. If an ambush was more effective, then it seemed clear differences in player stats were not going to be important in this event, so beginners and children could be just as successful as veteran players.

Above the head of the wombat in Nayuta's arms appeared a pop-up window saying CAUGHT. That meant no one else could take it away and earn the points for it. She felt bad seeing the other players trudge away in disappointment.

So there she was, capybara on her lap and wombat in her arms, gazing up at the sky.

Huh...? Wait, I can't move...

All she had to do was let go of the wombat, then push the capybara off her legs. She could do that whenever she wanted, but the sensation was so soft and warm and cuddly. If there was a good reason to do so, she would be able to free herself, but she couldn't see that reason right now.

Eventually, another capybara came and pressed itself up against her back. Two more hemmed her in on the left and right, and then she was truly surrounded.

As the wandering capybaras began to bury her, Nayuta came to an understanding.

People cannot resist the fluff.

Sweets can be resisted, due to the fear of gaining weight.

But there is no downside to fluffiness. You cannot fight it.

Prone, sideways, buried, sinking, drifting, rocking along, her soul adrift and melting into a plane of pure bliss.

...Uh-oh. This is bad...I think I'm stuck...

Her sense of the passage of time got fuzzy. Her vision was completely blocked by a wombat tummy when she finally noticed she had received a message. It was difficult even to move amid the sea of fur, but Nayuta managed to move the wombat aside and open her player window.

The message was from Koyomi.

H E L P M E

Nayuta considered this plea as the waves of warmth overwhelmed her. There was no doubt she was in basically the same situation as Koyomi.

I can't. I'm buried too. Also, I don't know where you are.
The response was prompt.
stuck in a bunch of fur
Yes, I know.
capybara bad news
I know that, too.
no wombats
I managed to catch one.
!!
It's resting on my head now.
traitor!
Why am I a traitor...? If you want to meet up again, why don't you log out? I think I can break free, but it sounds like you can't get back even if you try at this point.
You should come here, Nayu.
But I don't know where to find you...
I'll shoot off a signal flare, so you come bounding over the capybaras' backs. Please come now come quick come hurry hurry

When Koyomi's typing got weird, you had to be very careful about how you dealt with her. Nayuta quickly grew tired of the pointless back-and-forth and pushed the furballs out of the way to sit up.

She said "bound over their backs," but they're so soft, I don't think that's even possible.

As she got upright, however, she saw a little ball of fire the size of a fist rising from the sea of fur in the distance. Koyomi's Fire Escape technique was at a very low skill level, so it was almost completely useless in battle, but she'd found a good use for it here, at least.

Nayuta tried to get on the backs of the nearby capybaras and found they were very soft and almost useless as footholds.

Wait, but if they're considered impervious, then maybe...

On a sudden whim, Nayuta tried out the Unrivaled Leap skill. This was an advanced version of the Eight-Boat Leap, which improved one's jumping distance and caused one's feet to deal damage.

This would hurt any enemies you used it near, but in the case of an indestructible object…

There was a hard *clink* sound, and Nayuta bounced through the air again.

Oh! I think this will work!

It wasn't the capybara's back she had touched, but a pale barrier above it that indicated an indestructible object. They appeared when said object was the target of an attack, so it wouldn't have shown up if she merely jumped, but because it was Unrivaled Leap, she got an extra step to jump off.

Using this to glide through the air, Nayuta quickly sped to the area where she'd seen the fireball rise. The moment she came to a stop, she sank into the sea of capybaras, but she knew Koyomi was buried somewhere nearby.

The beasts were stacked three, four, five deep there, so even with Nayuta's height, her feet couldn't touch the ground. The ground sank lower there, apparently. As the poofy fur rose up to her head, Nayuta called out, "Koyomi, are you there? Say something if you hear me!"

"…Naaayuuu…Koyomi iiiis…down heeeeere…," came an elongated call from a few paces away.

Nayuta dove into the mass of capybara and thrust a thin arm in the direction she was guessing.

Her fingers poked into a squishy cheek.

"Oh. Is that your cheek, Koyomi?"

"Hweh? No…I don't think that's me."

"Eeek! S-sorry!"

Nayuta quickly withdrew her finger, afraid she had poked a total stranger. But there was no cry of protest or anger.

"…Hmm…? Is that you, Nayu? I feel something soft and dangly like a sleeve…"

Now it was Koyomi who'd brushed up against something. But nobody was touching Nayuta.

"No, I don't think that's me. Um, is there someone else there?"

There was no response, but it was clear that someone—or something—else was buried in the swarm of capybaras.

Nayuta parted the fur until she finally arrived at the answer. She also saw Koyomi's face peeking through from the other side.

"Oh! Nayu!"

"Koyomi! We finally found each other. But…"

There was another person between the two friends.

An unfamiliar girl wearing a long *kariginu* robe. Her eyes were closed, and she seemed to be sleeping—but there was one strange detail that definitely stood out about her.

Koyomi swallowed hard, and Nayuta was at a loss for words.

The little girl sleeping amid the capybaras had two little horns extending from her forehead.

§

"…And so you escorted her back here?"

It was evening at the Three-Leaf Detective Agency.

Klever had finished his tour guide reservation and returned to the office, and he seemed to be regretting not simply logging out of the game entirely.

In addition to the usual two, he was playing host to a silent young girl in a *kariginu* robe. She looked as old as an elementary school girl, but she had two small horns growing from her forehead, and her knuckles were spherical joints, suggesting she was a puppet or a doll of some kind.

However, the texture of her skin was the same as any other player, and her features were well-composed and adorable.

Koyomi gave the girl a little pat on the head and said, "I don't even know if you can use the word 'escorted,' because she's treated as an item, not even an NPC. She's registered as a tool. It's called a 'demon puppet.'"

This took Klever by surprise. "Demon puppet? I've never heard of that item before. Where did you find it?"

"She was buried in the capybaras," Nayuta explained. "Koyomi and I found her almost simultaneously...but because I touched her first, I got ownership. I don't even know how to use her, though..."

"What does the item explanation say?"

Nayuta read it off for him. "It just says, 'she still slumbers'..."

"Hmm. A key item for the event, perhaps."

It was still very strange to see this young girl dressed as an *onmyoji* be treated as an item by the game.

"Ya think Tora-tora would explain it to us if you asked?" inquired Koyomi, who was barely any taller than the girl. She leaned over and rubbed her cheek against the puppet's.

Torao, who could be found at the Cat-God Worship Research Society next door to the detective's, was an engineer on the development team. Nayuta and Koyomi had met him a few times, but it was Klever who was tied to him at the hip, because they were such valuable business partners.

"That might not be so easy. Mr. Torao explains things that are necessary to know for business concerns like playtests and error-hunting, but he doesn't tell me anything related to in-game strategy—not that I really want to ask, either. It's just not fair."

For once in her life, Koyomi looked to be deep in thought.

"Hmm... Well, I'm not begging to ask him, either...it's just... something seems weird about this..."

"What is it that's bothering you?"

"I just think...she was buried in the capybaras, yeah? Just dunked under them. Not in a treasure chest, no event activation. Isn't that weird? And it's a cosmic mystery, so there were tons of other people around, but it seems like Nayu was the only person in the entire place who'd found something like this."

Nayuta seemed perturbed by it, too. "I checked some strategy sites and message boards, but I didn't see anyone talking about finding something along these lines. Either I just happen to be the first person to find one, or she's a one-of-a-kind thing..."

"Or it's a developer error, eh?" murmured Klever. He couldn't just blame anything he wanted to on developer mistakes or bugs, but little things got corrected all the time in online games. This was probably something to tell Torao about. "All right. I'll give him a report rather than a request for information. If he doesn't respond, then it's probably as programmed, or they might make an adjustment without any announcement. Is that acceptable?"

"Yes, please do that. It's hard to say if this was meant to be public or not. If anyone asks me what that is, I don't even think I can tell them, and I'm technically the owner."

"Understood. I'm rather curious myself."

Klever added a screenshot to a simple message and sent it to Torao. He was just getting back to his desk to continue working when someone knocked on the door to the agency.

"Ah, it's good to see you again, ladies," a small, hunchbacked man wearing a Shinto priest's robes said, waving. On the other side of his round lenses, his sleepy eyes twinkled with mirth.

"Mr. Torao? Did you come over when you saw the message?" asked Klever, hurriedly getting to his feet.

"Yes, I just stepped out."

They were located right next door, but a response this fast was out of the ordinary. The cat-god priest, who also worked as the chief of the error-testing lab, patted the back of his own head and stood before the group.

"It's good to see you too, Mr. Torao."

"Hey, Tora-tora, wassup?"

"Glad you're both looking well," he said, waving off Nayuta and Koyomi's idiosyncratic greetings. Then he fixed the demon puppet girl with a look. "Here we are...I really didn't expect that you, of all people, would find her. Where was she?"

Klever looked to Nayuta. She and Koyomi had found the girl, and he wasn't even there when it happened.

Nayuta folded her hands in front of her and explained, as coolly as a receptionist, "At the capybara event that began today. She was buried under the swarm of capybaras."

Although her tone of voice was exactly the same, to Klever it sounded like she was softer and warmer than when she'd first met him. Part of that was just being more familiar with them, but it also seemed to him like she'd gotten over something, and was viewing the world with a more positive outlook.

Torao, on the other hand, had an awkward, guilty-looking smile plastered across his face. "Ah, I see. Where better to hide a tree than in the forest... Pardon me."

He flipped back the sleeve of the girl's robe to check a tag there.

"Demon puppet, support model, Onihime replica Number Eight—ah, yes, there's the missing Number Eight. Now..." He glanced back at the others over his glasses. "I assume you'd appreciate an explanation?"

Klever, Nayuta, and Koyomi nodded silently, eliciting a heavy sigh from the man.

"First of all, thank you for the report... I'm guessing you sent me that line because you were concerned this might be the result of a mistake on our part?"

Nayuta nodded, but Klever only grimaced awkwardly.

"No, I thought it might be a secret item or something tied to an event. I wasn't expecting a response from you, but the girls were suspicious, so just in case, I decided to send you that message," he said.

Torao nodded to himself. "Well, you're both right. We did make a mistake, but it is also an intended part of the game, you might say. This is very difficult to explain, because there are many twists and turns—you might say this state of affairs shows how much this current event is just a stopgap due to a lack of manpower...," he said, a roundabout way of prefacing his explanation. Klever could already sense this was going to be a long story, and snuck off to make more tea.

§

Torao's story about the early stages of the plan to implement the demon puppet could be broken down into a few bullet points.

- The "dare" quests that could only be done solo often had wild swings in advantage or disadvantage depending on the player's job. This had been viewed as a trouble point from the start.
- They were able to get away without much trouble by setting the enemies to be weaker, but as they got further into the second half of the event, the team decided they needed to include some heartier dares with stronger enemies.
- In order to mediate the difficulty gap between jobs, therefore, the team decided to introduce a "demon puppet" automaton to assist players in battle.
- Players in melee combat roles could have a support puppet, while support players could have a melee puppet, allowing anyone to tackle any dare quest with a heavy emphasis on combat.

That much was fine. The difficulty and twists and turns started after that point.

Torao sank into the sofa and stared up at the ceiling.

"The first argument was about how to handle the demon puppets. Do we treat them like mercenaries with a rental fee? Do we allow players to own them and customize them to their liking? How do we introduce them? How do you earn them? Which quests will they apply to? We had plenty of suggestions. But we don't have much time. And sure enough, there was some confusion between the senior management and the dev team."

They nodded, urging him to continue. The detective and Nayuta were listening closely, while Koyomi held a cat bot in her arms and was already starting to nod off.

Torao ignored her and continued: "Management wanted to use the demon puppets as the big tie-in promotion with a hot new clothing company. They got them involved in the design, drew up the reveal quest and tie-in details, and had a date set for the unveiling. While I can't tell you the name of the company...I can tell you they were bought out by a major corporation without warning in March."

"...Yikes..."

Klever face-palmed. He could easily imagine the kind of chaos and confusion that would result from an event like that.

Torao smirked. "Yes, as you can imagine, the other company had to change their internal strategy, and we had no choice but to shelve the tie-in project. But the team still wanted to up the difficulty on the dare quests and to have a means of counteracting that. We still needed the puppets, so we whipped up new costumers and prepared a debut event on our own this time. We'd hide a few inactive puppets in certain quests so players would discover them, and their curiosity would spread by word of mouth. Then, before too much time had passed, we'd throw in a quest about the puppets to introduce them formally."

Nayuta, who'd been listening to his story intently, considered what he'd just said. "It seems like a fine plan... So does that mean it was intended for me to find her the way I did?"

She looked across the room at the immobile puppet girl.

Torao's shoulders slumped. "We were preparing for that. It was a lightning-speed process after the tie-in went kaput...to the extent we even had to send a few members of the error-testing team to help. And that's when the higher-ups suddenly said, 'Let's not distribute the puppets with rare drops, but make them all store-bought items to juice up the income.' I'll be honest—I wanted to beat them to death with my own two hands."

He was normally a genial and aloof fellow, but now Torao had a dark smile on his face, and there was no mirth in his eyes. Klever and Nayuta avoided his gaze, and inadvertently locked eyes instead.

"Umm…it sounds like the dev team has had it tough…"

"You hear about it all the time…but when you're running a long-term event based on user-submitted entries, having a bunch of unexpected changes in direction must be an absolute killer," Klever added.

"So you understand our plight," Torao said weakly. "Honestly, it wouldn't matter as long as we had the time to do it. But when you don't have the time or the people to implement such a thing, the last thing you want is people changing their minds on a whim." It seemed their sympathy was helping to quell his anger.

His voice still dropped further, however. "We went along with their request. We had already sprinkled a few puppets around within quests, treating them like mystery items, on a timer that was set to reveal them around the start of the Golden Week holiday. But if they were going to be sold exclusively in the shop, we'd have to recover them all. Fortunately, it was easy to recover about ninety percent of them. We'd made their positions clear already, so it was a quick job. But that last ten percent, we were unable to recover. They went missing."

Klever raised his hand and asked, "If I'm guessing correctly, were the last ten percent under the purview of Mr. Endou, who got hired away from the company?"

He had personally known that engineer until April, when he abruptly took a job with a different company. They hadn't been in touch since then.

Torao pressed his fingers to his eyelids. "I don't blame him. He wasn't a full-time employee, had as much work as anyone, and got so much crap that anyone would be furious in that position… Basically, he was the only one who knew where the puppets he placed are hidden."

Nayuta was shocked by this. "You didn't share such an important piece of information among the team?"

"You've really hit on a sore spot," Torao said, hanging his head. "Of course, that would ordinarily be unthinkable. But we had an

extreme schedule, a small team doing consecutive all-nighters...
We couldn't keep up informing each other; everyone was focused
on their own work. So each individual person who hid the puppets was on their own. We had a broad outline of how the different quests broke down, but once they'd been divided up, the
boss wasn't asking us which quests, which locations, and which
requirements we'd set up for the puppets to be found. And just
after we'd finally hidden them all was when the order went out
to bring them all back in. There were a couple other reasons
involved, but that was the straw that broke the camel's back.
Endou threw a fit, deleted his work history and backup in a rage,
and quit just like that. He'd been getting offers for a while, and
I think it was an inevitable choice to make. If we could throw
more people at the problem, we could've found the rest, but realizing the mood around the team, leadership decided to give up
on searching and treated the last ten percent as missing objects.
Given the needs of the schedule, we canceled that process and
prioritized other jobs. I think that was a wise decision."

His outrage at the carelessness of the upper management was
palpable. Nayuta cast a sorrowful gaze at the adorable little puppet girl.

"...I'm sorry. The more I hear about this, the more you're
beginning to sound like a cursed item."

Inwardly, Klever agreed.

"And that's not the end of the comedy," Torao smirked. "We
settled on distributing the demon puppets by selling them in the
store, but now management and development are arguing over
that decision again. It's not about the cost of it, but how it will
affect the gameplay and balance. Makes me glad I'm sequestered
out here on QA."

Klever just patted him on the shoulder.

The fact of the matter was that *Asuka Empire*'s developers were
quite excellent at what they did. Their initial plans and ability to
act on them might have been overly ambitious, but despite the

concerns, the 108 Apparitions event was a success, and the business tie-ins they'd conducted so far were going well.

A group of incompetents would never have gotten this far, and Klever was very impressed with what they had achieved.

The problem was that not every single member of the company was top-class, and some of them managed to sabotage things with exquisitely bad timing. This was the sort of thing that happened inevitably with companies, and it was usually the development team or the players who took the brunt of the damage.

Torao patted the demon puppet on the head. "So anyway," he said, "we're still not sure what exactly we're going to do with her. The one you've found here is definitely one of the models we placed in advance, but they're not meant to be handed out to the players."

"Meaning...you've got to confiscate her?" Klever asked.

"If we forcibly removed items ordinary players had found on their own, it would affect public trust in the game," Torao snorted. "For one thing, it's not buggy or glitched, and we've decided we're putting them in the game. They're not strong enough to destroy the game balance, and they're not *that* useful. So...here's what I have to ask you, Kurei. Would you folks care to do a little live beta testing for me?"

Klever's ears perked up. There was no reason Torao would go on and on, revealing the embarrassing dirty laundry of the team completely unprompted.

I see. So he wants regular players to try out the puppet and get their feedback, which he can take to the negotiations between management and development, and get them to wrap it up...

In Torao's mind, he probably had an ideal solution to this quandary. He just lacked the evidence he could use to convince both sides of his wisdom.

Of course, there was no way they'd called the leader of the error-testing QA department to a debate like that, but he might be able to slip a report into a colleague's hands.

"...Very well. So you'd like us to use the puppet in live battle and give you a report on how it was? You're the owner of the puppet, Nayuta. Can you do that?"

"I don't mind—but I'm not sure how to actually use it. Will it move?" Nayuta asked.

Torao smacked his fist into his palm. "Oh, right! It's not clear, is it? Uh, if you look at the back of her head, there should be a coin slot right around the nape of her neck."

"A coin slot," Nayuta repeated skeptically, sensing something unpleasant was coming.

Torao innocently lifted up the back of the girl's hair. "It works for twelve minutes on ten sen and two hours for one hundred sen. The coins are handled digitally, so this is basically only for show. If you put your hand up to the slot, the coins emerge and are subtracted from your balance automatically. This is another thing we're arguing about now... Some people want to have the transactions use real money, but that's obviously going to severely diminish the number of players who use it. For now, this one runs on the in-game currency, so don't worry about the cost. If the puppets do end up being on a rental system, it'll probably be around one hundred yen for two hours."

"That sounds like it will earn an insignificant amount of money and a significant amount of hate from the players," Klever said frankly. Torao laughed.

"And the issue of usability and player sentiment is more important than the price. Forcing players to do a bunch of small transactions is a hassle that will backfire, and they'd make more profit by just selling them for 5,000 yen a pop or so. Personally speaking, I'd prefer the units themselves be free or rewards for finishing a quest, with custom parts and cosmetics sold for a price. It's an easier path to doing more business collaborations and more likely to get players to willingly spend money."

Nayuta stared at the coin slot on the oni girl's neck and frowned. "In any case, actually activating her requires you to put the coin in, right? That seems annoying enough on its own..."

"Well, it's just *too* convenient for them to be usable without any limitations," said Torao, scratching his head. "They're only supposed to be a support system for people playing jobs that are unsuited for solo play. We want them to be used only when they're needed, not all the time. For now, the time when you're walking around town or have them in your item bag won't count as active time. It'll only count down while you're exploring the dungeon or in combat. The idea is that it'll sit in your item list most of the time and only come out when a powerful foe emerges. There's a helpful tutorial manual that pops up on your first use, so make sure you read that. Also, two more warnings."

He held up two fingers.

"Demon puppets can't be used in PvP combat. They'll act automatically against CPU opponents, but they shut down when around other players. We can't have the presence or lack of a puppet playing an outsize role in the outcome of those fights. Also, you can only have one puppet active within a party during a single fight. You only have the one right now, so it doesn't matter, but if the other members also had puppets, you wouldn't be able to have two or more active at the same time. Otherwise you'd have all the puppets fighting and the players wouldn't need to do a thing. Anyway, that's all."

With his explanation finished, Torao promptly turned to leave. Klever sensed a further secret in his haste to disengage. There was something he hadn't said, or something he didn't want them asking him, clearly—but he wasn't going to tell them anything if they stopped him.

After Torao left the office, Koyomi's eyes finally snapped open over on the couch.

"Mwah...? We done talking...?"

"You were completely passed out for a minute there. Mr. Torao just left."

She rubbed at her sleepy eyes and set down the *nekomata* she'd been clutching to her chest.

"Ohhh…I was so excited about the capybaras yesterday that I really didn't get much sleep last night… Well, seems like the detective's job is done, so shall we get going?" she suggested, giving Nayuta a look.

It was always nighttime in Ayakashi Alley, so it could throw off your sense of time. Nayuta checked her clock and found it was after five in the afternoon.

Klever had been thinking it was time to go back to the real world and start making dinner, but the end to that interaction had left him curious.

"You're done with your work for the day, right, Detective?"

"…Well, I don't have any real plans," he said obliviously. The way the girls looked at him reminded him of carnivorous hunters that had found their next prey.

Nayuta beamed at him. "I forgot to mention this to Mr. Torao… but there was a hidden area where we found the demon puppet."

"Yeah, and it seemed like there was gonna be some *crazy* treasure there! And it's super-hard to find this spot, so I'm pretty sure we were the first to get there!"

Klever pressed his fingers to the bridge of his nose. This was a treatment he'd earned by raising his character in such a bizarre way.

"So, Detective…I think you'd be a huge help."

"Um…may we ask you to come along with us?"

The lucky detective, who could increase the chance of rare drops by several percentage points single-handed, may not have been much good in battle, but that day he was brought along as though he were a special bonus accessory.

§

Even after the sun had gone down in the real world, the map of the Beast Hunt: Genroku Capybara Scroll quest was blessed with beautiful sunny weather.

It was right around the dinner hour, so there were fewer people around than just after it opened, but it was still quite crowded.

Once again, the sheer number of capybaras out there was unchanged in its majesty. The waves of brown fur, rising and falling, revealed the limbs of players trapped in their midst like the souls of the dead drowning in the pools of blood in Hell.

Nayuta and Koyomi had already enjoyed the experience quite a bit, but the detective, who was seeing it for the first time, couldn't stop his cheek from twitching.

"I know huge swarms of creatures are a staple of panic-based horror...but this is just horrible..."

Koyomi, who was already in a state of bliss, nodded absentmindedly.

"...Yeah, I know. Uh-huh...they're so cute, right? It's so adorable...but even still, there should be a limit to these things..."

Nayuta, on the other hand, had been intimidated by the sight at first but was now getting used to it. She picked up a capybara that came wandering over to sniff her and turned to the detective.

"Is it true that men don't have much interest in cute things like this?"

"It depends on the person, but I would not say I do. Torao might be a cat person...but you can't even imagine me being surrounded by pets or animal plushies, can you?"

Nayuta considered this question and said honestly, "I imagine every plushie you'd have would be a fox."

"...I see. Well, it's very nice that you have such a rich imagination."

It was a rather adorable mental image, actually, but Klever did not want to admit it.

Nayuta hopped up and down with the capybara in her arms. It was a bit lighter than the "luggage" she intended to carry soon, but she got a good mental image of what it would be like to hold it.

She had the character build of a fighter anyway, so a little extra weight was not going to affect her ability to move. The detective watched her with skepticism, lifting a hand to his chin.

"Nayuta…are you doing warm-up exercises?"

"Something like that. There's a bit of distance until the entrance to the secret area, so I'm going to use Unrivaled Leap to bounce on top of the capybaras. Koyomi's light enough to swim over there, but with your stats, I think you'll be immobilized if you sink under the capybaras—so I'm going to carry you."

If this were *ALfheim Online*, they could fly as needed, but sadly, *Asuka Empire* did not offer that function.

Abruptly, Klever did an about-face. "I've just remembered something I need to take care of. You two continue on without me."

Nayuta wasted no time in grabbing the detective's collar. "Which would you prefer," she asked, "carried piggyback or like a princess?"

"Neither."

"It might be difficult to balance if I'm carrying you on my shoulders. And having you slung over my shoulder, butt in the air, is going to put all of the weight on one side… I think piggyback would be best."

"No. I'm leaving."

Because of his total lack of strength, he couldn't even shake her hand loose. It was a reminder to Nayuta that he really needed a minimum of battle ability just to be able to protect himself.

Koyomi glared at him bitterly. "How can you refuse her offer of goodwill like this? How selfish are you…? You'll never be blessed with a greater honor. You shouldn't even have gotten the first chance!"

"Then let's make that statement true and never let it happen once. At any rate, I'm not…"

Koyomi clicked her tongue and pulled up her item list.

"Hey, Nayu…I've got a large wicker hamper here. It should be large enough to fit one detective inside. Let's toss him in there and take him with us."

"Good idea. I'll take that from you."

"Wait! Are you kidnapping me?!"

"Stop whining!"

Koyomi brandished the wicker hamper over her head and leaped at the detective like a wild animal, shoving the open mouth over his head. Over his protestations, she quickly jammed shut the woven lid.

"Detective, if you try to log out to get away, I'm going to have Nayu wear cat ears to your office tomorrow, and whenever you have visitors, she's going to explain that it was all to satisfy your personal tastes—"

The detective wailed something in protest, but his voice was too muffled to hear.

"That was a really wicked idea you just had, Koyomi," Nayuta said.

Koyomi just cackled. "No worries. It's just to make sure the detective doesn't run away. It's gonna be heavy— You sure you can lift it?"

"I won't be able to make any huge jumps, but if I run along with Unrivaled Leap, I think I can make it…"

Their destination was visible from there, at least. If she fell down, they'd just have to plow forward the slow way.

"Okay. See ya there!" said Koyomi, leaping into the sea of capybaras.

A few moments later, Nayuta held up the wicker hamper before her with the detective trapped inside.

"There we go… Now, please don't struggle, because it'll be dangerous. We'll be there before you know it."

The movement inside the hamper abruptly stopped in apparent resignation. He was much heavier than the plushie-like capybara, but as she expected, it wasn't so bad she couldn't run along.

Just as before, Nayuta was able to run along with Unrivaled Leap, making her own steps over the indestructible capybaras. She wasn't getting much height, as she expected—it was all she could do to keep alternating her legs—but she was making good progress anyway.

If she stopped for even a moment, she would fall through, so she kept running atop the translucent barriers that appeared one after the other for nearly twenty seconds until she neared their destination, which had no marker or visual symbol. That was where Nayuta stopped using her skill and sank into the stifling herd of capybaras.

She opened the lid on the wicker basket and freed her captive. "We're here, detective. It's right around this area," she told Klever's grumpy fox face as it popped out of the hamper.

Within moments, the hamper vanished without a trace. They were consumable quest items intended to temporarily hide the user. You might use one to hide from a killer inside a mansion or eavesdrop on NPC conversations, or smuggle yourself among other cargo—but this usage was probably not intended by the developers.

Klever pressed his fingers to his eyes. It looked like he was dealing with a headache.

"Nayuta...is there anything else you ought to say before warning me that we've arrived?"

"Umm...you aren't feeling queasy, are you?" she asked, unsure of what he meant.

Klever hung his head in disappointment. "Ah, yes...that ditzy side of yours reminds me so much of Daichi. I didn't think you were all that similar...but I suppose you are brother and sister, after all."

"I thought my brother was more serious and well-behaved than me... Anyway, Koyomi hasn't gotten here yet. Let's look for the entrance first."

When she was alone with the detective, the topic of conversation sometimes drifted to her late brother. In most cases it was harmless chit-chat, but Nayuta liked that. It was a tangible reminder to her that there was someone else out there who remembered him.

"...I wonder, are the capybaras at the bottom all right?" the detective worried, looking up at the wall of capybaras stacked four or five high. You could just barely see a sliver of blue sky through them—if you were lucky. But he was already buried to the top of his head in fur.

"Well, it's a video game," said Nayuta vaguely. "If anything, the ones near the bottom are actually moving around more."

It only made the footing seem more perilous. The pressure of their weight wasn't that intense, but having everywhere you touched and moved be so soft and squishy made it very difficult to get anywhere.

Before she realized what was happening, they were being squished together like passengers on a packed train, and then she was pressed firmly against Klever. Her forehead was right around his collarbone because he was a head taller than her.

"…I'm sorry, Detective. I'm being pushed from behind…"

"I know it's not on purpose. I know that, but still…"

Inside a train, there would at least be poles and straps to grab. But there was nothing of the sort among the capybaras. Neither of them was even stepping on the ground.

They were so tight she couldn't help but be aware of his body temperature. It was then that Nayuta was reminded of the stealthy kind of horror contained in this quest.

He whispered into her ear, "Can you turn sideways, Nayuta? If we create a little breathing room, I'll climb up on top of the capybaras…"

"Oh…if you want to climb, I'm lighter."

"All right, then. Use my knees as steps. Right there…"

"Aaah!" she shrieked, surprised by a sudden shift in the capybaras surrounding them. She lost her balance as she tried to climb upward and ended up clinging to him with her arms around his neck.

Now they were aligned even tighter. Even calm, rational Nayuta was rattled by this.

Klever was tilted backward at an angle so that he was almost facing upward. Nayuta was resting on top of him, her feet not reaching any solid surface, unable to shift away.

"I-I'm so sorry…!"

"That's exactly what I wanted to hear from you when you released me from that wicker hamper," the detective joked. His voice sounded slightly strained. He was doing his best to remain calm and maintain his dignity, but it was clear he, too, was having difficulty with this.

Because of the capybaras moving across her back, Nayuta couldn't straighten up. She was frozen in place, her face beet-red.

Eventually, someone else came diving through the layers of fur, and they saw a familiar face.

"…I'll be honest. I had a feeling this might be happening… Just knowing your luck stat, Detective. If you were going to make a move, it was going to be now… And how many times is this?" asked Koyomi, direct and venomous.

He hastened to explain. "Are you talking about what happened at the resort hotel? First of all, that had nothing to do with my luck stat, and it wasn't intentional. Would you mind helping us?"

"I wonder…with you immobile like this, would it be possible to just slit your throat from behind, Detective…?"

A small blade glinted in Koyomi's hand.

"Koyomi, I would prefer if you set aside the serial killer solutions and pulled my arm instead. I can't push off anything with my feet," Nayuta explained, still red in the face.

Her friend cast a suspicious glance at her instead this time. "If I pull you toward me at this angle, it's going to create a special event in which your breasts slide directly over his face…and then Koyomi will be very, *very* cross."

The other two clammed up.

"Here's an idea," Koyomi continued. "Nayu, can you help me turn the detective over so he's face-down? Then I'll pull him this way and give him all kinds of annoying lectures while you kick him in the butt and insult him. Sounds like a good plan to me…"

"Um...this situation is my fault, so I'd rather we didn't do that... I'm sorry, Detective. Are you able to turn over?"

"Yeah. I should be able to rotate myself..."

Despite the wriggling capybaras all around them, with Koyomi's help, the pair were able to restore some measure of control over their posture. When Klever was feeling slightly more reassured, he reached up to wipe the sweat from his brow. All three were buried in capybara up over their heads.

"So the hole is deeper here, eh? It seems beneficial that the capybaras are no heavier than plush dolls...but this is a much more difficult trick than I expected."

"Was it soft, Detective? Did you enjoy it? Did it smell nice?" Koyomi asked pointedly with flat, emotionless eyes. Nayuta and Klever chose to ignore her.

"I'm just glad they don't stink like wild animals. Also, if we were squished this closely in real life, we'd all have suffocated by now."

"All right, I can tell you're trying to change the topic...but if anyone here smells like a wild animal, it's you, Detective. You almost went feral a minute ago, didn't you? Let's be a little more careful next time, Nayu, hmm?"

Nayuta felt around with her toe for the entrance to the hidden area and muttered, "Listen, Koyomi...both this time and last time were my fault, so I would appreciate it if you didn't blame him for it. He didn't do anything wrong. This treatment is getting to be cruel."

"Nayu...," Koyomi sighed. "Nayu, that soft side of yours is the problem! Listen...I'm not angry because I hate him. I'm angry because I'm jealous and envious and frustrated that it wasn't me. And the fact that you're so soft on him makes it even worse. If you just said, 'Detective, you're a brute! A sicko! A pig!'— Then I could intercede and say, 'Now, now, you don't have to be mean,' but instead, you just have this natural way of putting yourselves in flirtatious situations, and it's infuriating. I want to be flirtatious with you, too! I want you to blush and say, 'It's not Koyomi's fault!' through trembling lips, too! It's not fair that it only happens to him!"

Klever pressed on his forehead. "Koyomi…it's quite refreshing that you're so open and honest about your personality, but I think it's better if you just stop talking now. Notice how the smile is frozen on Nayuta's face?"

"Oh."

Nayuta humored Koyomi with a strained, confused grin. "I suppose I may have been spoiling you, Koyomi. I'll have to reconsider how I treat you, I think."

"No! Don't think! Please just be the same Nayu as ever! Be the wonderfully kind and supportive and gullible Nayu who always spoils exhausted Koyomi after she gets off work!" Koyomi pleaded, clinging to her sleeve despite their general lack of mobility.

It was hard not to get carried away because of her childish appearance, but Nayuta steeled her heart and said sternly, "First of all, please do not call me gullible right to my face. That is *not* a compliment."

Koyomi put her fingers to her lips and made puppy dog eyes at Nayuta. This was a grown adult with a job and everything.

"…But…but Nayu…you *are* so gullible…"

She was not going to concede that point.

The detective, who'd been checking around his feet, spoke up to say, "Oh, is this it? There's a shift in the grass. It dips a little bit. I think there might be a mechanism here."

"That's it! Do you feel a circle in the middle of it? If you pull on that, it'll teleport you to the secret area, but don't do it yet! All three of us need to be directly over it," said Koyomi, crawling toward him. Nayuta followed suit, and within moments they were bunched together.

In the place where the demon puppet had previously been stored was a chain attached to the ground with a circle on the loose end. Now that they were together, Koyomi used both hands to tug on the circle.

At the same moment, all of the capybaras that had blanketed the entire meadow vanished in a puff of smoke.

They were no longer in the open, under a bright blue sky.

Now it was the base of a mountain at night.

Instead of what they'd been looking at a moment ago, they faced an enormous torii gate and a long, long, *long* stone staircase on the other side. Stone statues depicting lazy capybaras lined the stairs, and at the distant peak of the mountain was a faint light.

The torii was the entrance to the stairs, and there was a sign standing right next to it. Nayuta and Koyomi had already seen it, so it was Klever's turn to read what it said.

"Let's see… Path of Encapyment, Trial Road… There are mid-bosses partway along the stairs… You have a chance at receiving rare loot… There is a final boss at the top… Good luck with the climb… Note: Real capybaras are very timid and peaceful animals, so do not strike or cut them… What the heck is this?" Klever asked, pointing at the very instructive and helpful sign.

Koyomi waved her hand easily. "Oh, it's because it's an event for beginners. They probably wanted to make sure kids could understand the stakes, too, ya know?"

"Hrm…and did you two already climb to the top?"

"We did," Nayuta replied. "In fact, we went twice."

"But not only did we not get any rare loot, we didn't get anything, period…so we realized we needed you here with us. That's why we were waiting for you to finish your work."

The detective rapped his walking stick on the cobblestones. "I see," he said. "Then you already know what kind of monsters are facing us."

"The Twelve Capybara Generals."

"…Hmm?"

He was taken aback by the brevity and unhelpfulness of her answer. Nayuta had mercy and gave him a more detailed answer.

"The first one was just a capybara wearing a mouse suit. It was very weak."

"Uh-huh."

That had been rather surreal because capybaras were not far off from giant mice to begin with.

"The second one was a capybara wearing a cow suit. It was extremely weak."

"...I see."

"The third one was—"

"Okay, okay, I get it. A capybara in a tiger suit, I'm guessing. Then a rabbit, dragon, snake, horse, sheep, monkey, bird, dog— and lastly, a boar."

"That's amazing! How did you know, Detective?" Koyomi exclaimed. He gave her an exhausted look.

"It's cosplay of the twelve zodiac animals... It would be strange if you *didn't* recognize the pattern. And what's at the peak?"

"Well...nothing showed up."

For just an instant, his eyes glinted.

"...Ahh. Nothing, you say? But the sign would suggest there should be a final boss."

"But nothing showed up. Do you suppose there's a condition to fulfill first?"

"If there is, we were hoping you could give us a hint."

Klever did not budge from the sign. He stared closely at what was written there, looked on the back to confirm there was nothing there, then inspected the torii gate, and at last turned to Nayuta and Koyomi again.

"This quest is a tie-in with a zoo somewhere, isn't it?" he asked.

Koyomi nodded. "That's what I hear. Something about supervision of capybara activities."

"So if they have that as a sponsor, do you really think that, even in a game like this, the developers would recommend players *harm* capybaras?" the detective pointed out.

Nayuta was stunned. She had assumed the capybaras that showed up were enemies and defeated them with that in mind. The presentation had been silly, and when they were damaged, their eyes turned to *X* marks and they lifted white flags in surrender. But now that he mentioned it, the whole thing had felt a little strange.

Koyomi's lips pursed. "But look at what it says on the sign! There are mid-bosses on the stairs."

The detective nodded. "Yes, mid-bosses. It doesn't say they are capybaras. And there's another curious point: 'You have a chance at receiving rare loot.' It doesn't say you can get loot for beating them; it just says 'you have a chance at receiving.' You could take that to mean someone will give you that loot. Lastly, it says, 'do not strike or cut them'... Does that mean you shouldn't fight them at all?"

Nayuta and Koyomi looked at one another. Silence passed.

They were both experts at tackling bloody and violent quests. Enemies were there to be defeated, and they'd never considered the possibility that there were other options for what to do with them.

To be honest, they had looked at the warning at the end of the sign, assumed it was meant to remind people not to attack capybaras in real life, and otherwise ignored it.

"...Well...I guess we can try it..."

"...Yeah..."

They had no real reason to argue against his suggestion, so Nayuta and Koyomi began to climb the steps.

Klever followed a few steps behind, rubbing his chin thoughtfully.

"Capybara versions...of the Twelve Divine Generals... Hmm, something sounds familiar," he murmured, loud enough for Nayuta to hear.

§

At a wide landing on the stone stairs, a capybara dressed up like a mouse slumped on its side on the ground. It was about the size of a large dog, but with shorter legs and a larger head.

There was another sign at the side of the landing that even told them TWELVE CAPYBARA GENERALS: MOUSE.

"And we're *not* supposed to beat it…just ignore it and keep going?" Nayuta asked.

The detective shook his head. "You're not going to get the rare loot that way. We probably have to do something that isn't fighting it."

The mouse-disguised capybara waddled over to Koyomi and started to whack at her lightly with its soft feet. It barely did any damage, but it did count as an attack. Despite its weakness, it seemed to be raring to fight and had no intention of fleeing.

Koyomi held back the mildly raging capybara and asked, "Umm…so what am I supposed to do about this?"

"Spend some time with it and don't fight back. We'll look around the area in the meantime. Nayuta, you check out that side."

With Koyomi occupying the capybara, Nayuta and Klever split up to check out the stone steps. There were more capybara statues here, but one was different from the others.

"Detective, this one is the only statue with a nameplate on the base. Is that Bi…kara?"

There was a metal plate with some difficult-looking kanji etched on it. Despite the similarity in sound, it was not a kanji version of "capybara." And upon closer inspection, the statue itself was closer to a simple mouse than an actual capybara.

The detective trotted over at once. "It says *Vikala*. That's one of the Twelve Divine Generals in Buddhism. I'm guessing there's a mechanism here…"

Nayuta's fingertips brushed against the plate on the stone statue.

Immediately, the landing on the stairs, which was not especially big, extended outward in all directions. It formed a circular arena where a red light shone in the center. The capybara dressed as a mouse spooked and ran behind Koyomi to hide.

Eventually, they were greeted by a fierce warrior holding a

halberd and clad in sturdy armor. Its head was that of a mouse, however, and its glowing red gaze was full of hatred and menace. A gut-rumbling voice boomed down at them from the heavens.

"I am Vikala of the Twelve Divine Generals. Man-children, protect that beast from the threat of my halberd!"

Nayuta and Koyomi assumed battle positions at once. The detective called out, "This must be the real mid-boss! I suppose the chance to get rare loot comes by protecting that capybara until the end of the battle. Be careful!"

Based on appearances and aura, this enemy was no slouch at all. There was no easy opening to exploit in its halberd stance, either.

Koyomi tried taking the initiative. Using her speed and small size to her advantage, she zipped up close, drew her ninja blade, and thrust it at the enemy in one motion.

Mouse-headed Vikala spun around to dodge and struck the butt of his halberd against the stones.

"Fwah—?!"

The stone rumbled and cracked, sending shards of rock upward to pelt her.

"Koyomi!" Nayuta cried, momentarily panicked. But Koyomi jumped backward to soften the impact and put space between her and the enemy. She'd taken a fair amount of damage, but it wasn't fatal.

There was no time to be relieved, however. Nayuta bounded forward. She had to draw Vikala's attention toward herself before he could attack Koyomi again.

Vikala turned toward Nayuta's bold charge and swung his halberd at her from a distance at which it couldn't possibly reach her. As it swung downward, a lightning bolt came plummeting down toward Nayuta.

"Argh!"

She just barely managed to dodge it at the last split-second, clenching her fists. The bolt gouged a huge chunk out of the ground as it boomed. With her minimal armor, Nayuta would probably have lost most, if not all, of her health.

The sooner they could defeat the boss, the better, but this was not an easy enough foe that they could simply smash away at his weak spots.

First, she would land a Purifying Blow somewhere on his body, and based on his reaction, she would try to find out what his weak elements were. If he turned out to be weak to spiritual damage, he would falter, and if he seemed unfazed by it, then she'd have to switch to physical attacks like Smashing Palm.

But first, she just needed to hit it. She wouldn't learn anything without that.

"Keep that capybara safe, Detective!" she called out, and sped through the gap toward her opponent.

Vikala deftly spun the halberd and swiped it across in a horizontal swing as Nayuta charged at him. It was quick and heavy, but she leaped into the air to jump over it. The weapon jerked upward, trying to follow her, but the shift in direction caused a drop in power and speed.

I think my timing is right!

After the big halberd swing, there was a brief but undeniable opening to strike at Vikala's side. She was just about to take advantage when she heard Koyomi shriek, "Nayu, no! He's got paralyzing breath!"

Her warning was a split-second too late.

Nayuta rushed directly into a colorless, translucent breath attack straight from Vikala's mouth. By the time she realized her mistake, she was already suffering an instantaneous paralyzing effect.

Then Vikala made a mudra with one hand and unleashed a shock wave that completely knocked Nayuta off her feet. While Koyomi was just barely able to stand, she wasn't in any condition to move, either.

The paralysis effect had multiple stages.

Light paralysis recovered on its own in ten to twenty seconds but couldn't be recovered from with techniques or items. Or, in other words, it would heal on its own before either techniques or items would work on it.

Medium paralysis took about thirty minutes to dissipate, but a single mild breath attack wouldn't lead to that. It was easiest to fall into this state when poked with a paralysis needle.

Heavy paralysis, meanwhile, only occurred after suffering multiple rounds of paralyzing attacks, and would not recover naturally. You could only get rid of it with a technique, a healing item, or by leaving the quest.

For both Nayuta and Koyomi, this was only light paralysis. It would go away in a few seconds, but those were seconds they desperately needed.

Attacks that they might have survived with heavy armor were downright fatal when you were as lightly armored as they were. But Vikala did not so much as spare a glance for his paralyzed opponents, turning to run straight at the capybara instead.

And right next to it, Klever.

"Detective, run!" Nayuta screamed.

He just clicked his tongue. "Dammit…the capybara is his top target!"

Klever readied his cane. But rather than using it to fight back, he used the handle to hook the edge of the capybara's costume, hurling it around with centrifugal force before tossing it free.

The giant rodent, which was only as heavy as a plush animal, flew in a gentle arc to land next to Nayuta.

Vikala spun around, intending to follow it, but the detective's cane caught his leg.

It was just a few seconds until Nayuta would recover from the paralysis—but buying those few seconds, with all of his stats aside from luck still where they were at level-1, was essentially an act of suicide on Klever's part.

Vikala turned again as he toppled over, stabbing his halberd accurately through the detective's body in less than a second's time.

"Detective?!"

Klever vanished in a flash of light, but not before one final message.

"Nayuta! Use the pupp—"

The last bit didn't make it.

Koyomi recovered from the paralysis a split-second earlier than Nayuta did.

"One hit...?! I guess that makes sense... Well, time to avenge him!"

Given his statistical handicap, they just took for granted that Klever would stay out of battle like he always did. But in this case, he made a calculated sacrifice to protect Nayuta and the capybara.

Rather than carelessly leaping at the opponent this time, Koyomi stayed back and threw a kunai at Vikala. He spun his halberd like a propeller, knocking the projectile aside. His rat eyes glinted red. Koyomi made the mistake of looking right at him, however, and slumped to her knees.

"N-now it's an Evil Eye?! These status effects are brutal..."

With Koyomi weakened and immobile, Vikala disengaged and started rushing for the capybara again. From her item list, Nayuta chose Demon Puppet Onihime.

"Onihime, battle readiness!"

The horned girl *onmyoji* responded to its master's call by transitioning into battle mode. The demon puppets moved on autopilot for the most part, but by using certain preset keywords, you could give them simple orders, too.

"Battle readiness" was the switch to transition to fighting mode. Once the order was given, the activity counter would engage.

The little *onmyoji* girl's eyelids slowly rose.

The eyes behind them were a deep blue and faintly glowing.

Immediately after her activation, a white strip of paper flew off Onihime's slender arm as swiftly as a swallow. The strip smacked onto Koyomi's shoulder near her neck and began to counteract the effect of the Evil Eye.

Meanwhile, Nayuta leaped in front of the terrified capybara and took a fighting pose. Vikala thrust his halberd at her with lightning speed.

While his main target was the capybara, it seemed if there was a player in the vicinity, he would attack them first.

Wary of his paralyzing breath, Nayuta stepped backward and deflected the halberd edge.

"Onihime, increase paralysis resistance!"

This was her first time testing it, so she didn't know if this would work, but she figured she'd go for broke and treat the puppet like she would an ascetic-type party member and ask for help.

From the rear, Onihime sent another paper seal flying, this time toward Nayuta. But it flew in a straight line, and as Nayuta was busy fending off Vikala, it went right past her.

So it didn't have a homing ability. You'd have to wait a moment after giving the command to ensure the seal actually hit you.

"Nayu, I'll switch with you! Then you can get it!"

Koyomi, having recovered from the Evil Eye's effects, threw a series of kunai. Angered by a third interruption, Vikala roared with anger—in a high-pitched ratty voice.

With his attention turned to Koyomi, Nayuta stood still and gave her order.

"Sorry, Onihime! One more time, paralysis resistance!"

The onmyoji girl threw a white strip of paper. It flew as straight as an arrow and stuck to Nayuta's back this time, conferring its protective power to her. It felt like a pleasant, spreading warmth.

Trusting in the defensive boon, Nayuta leaped forward into battle. Vikala sensed her approach and turned to face her.

The tip of his halberd grazed Nayuta's cheek as he swung it by, his paralyzing breath surrounded her, and she felt a chilling, prickling pressure shake her very soul.

But none of that prevented the full motion of her limbs.

With a shrill bark, she drove a powerful fist into the armored solar plexus of her target.

The feedback was immediate.

A shock wave ran back through her fist, and was still reverberating there when from high in the heavens above, there was the crash of a gong to signify the battle had reached a conclusion.

§

On the last day of the holiday week, Nayuta was lazily brushing Koyomi's hair at the Three-Leaf Detective Agency office.

"*Nya-fuu...* This is Paradise...," burbled Koyomi as the brush passed through the brown hair that covered every inch of her body.

The rounded silhouette, the short limbs with padded feet, the huge head with sleepy black eyes—anyone would recognize it as nothing else but the noble, lovable capybara.

While there was a little peek at her human face through the capybara's gaping mouth, it was still mostly blocked by the upper and lower jaws, and wasn't very noticeable.

Nayuta was not the only one who was busy brushing the capybara Koyomi.

There was also a puppet dressed as an *onmyoji*, devoid of expression, brushing the capybara from the other side.

The owner of the office, Klever the detective, was doing his very best to avoid looking at the bizarre spectacle happening before him.

Out of consideration for him, Nayuta chose to say nothing.

There was a knock at the door, which promptly opened.

"Ah, you're all here. And how is Onihime doing?" Torao from

the error-testing department asked genially, giving Nayuta a little bow. She did not stop brushing the capybara.

"Good afternoon, Mr. Torao. Onihime is incredible. She doesn't have much in the way of firepower, but she's a gifted backup member. We were able to beat the Twelve Divine Generals up to the sixth one. As you can see, Koyomi is very pleased with the capybara *kigurumi*."

From atop Nayuta's lap, the face-down Koyomi waggled her tail to display her mood.

"Yep. Sure am. Capybaras really are the best... I think this capybara suit is going to be a lifelong treasure of mine... All I have to do is wear it for Nayu to spoil me rotten, and other players are nice to me, too, and the *keukegen* treat me like one of their own. Maybe I should change jobs from ninja to capybara..."

Of course, despite her buoyant mood, that was not possible. The *kigurumi* costume was a very rare drop. At the very least, of all the people on Nayuta's friends list, Koyomi was the only one who got it, and it was making her a popular figure; people gathered to see her just walking around with it on.

Onihime—who was busy brushing away—had also gathered quite a bit of attention. The demon puppets the dev team had failed to recover had already wound up in the hands of several players.

There were less than ten in total, most likely, so it was still a minor story, but strange rumors were already beginning to spread in the manner of an urban legend.

Such as: They're putting in battle androids that run on AI.

Such as: It's a top-secret test meant to collect battle data for clients in the weapons industry.

Such as: A hacker with a penchant for dress-up dolls dropped something weird into the game files...

If they hadn't heard the truth from Torao already, they might have enjoyed hearing those rumors for themselves.

As for him, he happily took an empty chair. "Well, you've been a great help. Thanks to your battle data and report, we've managed to air out some of the problems with the demon puppet implementation. We weren't in time to do it this week, but it looks like we'll be unveiling them to the public with the next update. As for the monetization, well...I think they'll end up settling for the least harmful choice."

Klever smiled weakly. "I'm glad to hear that. So your suggestion made it through, then."

"No, no, it wasn't my suggestion—at least, not publicly," Torao said with a smirk, patting Onihime on the head. "Although I didn't tell you, this one's a bit of a soft spot for me. One of the other folks who joined the company at the same time I did designed the base for the demon puppets. A bunch of people took part in the process, but I know how much trouble it was, so I'm hoping the puppets see the light of day in the best shape they possibly can. Take good care of this one, will you, Nayuta?"

Nayuta smiled and inclined her head. To her and Koyomi, who fought on the front line, a support member in the rear was a true lifeline. Onihime being summonable from the item list at any time made her the perfect party member.

But something about her was still a mystery to Nayuta.

"Mr. Torao, does she have her own learning function? I started brushing Koyomi, and then she started copying me. I'm just a bit surprised, because I thought these were simply combat companions."

"Yeah. They can't do anything complex, but they can learn enough for a little monkey-see, monkey-do. I don't know exactly what that means in the long run, but we've seen them perform shoulder massages, for example. But...I have a question for you, too..."

Torao took a quick look around the office. Normally, the Three-Leaf Detective Agency was staffed with black cat bots that milled around. But the bots were currently stationed atop the cupboard, carefully watching the swarm of creatures below.

One capybara plodded over and started a pleasant nap, using Torao's foot as a pillow.

A wombat was seated on the detective's lap as he worked,

acting as though it owned the place, while large, round furballs filled the space around Nayuta, Koyomi, and Onihime.

The rare capybara *kigurumi* that Koyomi had earned contained a special skill called Summon Furball. While the player was in town, where battle could not happen, it had the powerful effect of summoning a random selection of capybaras and wombats, within a certain limit.

For the past day, Koyomi and her minions had taken over the Three-Leaf Detective Agency and caused its owner, Klever, no small amount of anguish. This situation was the very matter that Torao was curious about.

He pointed at the wombat on the detective's lap and asked, "Kurei...isn't that interfering with your work?"

"......It just climbs back here, no matter how many times I push it off, so I've finally given up."

You would think the solution would be as simple as to leave the VR space and go work in a real-life office, but sadly, he had a guide job lined up that day. He was currently waiting for the client to arrive and organizing some papers while he had the time.

After Torao left, Klever narrowed his vulpine eyes and managed a dry, exhausted-sounding chuckle.

"So...even though this wasn't a playtest, Mr. Torao certainly got everything he wanted from us."

"Are you talking about Onihime?" Nayuta shot back quietly.

"Yes, there were reports to file, but I think it was worth it..."

"Maybe so...but I also mean the Twelve Divine Generals," Klever yawned. He'd been forced to help them in their quest to beat the Twelve Generals after work for the last several days, thanks to his boosted drop rate.

Unluckily (or luckily), they'd been taking a break since the day they were forced to retreat, but after several days of this, the fatigue was starting to get to him.

Nayuta petted Koyomi, who was purring happily, and asked, "Twelve Divine Generals? What do they have to do with Mr. Torao?"

"You couldn't tell from fighting them?" he asked. "Those generals were clearly programmed to be a test of the demon puppets' battle abilities. They came equipped with a variety of behavioral patterns that were designed to make the puppets' support easier to use, and to get players to experiment with them and learn the ropes."

The Twelve Generals were formidable foes, but you didn't need to whittle them all the way down to zero— Just land a critical hit on their weak point when it was exposed, and the fight would end.

If you won, the general would retreat, and the Chinese Zodiac-themed capybara would give you a rare item as a prize. If you failed to protect the capybara from the general, the trial would end right then and there.

Although they didn't realize it until it was pointed out, in the Twelve Divine General fights up to that point, they had relied largely on the demon puppet to win.

"So my personal theory is that originally, all players were supposed to find out about the puppets at the bottom of those stairs. Then you'd temporarily work with one to conquer the Twelve Generals, then the final boss, and lastly be awarded your own demon puppet—and I think that's what Mr. Torao is trying to get them to reinstate. After all, it's hard to know what to do with such a tool if you just stumble across it, and the fights with the Twelve Divine Generals are something of a tutorial. We haven't finished it yet, but I think he's gotten exactly what he wants. His good mood must be on account of some very good data we gave him," Klever said, grinning like a fox.

Nayuta sighed. "Next time, explain that when you figure it out. Now I feel foolish for doing those fights without thinking any of it through."

"I think he *wanted* you to fight them without conducting any theorycrafting beforehand. You should be proud to have done such a good job."

She considered this for a while, her brow furrowed. "It still doesn't sit right with me...but are you saying it was Mr. Torao's doing that we got Onihime in the first place?"

The detective put a finger to his lips. "That was surely a coincidence. He could have gotten his data secretly from other players. But at least according to my own irresponsible speculation...I think their failure to recover all the demon puppets was actually on purpose." His voice dropped in volume. "After all, if they actually got them all back, senior management wouldn't be blamed for their decision. This whole incident needed to be an unnecessary and chaotic wrench in the works thrown by the bosses' unfair decision to change directions. Then the devs could use that fact as a cudgel to win their argument over the implementation of the puppets. At least in my opinion."

His "irresponsible speculation" had a strangely convincing ring of truth to it.

"So it's like...a factional rivalry within the company?"

"That could be part of it. I don't know the finer details...and I'm too afraid to stick my nose into their business."

Nayuta was stunned. If Klever's suspicions were correct, then this whole thing was one big farce from start to finish.

"But surely that's not true..."

"No, it's not. It can't be. Like I said, all my own speculation," he admitted, and returned to his work with a smug look on his face.

Unsatisfied and frustrated, Nayuta resumed brushing Koyomi. Before long, the capybara-suited girl began to snore. Lulled by the sound, Nayuta found herself starting to nod off as well.

At this point, Onihime stood up and began to silently comb Nayuta's hair instead. Her motions were gentle and careful, as kind as a mother cat licking her kitten.

Watching this heartwarming and strange sight out of the corner of his eye, the detective with the wombat in his lap continued tending to his work, fighting back against the fatigue that threatened to consume him, too.

Ayakashi Alley's Railway System

The large town of Ayakashi Alley, which opened to host the 108 Apparitions campaign, features multiple streetcar lines.

The Yamanoke Line runs in a big loop around the town, while the Somu Line goes straight from east to west. The Saikyo Line passes through to the north, and the Yurikarasu Line runs along the coast. However, all of these are essentially just portals taking the form of trolleys, and their "train stations" are more like simple bus stops than anything.

"But this will make it difficult to implement a railway apparition quest," some developers protested last October, just before the 108 Apparitions event launched.

Some of the user-submitted quests were set in stations or trains. In order to deliver those quests to players without feeling anachronistic, a modern railway and station were necessary, so the eastern end of Ayakashi Alley, known as Ueno, was chosen for the location.

The subterranean part of the station is a complex and winding dungeon, but for players who want to use the station without a dungeon-crawling experience, an elevator will go straight to the platform. Security systems and warnings were made clear to prevent players with travel tickets from accidentally wandering into the dungeon.

This station is the terminal to various rail-related quests and likely to play a larger part in the future of the game.

Chapter 3

The Book of Onihime, Part One

Tooru Endou the game programmer was at a loss for what to do about the dead body at the bottom of the tub.

It was clear what he ought to do.

He should call at once for an ambulance or the police—even a man naive to the practical ways of the world like himself was smart enough to know that.

But once I call one of them...how do I explain myself...?

His wits, muddled by the all-nighter, struggled to form rational thoughts.

His vision wobbled and warped.

Actually, it was his knees that were doing that, not his eyes.

He leaned back against the wall, sat down, and put his hands over his face.

"Why...when we're so damn busy...why did you have to go off and *die,* you moron...?"

Maybe this was just a nightmare, and he was the only one who didn't realize it. He'd fallen asleep, and when he woke up, the body would be gone. In fact, *all* of his life would've been one big bad dream, and he'd get to start over from primary school, he imagined—fleeing into the comfort of an impossible fantasy—as he tried to get the body out of the bathtub.

But the large, heavyset corpse was much too bulky for Endou, whose muscles were weakened from overwork and not up to the task. On top of that, his limbs were trembling, and he couldn't tense them or will any strength into them.

In a state of sheer desperation, he ultimately drained the tub, put towels around the body, and pretended he hadn't seen it.

Then he crawled to his bedroom and fell onto the bed. For the moment, he just wanted to sleep deeply and—most importantly—mindlessly.

He could think when he woke up again. He very much doubted he would awake with an inspired solution, but for the moment, he couldn't even keep his eyes open.

Fatigue so heavy it paralyzed his judgment, his heart, and even his common sense ripped his consciousness away from him.

By tomorrow... By morning...

The next morning, the body was still in the tub.

§

Dogs belong to the family Canidae, in the suborder Caniformia of the order Carnivora. In Japanese, Carnivora is sometimes referred to as "the cat order."

Therefore, if you view it through a wide enough lens, dogs are cats.

Bears belong to the cat order, and pandas are called "large bear-cats" in kanji, so they're relatives of cats, too.

Seals, walruses, sea lions, and otters are in the cat order, too. Despite being marine animals, they are broadly categorized as cats. At the very least, they're more cat than human.

The black-tailed gull is a bird, but given its name in Japanese is *umineko* ("sea-cat"), one cannot deny the possibility that it is a member of the cat family.

One sometimes hears bizarre theories such as "the Chinese Zodiac has no cats." This is nonsense because tigers and dogs are basically cats, and when it comes to birds, it is possible to interpret *some* birds as being cats as well…

"…and that's the sort of thing Mr. Torao will say with a straight face."

"That reminds me: Foxes are in the Canidae family, too."

It was Sunday at the Three-Leaf Detective Agency. Or more accurately, in the office of Clover's Network Security Corporation, Kaisei Kurei's home, where Klever and Nayuta sat at the lunch table.

Their menu was mixed rice, miso soup, pickled vegetables, and cabbage rolls—a fairly well-balanced meal. Nayuta had brought the rice and cabbage rolls, and she'd whipped up the miso soup and pickles in a jiffy in the office's kitchen.

She'd been good at domestic chores since before she lived alone. She was deft and brilliant in the kitchen, and the food tasted great—but given her age and appearance, there was an undeniable problem with this situation.

In the real world, unlike her brave and bold warrior priestess appearance, Nayuta preferred to wear reserved, plain clothing. That day, she was in a simple summer sweater and a long skirt, but unfortunately, due to her remarkable figure and good looks, it still looked anything but plain on her.

…If anyone ever finds out about this, I'm going to be arrested…

It was a thought that often occurred to Klever when he engaged in small talk with this teenage high school student in his own home. He could swear upon Heaven and Earth he was doing nothing wrong, but there was no way to ensure anyone else believed him.

Whether she was aware of the existential terror that gripped Klever or not, Nayuta sat up straight, chopsticks in one hand, and gave him a very graceful smile.

"Putting aside the theories of the high priest of the cat-god religion…I think that foxes are closer to dogs than cats, but the way they curl up when they sleep seems rather catlike to me. And I feel like the way they take to humans is closer to cats than dogs. Like, either they don't let their guard down, or when they do, they pretend they don't care."

"I'll admit, I have a hard time imagining a fox wagging its tail or jumping around after a ball," he replied.

In the sense that he could still enjoy idle chit-chat like this at the table, Klever was getting used to the situation. Both of them were living alone, and before this, he tended to forego good cooking for other concerns.

According to Nayuta, cooking "just isn't as enjoyable if you don't have someone else around to eat it." She started off with light items like sandwiches, but at some point, she began taking over his kitchen area.

There were now spices in there Klever could not remember buying, and he was starting to feel a little bit weird about it, like he was being tamed or fattened up, but Nayuta probably did not realize what she was doing.

To her, she was just returning the favor of receiving some school exam tutoring sessions.

"It's about the same amount of work to cook for two people as for one, and I'm mostly using you as an excuse to cook the things I really want to eat. Please don't fret about it," she told him. He couldn't see a good reason to spurn her offer.

It was true that VRMMORPG players tended to neglect their diets in the real world. All those delicious in-game sweets that didn't make you gain weight were, on the other hand, just simulated food with zero nutritional value. You could feel sated eating them in-game while your actual body just got weaker and weaker.

Naturally, this had given VR games a reputation of being "good for dieting," which led to a major increase in female players, but it also created an unfortunate class of people who suffered from malnutrition and anemia.

When Nayuta said she often got lazy with cooking when she was alone, it wasn't a joke. College students and young adults living alone who ruined their health after getting into VRM-MORPGs were a fairly common phenomenon.

Even Klever had admittedly sometimes put in an order of Nyanko Soba within the game to tide him over when he was really busy with work so he didn't have to log out.

It was after Nayuta witnessed him doing that very thing at the agency that her little snacks and treats turned into full-blown meals with him.

While it was pathetic to admit this, as an older adult, he was honestly grateful for the help. And he made sure to pay her back extra for the cost of the groceries.

"Oh, and put the mixed rice into onigiri. They're in the freezer, so go ahead and take them out to thaw when you need a late meal."

"...Thank you. I appreciate that."

Apparently you could tame foxes with food.

Nayuta sipped her miso soup politely and noted, "Back to the earlier topic...even though foxes' faces and figures are closer to dogs', they just *look* more like cats. It's almost like foxes exist in the gap between dogs and cats...or is that just me?"

He couldn't help but grin at that thought. It was adorable.

"So we're just talking about the general image they have? I understand what you mean. Dogs are animals that faithfully serve mankind, while cats are animals that refuse to serve anyone but themselves. Both are pets that live in the vicinity of humanity, but have opposing images. As for foxes...their image is that they don't take to humans, but are animals that serve the gods. That's due to the influence of the god Inari in Shinto. As a result, they are similar to dogs in that they are animals that serve something, but are similar to cats in that they don't serve mankind. That seems to match the mental image that you have of them. What do you think of that?"

She put a hand to her mouth in surprise. "I...I think it makes sense now. Yes, the image that I have of foxes is closer to the Inari fox familiars than actual wild foxes. Koyomi says foxes are like dogs and not at all like cats. I always found that difference of opinion to be strange…but I think that to Koyomi, foxes are just cute animals that look like dogs. They have big mouths, pointy snouts, and more general facial similarities to dogs than cats."

A wry smile tugged at a corner of Klever's mouth. "If we start analyzing wolves, bears, and lion dogs, too, we're going to get deep into folklore studies. And then there are people like me who have normal mouths and noses but are for some bizarre reason treated like foxes simply for having narrow eyes. Perhaps the mental image we have of humans is much less defined than we'd like to think."

"Oh no," Nayuta said, instantly shaking her head, "your foxlike qualities aren't just your eyes. It's your slender figure, the unmistakable aura of sketchiness around you, the otherworldly fastidiousness, all things that make you seem like a transforming fox doing its best to pass itself off as human… So it's a combination of many features, and not simply because you have narrow eyes."

"…Please don't pile them on one after the other. I can't possibly offer a rebuttal to all of them at once."

This was all just Nayuta's subjective impression of him, so it wasn't really the kind of thing he could argue against, but even still, it was hard to take.

She giggled at his anguish. "Still, I think you've helped improve my mental image of foxes. And also taught me that I shouldn't judge someone based on how suspicious they look…at least, that's what I tell myself."

Klever sipped his tea. He looked at her quite seriously. "No, looks are very important… Of course, you don't want to trust someone at first glance, just because they seem appealing, but if someone seems just a little fishy or up to no good, you should trust that intuition. As I'm sure you know, being raised in a police family, there are plenty of bad people out there, and young girls like you are the most popular targets. You seem to trust me, and I have zero intention of betraying that trust, but you shouldn't forget your sense of caution."

"I understand what you're saying," she said, her smile fading a little, "and I'll be careful. But if I'm overly cautious about everything, then I really will end up having to fend for myself for my whole life…"

She was absolutely right about that, Klever had to admit.

"…That's exactly right. Knowing where that fine line exists is hard. Anyway, if anything happens, you can come to me for advice. And if you can't say it to me, ask Koyomi. I can't help but notice that in the last few days, you've had something gnawing at you," the detective said, knowing it was rude to bring up but saying it anyway.

Nayuta's eyes went wide with shock.

"…Huh? You have? Was it that obvious…?"

"So you *are* worried about something. You seemed like you were forcing yourself to be cheerier than you really felt. It was just a guess on my part."

He didn't know for sure. He'd just taken a stab at it, thinking that it could be worth a brief chuckle if he was wrong.

She wiped a hand across her forehead. "Ahh…yes, I forgot. That's the kind of person you are, Detective. I mean, it's not really something worth worrying about…but…"

It was rare for her to trail off in the middle of a sentence like that. Klever poured more tea into her cup and waited patiently for more.

"…The truth is…the other day, when we were shopping at the supermarket together…a friend from school happened to see me…"

"…Hmm?"

He froze. She'd said one of his alarm phrases.

"…Of course, none of the teachers know," she said, her voice getting quieter, "but at some point, people decided that I have an older boyfriend…and they also snapped a picture of the two of us together…"

His face had gone totally pale now.

"…B-but no. We were just buying ingredients. There was nothing salacious about that situation."

"That's what I thought, too…but in the picture, we looked much closer than I would have thought…and I was like, 'Wait, do we look like this to other people?' It came as a bit of a shock… I'm sorry. It's not really worth discussing with you for advice, but it just popped into my head. Oh, and I made sure to explain that you were a friend of my brother, so I think we're fine," Nayuta said, putting on a brave smile, although the reassurance did not reach her voice.

Hesitant and dreading the answer, Klever asked, "And…did that answer clear up the misunderstanding?"

She looked away without saying anything and popped a bit of pickled turnip into her mouth.

"Hmm…maybe I didn't quite flavor these enough. Do you prefer your pickles a bit more sour?"

"…No. This is just right for me."

Neither one of them wanted to face reality, so the conversation ended there.

The awkward mood, which promised to last well through their meal, shattered with the surprise ringing of the doorbell.

He wasn't expecting any other visitors. It was Sunday, so the home office was closed.

"Oh? Who's that?" Klever asked, relieved to have an excuse to stand up.

He checked the display on the intercom system and saw an adorable little girl who looked to be of elementary school age. He did not know her. But she seemed familiar to him somehow.

Who's that…? The daughter of a previous client, maybe? Or someone's relative…?

Visitors were not especially rare. But it was always one of a number of acquaintances or someone from a business partner coming on official business. This was not the sort of place a young child would come to visit.

He leaned toward the mic and said, "Hello, Clover's Network Security. Did you want something, little lady?"

"Yo, Kurei, it's me. Hey. Wanted to ask you for something. Can you let us in? Sorry, I know it's the weekend."

From beyond the camera's view, he could hear a rather casual male voice. The girl shifted her gaze to the side. Klever let out a sigh.

"Is that you, Narafushi? What is it today?"

"...C'mon, Kurei, don't be mad at me! I said I was sorry for puking in your house last time!"

The owner of the voice, Yahiko Narafushi, was a classmate from college. He knew Nayuta's brother as well, but he was not an SAO survivor. In fact, he had little to do with games at all. While they were trapped in a game of death, he had been busy day and night at his job.

Now he was the kind of guy who showed up now and then to get drunk and complain about work.

"I'm sorry, Nayuta. A friend has shown up. Do you mind if I let them in?"

"Of course I don't mind," she said. "Should I leave, then? Am I going to be intruding?"

He'd tutored her in math before lunch, so if they called it a day now, it wouldn't be the end of the world. But Klever decided to hold her back.

"Actually, he won't be long, I think. And I'd like to introduce you to someone who was a classmate of Daichi's and mine in college."

Nayuta's shoulders twitched.

At the funeral of her brother, Daichi Kushiinada, Narafushi had wailed at the top of his lungs, regardless of who might be watching. Klever, who was still trapped in the game, couldn't be there, but he eventually heard the story from someone else who was there.

If anything ever happened to me, would Narafushi be able to help her out?

He wasn't anticipating such a situation, but between traffic accidents and acts of God, you never knew what might happen in the future. And having trustworthy contacts in case of an emergency would be a good insurance policy for Nayuta.

Klever left her to clean up the dishes and went to the door to welcome his friend in.

"Listen, Narafushi, I've got a guest over now. It's Daichi's little sister."

Yahiko Narafushi was a scrawny young man with glasses. As he shook his shoes off in the entrance, he gave Klever a bewildered look.

"Huh? Daichi's...? What? I mean, why...? You know each other?"

"I'll fill you in on the how and why later. Just don't be shocked. I am not trying to pick up teenage girls here, so save your tasteless jokes, all right?" he growled.

Narafushi murmured, "Well, uh...I think she was in the hospital from the accident during Daichi's funeral... But she's all better now?"

"Yeah. She's leading an ordinary life. And...who's this? A relative of yours?" Klever asked, glancing at the little girl Narafushi had brought with him.

"No way. She's a popular child actor at our agency. You don't recognize her?"

The girl bowed politely. "It's nice to meet you. I'm Mahiro Kirihara. Mr. Narafushi's been very good to me."

Narafushi worked at a midsize talent agency. Naturally, he had never once brought any of the company's talent to the office. Suspicious, Klever nevertheless gave the girl an obsequious bow.

"That's very polite of you. My name is Kaisei Kurei. You'll have to forgive me; I don't have much time to watch TV, so…"

The child actor promptly replied, "It's fine. Most of my work is for children's fashion magazines and shows, and the occasional work as a child extra. I wouldn't expect you to be familiar with me."

For a child her age, the girl's voice was extremely calm and subdued. She wasn't sucking up to him, and she wasn't nervous, either.

Klever pressed his fingers to his eyes. "I see. A children's fashion model… So Narafushi, now the question is…why did you think I would know her?"

"Uh, because you're a lolico—"

"Leave. Now. I have nothing to say to you."

He turned his back. Immediately, Narafushi reached out and began to beg.

"S-sorry! I'm sorry, Kurei! Fine, I'll admit it—I lied! Look, it's just…you're a handsome guy, but you never seem to have any female connections! So that leaves three options: Either you're gay or a lolicon, or only into 2D girls, right?! I know you're not gay and I don't think the 2D thing is the case, so by the process of elimination… Oh! Unless you're a…*furry*…?" his friend said, lowering his voice to a conspiratorial hush.

Klever gave him a frosty look. For some reason, he had a mental image of Koyomi laughing mockingly.

"…In recent days, I've gotten to know a woman who really matches your wavelength. I can tell you'd just be unbearable together, so I hope I never introduce the two of you…"

"Seriously?" Narafushi cackled. "If she's my type, then she must be a hot babe with a nice personality, a good sense of humor, and just an all-around perfect doll. Damn, wish I could sign her to the agency."

He was probably seventy percent joking, thirty percent serious. Klever tried to contain his headache.

"…Aren't you just a manager? You're not an actual talent scout."

"Yeah, but I can still pitch people on joining. We're short-handed right now. Not that it's ever worked…for…me…"

As he came inside, Narafushi trailed off. Behind the glasses, his eyes were wide with shock.

Nayuta seemed similarly surprised by what she was seeing.

They broke the ensuing silence simultaneously a few moments later.

"…Miss! Do you have any interest in showbusiness…?"

"…Huh? Onihime…?"

With a start, Klever looked at the little girl again—Mahiro Kirihara, the child actor Narafushi was accompanying.

At last, Klever recognized the source of the strange sense of déjà vu he'd felt seeing the girl's face.

The demon puppet named Onihime that Nayuta had found in *Asuka Empire* during the holiday week in May looked just like this little girl.

Onihime seemed a little bit younger in appearance, but that was probably thanks to her clothing and facial expression. But when it came to the look in her eyes and the shape of her mouth, the resemblance was startling.

Stunned by this inexplicable coincidence, he could only share a shocked look with Nayuta.

For her part, the child actor seemed befuddled and stood there in silence—just the same way Onihime so often did.

§

"This is a shocker… Who knew Daichi's sister was so beautiful…? He never ever showed us any pictures or anything, right? I just assumed it meant she was ugly, but clearly it was the reverse… She's so hot he hid her from me, knowing I'd bug the hell out of him to introduce me to her," Narafushi grumbled once they had finished their introductions.

"No, that's not true… I'm very plain and boring, and shy on top

of that," Nayuta said, forcing herself to give the detective and her brother's friend a smile.

Narafushi misunderstood the smile and leaned over the table. "Miss Kushiinada, are you *sure* you don't have any interest in showbiz…?"

"No interest. Not in the slightest," she replied instantaneously.

He was stunned. He hadn't expected such a quick response. The detective burst into laughter.

"That's just what I expected you to say, but he's not going to give up if you don't explain yourself. What's your reasoning?"

Nayuta answered, "My reasoning…? Well, I'm not interested, and I hate standing out. I don't want to sing or act. Also, I find forcing myself to act friendly and put on a good face is very stressful, so I'm colossally unsuited to that line of work."

It wasn't the sort of career you could do without a lot of determination. Not only was she not determined, she didn't even want to be involved. Hence the severity of her answer.

"B-but you could at least come and check it out…," Narafushi pleaded, not even trying to hide his disappointment. The detective gave him a foxlike grin.

"Give it up, Narafushi. I'm against it, too. I'm sure you're thinking of getting her into a swimsuit shoot, but Daichi would've never let you do it."

"I don't even like being in pictures, period, much less in swimsuits," Nayuta added. "And I don't want to have to quit coming here… Just the fact that I'm visiting a single man's home like this would be forbidden as a female performer, right?"

Now it was the detective's turn to freeze up. Narafushi fixed him with a baleful glare.

"Kurei, you son of a bitch… Listen, I'm more forgiving than most about this stuff…I'm not gonna quote any laws at you, and I don't sell my friends out to the cops…but you know what? You shouldn't do anything you'd be ashamed to tell Daichi about…"

"I haven't done a single thing, so shut your mouth. We're in the presence of a child."

The child actor, who was drinking tea quietly off to the side, gave them a very forced smile that did not reach her eyes.

"Please don't mind me. I can wait until you're done with your conversation," she said. It was clear that she was completely uninterested in whatever stupid topic the adults were discussing.

That cynical, subdued expression really was very much like Onihime's. She had a different hair color and eyebrow shape, but her eyes and mouth were very recognizably similar.

"I'm sorry for making you wait," Nayuta told her. "This conversation was done the moment it started… Can you tell us why you're here?"

Mahiro Kirihara straightened up. "I'm looking…for my missing father," she said softly.

Nayuta was stunned. The detective's eyes narrowed, and he glared at Narafushi.

"What does this mean? You should be taking her to the police, not me…"

Narafushi shrugged and gave her a look that urged her to elaborate. Her expression turned a bit withdrawn.

"My parents are divorced. I live with my mother and I stay in regular contact with my father through text messages. But about a month ago, he sent me a message that he couldn't see me anymore, and I haven't heard from him since…"

The pain this caused her was clear from her voice.

"I tried talking to the police, but they couldn't help. They told me they couldn't start a search for someone who's vanished of their own accord. So I thought maybe I could ask a private investigator for help…"

Klever sighed. "I'm sorry, young lady, but this isn't—"

"Wait, Kurei, wait," interrupted Narafushi. "You're gonna tell her that your agency is only in the game, and you don't do investigations in real life, right? I know that. We don't want you to

investigate this…we just want your advice as a former police-
man. Is this the sort of thing a private eye would be able to get to
the bottom of, for example, and how do you tell a good detective
from a bad one, and so on… If you happen to know any consci-
entious detectives, I'd love to get some contact info. That's why
we're here today."

"…Let me answer those one by one," Klever said, stroking his
chin thoughtfully. "First, I can only say finding missing persons
is a case-by-case matter. It's highly dependent on the state of the
missing. If they've run off to their parents' or friends' home, it's
easy to find them. If they've fled overseas, or…well, it might be
insensitive to mention this, but if they've gotten involved in some
kind of incident that caused them to pass away, they can be very
difficult to find."

Despite bringing up the topic of death, the girl did not flinch.
She just nodded silently.

"And I do know another detective…but he works in investi-
gating adultery and performing background checks. Searching
for missing persons is tough. I suppose I could ask him to put
you through to someone else, but I honestly wouldn't recommend
it."

Klever's narrow eyes looked away.

"If the police aren't acting," he continued, "then it's a case that
doesn't include any danger signs like the possibility of suicide.
For whatever reason, your father indicated he was disappearing
of his own accord. When a grown-up with a certain level of intelligence and determination makes the decision to hide, it's not
easy to uncover them."

Mahiro's lips pursed. Narafushi reached down to pat her on the
shoulder, then gave Klever a pleading glance.

"Come on, have a heart… Is there really nothing you can do?
It's her father. This sweet little girl is looking for her father, and
he has no idea. Don't you want to do something to help her? Anyone would," he said.

Klever grimaced quite dramatically. Nayuta sensed his train of thought and felt sympathetic.

She said her parents were divorced, which means...

As painful as it might be to imagine, her father might have started a new family and chosen to cut ties in order to hide them from her.

"Your father is trying to distance himself from you."

It was just too cruel to be so blunt with a young girl who was only trying to find her father. The detective was trying to move the conversation forward without making that clear to her.

Narafushi probably hadn't realized this point yet—or if he did, he wasn't thinking about why the man would have done what he did. He was helping the girl out based on a very simplistic motive: *Her father is missing. Therefore, we have to help.*

Klever fixed her with a very intent look. "What is it you want to do by finding your father? Do you just want to talk with him? Do you have something to ask him for? Do you just want to know he's all right...? Think it over and give me the honest truth."

She looked confused. "Is it that strange for a child to want to see their daddy...?"

"I'm sorry, that was a bad way to ask you," Klever admitted, squinting a little. "Let's say he's had to move to another country for work, where he can talk to you on the phone but can't see you in person. If that's the case, would you only want to know he's safe—or would you want to go overseas to meet him?"

Mahiro clammed up. She hesitated about what to say, but ultimately couldn't bring herself to say anything and thought in silence.

In her reaction, Nayuta recognized something. In this day and age, there was a special piece of infrastructure that meant the distance across the sea was no big problem.

"Mahiro...were you meeting your father all the time...in VR?"

She twitched, and Klever was satisfied with that reaction.

"Yes, I see... Maybe having face-to-face meetings would break the terms of the divorce, perhaps? That's often a thing. And it's why you didn't want to discuss details."

In many divorces involving child custody, certain terms such as "one meeting every two months" were common.

"Don't worry—I won't tell your mother about that. I won't tell anyone, in fact. Just explain the truth to me. And depending on what you tell me, maybe I'll have better advice for you," he said, kind and reassuring. Nayuta was oddly impressed, and realized that maybe he was better with children than she would have expected.

Mahiro thought it over for a moment, then said, "I met Daddy in games a lot. Right before they got divorced, he slipped me a piece of paper with his phone number. He said it was so I could reach him if I needed help. When I got lonely and called him, he said we could meet in a game anytime. Mommy doesn't know about this. She thinks I haven't seen him in over a year."

Klever's gaze sharpened. "And would that have been in *ALf-heim*? That's a popular game. Or maybe..."

"*Asuka Empire*," she replied, sure enough.

Nayuta and the detective shared a look. Now there was a connection between the girl who looked like the demon puppet Onihime and *Asuka Empire*—and it couldn't possibly be a coincidence.

"Um...even if I can't see Daddy in person, I'm fine with seeing him in a game, just to know he's doing all right. But I couldn't even tell anyone I was meeting him once he went missing...so I thought...I have to look for him myself..."

Even Mahiro, who had seemed so self-assured and in control, started to slow down and lose focus. In other words, she was thinking about her answer and unsure of where to take it. She wasn't able to hide the fact that she *did* want to see her father in person, if possible.

The detective grinned. "I see. So the adults in your life think your father chose to disappear and hasn't seen you in a long while. So does that mean you *didn't* go to the police…?"

"No, that part is true. Mr. Narafushi escorted me there, rather than Mommy…"

Narafushi nodded and scratched at his head. "But when we explained the situation, they said it wasn't possible to search for him. They said she needed to discuss it with her mother… And, I mean, that makes sense. But if that were an option, she wouldn't have gotten me involved, would she?"

A bitter smile crossed Mahiro's lips. "Mommy's already divorced, and she doesn't want anything to do with him. I can't bring Daddy up at home anymore. If it wasn't for Mr. Narafushi, I don't think I could have asked the police for help, either."

"All right." The detective clapped his hands. "Tell me more about your father. Let's start with his name and a picture of his face. Plus the last messages you traded with him."

"Ah. Um, just a minute." She went into her bag to get out her phone. "His name is Munemitsu Yamashiro. Thirty-five years old. He does some kind of digital-type job, like systems engineer or programmer or something. Here's a picture of him."

She handed over a smartphone displaying a picture of a friendly-looking young man holding an even younger version of her. The detective examined it and frowned slightly. He'd noticed something, but didn't say what it was.

To give him more time to think, Nayuta filled the gap by noting, "He seems very young. How old were you in this picture…five years old or so?"

"Yes. It was before Daddy and Mommy got divorced… He wasn't home a lot of the time because of his work assignment, but when he was, he would play with me all the time. He's a very nice daddy," she said sadly. It was apparent just how worried she was.

"…May I take a look at your texts, too?"

"Yes. Umm…here."

Nayuta leaned over his shoulder to see the message.

*   *   *

Mahiro, I'm going to be too busy with work to stay in touch for a while. In fact, let's just stop seeing one another at all. I can't keep breaking my promise to your mother. Take care of yourself. 13, B6P, Munemitsu

The content of the message itself was pretty much what she expected. The issue was the bit of text at the end, which was clearly some kind of code.

"What are these letters and numbers, Mahiro? 13, B6P..."

Mahiro looked confused. "I don't know. I thought, based on their location, he might have typed in a date wrong...but he didn't write a date on any other messages, and when I asked him about that in a response, the message got returned to me. It seems like he deactivated that address after sending this text."

Nayuta peered at the detective. He was deep in thought; his profile had the smoldering look of a star actor.

"13...B6...P... Wait, but his other messages end with 'From Daddy.' This is the only one that he signs with his name, Munemitsu."

"Yes, I thought that was strange, too... It almost made me wonder if this was a fake message someone else sent to me..."

If that was the case, however, you'd think they would want to make the message uniform with his others. There wasn't a lot of reason to change his format.

"Yeah, exactly, it doesn't make a lot of sense," Narafushi said, pouting. "Doesn't it seem weird that the cops wouldn't budge for this? I know they don't want to get involved in domestic affairs, but they really should be searching for missing people; that's one of their main jobs."

"I'm not so sure that's true," Nayuta pointed out. "There are many instances where searching for missing persons is very delicate. It's one thing if the person searching has good and moral reasons, but they could also be a domestic abuser or a stalker trying to track down an escaped victim. Even within families, there might be people who go missing and don't want to be found because they've taken on debt and they don't want the collectors going after their relatives. That doesn't seem to be the case here, but it goes to show there are many reasons a person might want to hide..."

She clammed up after that. There were other, more unsavory possibilities she didn't want to discuss in front of Mahiro.

"...All right. I've got it," Klever said, saving Nayuta from embarrassment. He went into his desk drawer and pulled out a business card, which he handed to Mahiro. "Here's my card. When you get the chance, send me copies of that picture and the last text message. My e-mail address is on the card."

"Are you going to introduce me to a detective?" she asked, her voice brimming with hope.

Klever winked. "No, I've changed my mind. I will undertake an initial investigation of this one. I can get you to a real detective after that. If I give him everything I've learned, it should compress the amount of time he'll need to spend quite a bit. And on that subject, what is your budget for this investigation, Miss?"

She lifted her hands from her knees. "Around a 100,000 yen, for now... If it takes longer, I have access to about 600,000 in total."

Klever whistled softly. "Well, that's certainly enough to hire the real thing. Keep that money for when you really need it. There's nothing wrong with holding on to it for later. As for my costs...I'll bill Narafushi for them. You're man enough to cover for her, right?"

"Huh?" Narafushi blanched. "I...er...w-well...as long as you give me the friends and family discount..."

"It's fine, Mr. Narafushi. I'll pay for it," Mahiro whispered reassuringly. Narafushi adopted an awkward grimace and beat his chest.

"N-no! I'm fine! I was the one who brought you here, and he's not gonna rip me off or anything! I think... You're not gonna do that, are you?"

Klever chuckled to himself. "There was a customer who hired me for a job recently who gave me 1,000,000 yen just for a successful result. Including the exclusivity contract and after-service follow-up care, I ended up making 2,000,000 yen in total."

Nayuta rolled her eyes. He was talking about Yanagi.

"Did you really get that much from him? That seems crazy," she said.

"Yeah. And I insisted I couldn't accept more than what we agreed upon in the contract," Klever said with a shrug. "But he said the extra wasn't a payment for the job, but a special fund for me to set aside for when I want to help someone else, and that person doesn't have the funds to pay for my services. That was his last will to me, which I accepted with the money. I couldn't refuse that. People like him are just pure of heart."

It sounded like the exact sort of heartfelt thing Yanagi would do. Nayuta felt her eyes well up with tears. The detective quickly turned to grab Narafushi's attention before he could whip out a handkerchief for her.

"But that aside, I *will* be accepting payment from you, so don't worry about that. I think the housecleaning fee from the last time you threw up in here should be included in the bill, too."

"Ah-ha-ha-ha...ha-ha...yeah. Sorry about that..."

Mahiro just watched them with a faint little smile on her lips. Her gaze had seemed cold and subdued when she showed up, but there was more of a natural childlike relief there now. When she noticed Nayuta looking at her, she murmured, "Um...were you saying something when I showed up, Nayuta? Oni-something..."

For an instant, Nayuta hesitated, then remembered she was also an *Asuka Empire* player. So there was a good chance she'd already heard about the demon puppets.

"Well, um, have you heard about the demon puppets people are talking about in the game? I'm in possession of one named Onihime, who's a little girl puppet right around your age... You remind me of her a little bit, so I was just startled to see you," she explained. The girl just looked confused, as did Narafushi.

"You didn't have any jobs relating to that, right, Mahiro...?"

"No. It's a puppet that looks like me, you're saying?"

"Yep. Would you like to meet up in the game and see for yourself? And if there are any quests that are bothering you, I can help you out with them," Nayuta suggested, hoping it might alleviate some of Mahiro's stress.

Before the girl could respond, however, the detective interjected, "Yes, I would ask that you do that as well. I think you're going to have to tackle a rather annoying quest."

This came as a surprise to Nayuta. "Huh...? Um, Detective... does that have anything to do with her request?"

"For one thing, my detective work is limited to the game itself," Klever said, winking at her. "Real-world investigations are outside of my area of expertise, and I have no plans to change that. Also, the reason I accepted her request is because I believe the hint related to her father is going to be found inside *Asuka Empire*."

When they looked back at him blankly, Klever wrote the number *13* on the wall-mounted whiteboard.

"At the end of his final text message. I didn't know what it was at first, but then something occurred to me. You and your father met all the time in *Asuka Empire*, didn't you? Well, in the ongoing event called 108 Apparitions, the thirteenth quest to be released was the Thirteen-Floor Underground Labyrinth."

Nayuta gasped softly. The Thirteen-Floor Underground Labyrinth was an infamously difficult quest that was the hardest of those revealed in the early stages of the event. Not only was the fright index rather high, the mid-bosses were very tough to beat, and the labyrinth itself was extremely large and deep.

This wasn't the kind of maze you beat one floor at a time. It had stairs that went up and down constantly, meaning that in order to keep from getting lost, you needed a three-dimensional understanding of the pathfinding involved to get from one place to another.

"13, B6P—I believe B6 stands for the sixth basement floor. The map for that quest is split into tiny sections from A to Z for each floor. There's usually a save point in section A and X, while the boss of that floor is in section Z…but the stairs aren't placed only after the boss, so you can go all the way down to the twelfth basement floor without beating any bosses. In order to get into the sealed bottom floor, you have to beat all the bosses first, but we'd be going to section P of the sixth floor, where I assume we'll find something. Maybe I'm wrong, and we're just going to be wasting our time, but we won't have to fight any bosses to get there, and I think that's the best place to go first."

"Just a minute," Nayuta hastily interrupted. "I don't understand. How can he hide a hint inside the game unless he's one of the develop…oh."

Mahiro's eyes shot open.

Was Mahiro's father a member of the *Asuka Empire* development team? That possibility allowed many lines to reach a single point.

"Was your father the one who instructed you to use *Asuka Empire* as a meeting place with him?" Nayuta asked. The girl nodded.

The detective folded his hands and steepled his fingers. "This is all purely speculation. But given his job in programming, the meetings he suggested using *Asuka Empire*, the Onihime puppet who looks just like you, and the blatant use of a mysterious code, I think all these things are too aligned to be a coincidence. I've decided it's worth digging into this as the first step of our investigation."

Mahiro fixed him with a tense look and lowered her head.

"…Please, sir. Help me find my daddy."

Nayuta gently put her hands on the girl's shoulders from behind. "It's all right. He might look fishy, but you can trust him. I know he'll manage to solve this for you," she whispered, placing an extra bit of pressure on the detective.

Meanwhile, Narafushi seemed crestfallen at this interaction.

"Hey…Kurei, man… How did you manage to get this babe of a high school student to put so much trust in you…? It makes no sense at all… What was it? Did you use hypnosis? Are you blackmailing her?"

"It is a reflection of my virtuous behavior. Also...I've been told I look so obviously sketchy that I seem more like an NPC than a person. Perhaps that makes people lower their guards a bit," he joked. It caught Mahiro off-guard, and she laughed.

"I...*cough!* I'm sorry...I didn't mean...!"

"I didn't go *that* far when describing you. It's just that my first impression of you was of the monster fox trying to pass itself off as human in The Fox's Wedding Parade, that's all."

"*Pfft!*"

One of the 108 Apparitions quests, The Fox's Wedding Parade, featured a very folkloric theme of protecting the bride from harm when the wicked fox took the form of a beautiful young man. Mahiro must have played this quest, too, because she was quite tickled by the comparison. She covered her face with her hands, shoulders twitching, eliciting a lukewarm look from Narafushi.

"...The thing is, while Mahiro plays it cool most of the time, she can be a bit of a gigglepuss. We'd be happy to give her more live TV appearances if she could just get that under control. Instead, she's more likely to cause a minor controversy..."

Nayuta rubbed the back of the helplessly convulsing girl, somewhat perplexed by the difference between this version of her and the one who'd walked in the door.

Onihime the demon puppet never smiled, but she looked like a smile would suit her face well. When that very similar face on Mahiro burst into laughter like this, she seemed even more endearing.

Even Klever, who watched the scene unfold with bemusement, couldn't hide the upward curl of his mouth.

§

After Narafushi and Mahiro left the office, Nayuta washed the dishes in the kitchen with Klever. She whispered, "Detective... what were you hiding in that conversation?"

With his hands covered in suds, the man remarked, "I think you'd be a better detective than I would. Or am I just that sloppy?"

"I think you'd be surprised at how quickly your face lets on when you're flustered. But if you don't want to talk about it, I won't pry…"

Klever shook his head. "No, no, I'll tell you. But first…did you pick up on what kind of lie I told?"

"I have a feeling you know her father personally. You froze up when you saw his picture."

He laughed until his shoulders shook.

"If you ever challenge me to a game of poker, I'm running the other way. The man in the picture she showed me looked *exactly* like an engineer I know named Endou. He was part of the development team for *Asuka Empire*, but from what I hear, he left the team back in April."

The name sounded vaguely familiar to Nayuta.

"Isn't that…the person Mr. Torao was talking about a while ago? The one who was angry over the confusion with the demon puppets, and quit to take a job with a different company…"

The colossal boondoggle behind the scenes of the demon puppet implementation was very fresh in her memory.

"Yes, that's the one. In Torao's story, he was angry over his treatment and decided to leave…but after hearing what the girl just said, I have a feeling that story doesn't really explain the whole thing."

"And he's not just a coincidental lookalike? Based on the picture, her father didn't look particularly memorable to me…"

"It's certainly possible; I wasn't particularly close to him. Which is why I didn't say anything earlier…but I am a former police officer, after all. I had to take lessons on recognizing features to ensure we didn't have any mistaken identities when it came to tracking down culprits."

"In that case, I'm sure it's him. The different last name might mean that he remarried and took his new wife's name."

If that was the case, then it might explain why he wanted to distance himself from Mahiro.

But the detective's eyes narrowed. "The thing is, it's not just his last name, but his first name that's different, too. The software engineer I know is named Tooru Endou."

Her hand stopped in the middle of wiping a saucer clean. It was going to take her a bit more time to understand the meaning of what the detective had just said.

"...And it's not a pen name or creative name of some kind?"

"We'll need to confirm with Mr. Torao and the staff first. But based on what little Mahiro said...it kind of feels like he's in some bad business. That's just a hunch, which is why I didn't bring it up. Maybe I'm worrying for nothing."

The disappearance of a programmer with the same face, but a different name...

Having grown up in a police family, Nayuta's instincts told her nothing but bad things about this.

"Detective...you don't think this might be something for the police...or the Public Security Intelligence Agency, do you?"

Agents from other countries abducting or murdering Japanese nationals to assume their identities was the kind of spycraft that really did happen.

But the detective wasn't quite ready to leap to that level of danger.

"I'd like to think we're not dealing with something that serious, but it's a possibility to take into account. Personally, however, I'm eyeing the angle that he might be a fugitive."

Nayuta's brow furrowed. In the background, water trickled from the faucet. If he turned out to be a fugitive from a real crime, then the police wouldn't just let him go.

The detective took note of the alarm in her eyes. "I considered the possibility of him being an industrial spy, but *Asuka Empire* isn't all that technically advanced, and I don't see the merit in sending him to a company like that. Seems like a much lower price-to-performance ratio compared with a pharmaceutical corp or military-industrial company. Which means either he's fleeing a crime that hasn't been uncovered yet, or he's involved in a crime that won't be made public, and had to assume another name to work undercover," he said smoothly, rapidly running through the list of possibilities. "Maybe he got into money trouble with organized crime or a dangerous cult, and he needed to hide himself. If that was the reason behind the divorce, then it would make perfect sense that the mother would want to cut off her daughter from contacting him. Maybe it's simple embezzlement or theft. Or he caused a major loss of investment or committed fraud against a mafia front without realizing who it was. Any of these seems possible."

Nayuta shivered. From what little hints could be gleaned from the short conversation with Mahiro earlier, Klever had formulated so many ideas. It was all just speculation and imagination, but it made logical sense.

"If he's vanished because of a reason like that, then it would be poor form to hire a private investigator to look for him," Klever continued. "It's possible the people who are after him would have access to the detectives' network of intelligence. If Mahiro introduces some very potent new leads...well, I don't want to think about what might happen."

A chill ran down Nayuta's spine. She glanced up at the detective at the sink next to her. "So the reason you convinced them not to just hire another detective is..."

He nodded gravely. "Right. It's not because the detective would be useless. You never know the skill of who you're going to get, but you should never count out a detective's ability to search for information. Many detectives are former police agents, and some of the larger agencies have multiple offices with the resources to work quickly. And the most serious angle of all is that they are faithful to the nature of their clients' requests. There are things they can and cannot do, and PIs are subject to their own regulations…but there are individual differences in ethics and legality depending on the vendor."

He handed her the last dish. Nayuta took it and wiped it with the cloth.

"How much confidence do you have in your current speculation?" she asked.

"Not much. I don't have enough information, and as you pointed out, it could just be a creative alias. So, Nayuta, I want you to keep all this a secret from Mahiro. I'd like to hear about the situation from her mother…but I can't imagine she'd tell a stranger something she hasn't even told her own daughter. It'd be a waste of time to ask. I'd rather follow that encoded message to the quest first. My hunch is that he might have hidden a letter there that contains an explanation for her about why he disappeared."

But something about this struck Nayuta as vaguely *wrong*.

"An explanation…? That seems like the sort of thing he should tell his daughter directly rather than utilizing a code."

"I can understand why a father might not want to expose his weakness and shame to the daughter he loves," Klever said, grimacing. "It's a father's dilemma—not wanting her to know, if he's being honest, but not something he can simply hide from her, either. Maybe he wanted to leave a hint for her, no matter how obscure it seems."

It was there that Nayuta finally realized the worst-case scenario that Klever hadn't mentioned yet.

"…It's not going to turn out that what he's hidden there is his last will and testament, is it?"

"If that's the case, then we're already too late. It's been over a month since he vanished. But…if it's a will, then he wouldn't hide it in such a convoluted way. If you're going to die, then just leave it in your apartment. But mainly, I just really don't want to see that situation play out," Klever said, his voice toughening. It happened very briefly, though, giving way to a bewitching smile. "Of course, it's silly to allow your predictions to be swayed by emotion. But it's also a problem to assume the worst and give up early on account of it. Maybe it'll turn out that he's gotten sick of his normal job, and is just hanging out and sleeping in some cheap net café right now."

Nayuta nodded, knowing full well this was a very unlikely possibility. "Sometimes it's better to just do something rather than sit back and have anxiety over it. I'll put my hope in your luck stat."

"That's a lot of responsibility. Now, you might not be in the mood for an English lesson at the moment, but what do you say? Shall we spend an hour on it?"

The only reason Nayuta was coming there was to get lessons to prepare for exams. The cooking was just her way of paying him back for the trouble. She'd already had an hour of math lessons before lunch, so it wasn't a total waste of time if she left now.

"No, I think I'll head home. I'm sure you want to get started on your preparations as soon as possible. I was thinking of coming back around Wednesday. Do you have any meal requests?" she asked out of consideration.

He made a face. "No, not really…"

"Then I'll make beef stew, since that's what *I* want to have."

She could already guess what he wanted to say to this, but she headed him off with a dazzling smile.

Diet was important. Nayuta enjoyed eating with Klever much more than she did having a lifeless meal alone. Coming up with meals gave her something to look forward to and a fulfilling reason to get through the day. She'd cleverly earned this privilege over time, and she had no reason to give it up now.

"Oh, and Detective, are you a fan of green peppers? I put them in my beef stew, but I know not everyone likes them, so I thought I'd ask—"

"I've got no issues with green peppers… You know, maybe it's just me, but I feel like there's a more fundamental issue here. Yes, I tend to neglect meals, and I'm certainly grateful for this…but how is it you make such a good housewife at your age?" he said with wonder.

"I do?" she asked. "I've been living alone for long enough that I think I'm just used to taking care of myself. I get lunch at school, so I need a proper dinner at night—and if my guess is correct, I think you often get the laziest option for each meal of the day."

"...There you go with the housewife thing again," said the detective weakly, aware that he was being swept along without an oar. Nayuta ignored his complaints and left the office behind.

It was less than thirty minutes, combining trains and walking time, to get between Klever's office and Nayuta's apartment. If she was over too late, he would drive her home in his car, which was why she made sure to finish up at a reasonable hour so she didn't interrupt his work for too long.

He sent her a message while she was on the train home.

Mahiro asked me about my schedule. It looks like we're going to try that quest Wednesday night. Narafushi won't be there, so we can invite Koyomi and go as a group of four.

She started to respond, and a mean-spirited tease popped into her head.

In that case, I'll bring over the food and my AmuSphere. Will I need supplies for a sleepover?

If it comes to that, I'm spending the night at a nearby net café.

Impressed with his inopportune fussiness, she set down the smartphone and giggled to herself.

§

Monday and Tuesday were uneventful and passed slowly for Nayuta, until at last it was Wednesday night.

On the table between them steamed two bowls of beef stew.

"Just a dash of red wine makes a huge difference, even to the store-bought roux mix. It's nice, since I can't buy alcohol as high schooler. And substituting cooking mirin just isn't the same."

He exhaled, spoon in his hand. "You really can do every-thing... You're quick and precise, and the flavor is perfect. I can't believe it's possible to whip up a legitimate beef stew in such a short amount of time."

"Anyone can make this with the right ingredients and a pressure cooker. In my case, I just couldn't make it because I couldn't buy the wine…I considered trying it with grape juice and mirin, but it didn't seem worth the effort."

"A wise choice. Cultivate that sensibility in yourself," the detective said gravely. Nayuta found it funny that he could be so serious about such silly commentary.

"It really is delicious, though," Klever remarked. "You didn't put some secret ingredient in, did you? Like chocolate or herbs, or…"

"Nothing, really. Oh, and don't worry—the secret ingredient isn't something clichéd like 'love,' so you can eat without fear," Nayuta joked. He gave her a dry, obliging chuckle.

When their dinner was over, the detective made a show of rolling up his shirtsleeves. "All right," he said, "we've got a bit of time before our meeting with Mahiro. I'll clean the dishes, so you head home now while you've got the chance—"

But Nayuta was already pulling her AmuSphere out of her school bag.

"I appreciate you doing the cleaning up. I'm supposed to be meeting up with Koyomi to explain things first, and it's time for me to get going, so I'll just log in from here," she said. Before he could say a word, Nayuta was already connecting her device.

"Uh, hey, wait…," he protested weakly, but she was already lying down on the couch, and gave him a sidelong glance.

"Don't worry, Detective. I don't act this trusting around anyone else. Consider that a reflection on how I feel about your character."

During a full dive, her body was essentially in a state of unconsciousness. Unlike with a NerveGear, the AmuSphere's safety settings would respond to some level of external stimuli, but she wouldn't wake up from, say, gentle contact against her chest. This was the sort of tool that ought not to be used around people of the opposite sex who were not your family or intimate lover.

"That kind of unconditional trust is blind faith. Just wait. At least go to a room that locks from the inside..."

"Link Start," she said, cutting her mind off from reality and sending it to virtual space. The last bit of vision in the corner of her eye had resembled the detective with his head in his hands, but she wasn't concerned with that now.

After logging in, she was at the cat-god shrine on Yoiyami Street of Ayakashi Alley. You could choose to start from pretty much anywhere in a town you'd visited before, but she often found herself logging in here these days. It was the closest spot to the Three-Leaf Detective Agency, and it was less busy than the main street, so it was easier to meet up here.

There was Koyomi, standing right below the torii gate.

"Oh! Nayu! Hya-haaa!" she said, launching herself onto Nayuta, who beamed. Koyomi the ninja was small enough to barely be taller than Mahiro, a grade-schooler, but she was, in fact, a company employee who was older than Nayuta.

"You beat me here. Were you waiting long?"

"Nope. I logged in about ten seconds ago, and I was just thinking about whether to message you or not. Is this Mahiro girl here yet?"

Nayuta had given Koyomi a general rundown of the situation when she had invited her to join this mission.

"She should be coming to the Three-Leaf Detective Agency in about thirty minutes. Shall we talk in the office?"

"Hmm...oh! I know, let's go get Nyanko Soba! I was just having sweet and sour pork for dinner, so I could really use something light and refreshing to cap it off. What did you have for dinner?"

"Beef stew. I used a pressure cooker," she explained. She couldn't reveal that she was at Klever's house right then.

As they strolled down Yoiyami Street, Koyomi bounded along with such excitement that you could practically see a tail wagging.

"Ooh, beef stew, huh? Ooh, I wish I could have some beef stew. That's really laudable of you, Nayu, making such an involved dish when you live alone."

If she were alone, Nayuta would have been much lazier. But if she said anything to that effect, it would lead to Koyomi finding out about everything with the detective. Nayuta didn't like keeping secrets from her, but this affected Klever's reputation as well.

The Nyanko Soba shop, run by two-tailed *nekomata* cats, was right near the Three-Leaf Detective Agency. They went in and sat in the booth at the back, where Koyomi got a fresh tray of *zaru* soba for dipping and Nayuta got soba ice cream for dessert— which was just buckwheat-flavored.

"There are more toppings in the self-service area now. Fish cake, sakura shrimp, chicken tempura, crunchies...crunchies?" said Koyomi.

"Oh, that's for the staff. It's basically dried cat kibble," replied Nayuta.

Honestly, something like that really shouldn't be offered in a list of toppings at a soba restaurant.

Koyomi dug into her serving of soba noodles and Nayuta scooped her ice cream as they settled in to discuss their mission for the evening.

"...So basically, this child actor girl's father is named Yamashiro, and Yamashiro started passing himself off as a programmer named Endou, but now he's gone missing... So that makes me ask, what happened to the *real* Endou?" Koyomi asked. It was a perfectly valid question to have, but Nayuta froze.

To pass oneself off as another person required that person's identifying information. If he was working at the company under that name, then he needed some kind of government-issued ID. You couldn't just call yourself a stranger's name and expect it wouldn't hit snags with the bureaucracy.

They had been hired to search for Mahiro's father, but they still knew nothing about the man whose identity he was assuming, Endou.

"...Where could he have gone?"

"Right? It's a good question."

There were times when Koyomi picked up on things that Nayuta completely overlooked.

So we've got two missing people, actually, Nayuta reminded herself as they left Nyanko Soba, satisfied.

The nearby Three-Leaf Detective Agency was set up on the second floor of a building. They took the stairs up and were greeted by a giant black cat-Buddha statue that was at least ten feet tall. This very odd statue was somehow in a different pose every time they saw it. In this instance, it had a cone of soft-serve ice cream in one raised hand, while the other cradled a manga magazine to its chest.

"Oh. The Statue of Liberty."

"If you ask me, this cat seems to have a little too much liberty."

They walked past the smug cat-Buddha and opened the door to the agency office. Klever and the girl were already inside, and the room had the scent of tea.

"Ah, there you are. Right on time," the detective said, waving at them from his desk. Seated across from him was a girl dressed in samurai armor who looked very similar to Onihime. She stood up from the couch and bowed to Nayuta and Koyomi, then spoke in the tones of a child actor who was used to projecting.

"Good evening. My name is Mahiro. Thank you for helping me today."

Koyomi couldn't handle that greeting and lost her composure. "Sh...she's so *cyoot!* Wow! And she really looks just like Onihime! Wow! So cute! So cute! Nayu, she's so cute!"

Nayuta gave Koyomi a forced smile and said nothing about her lack of vocabulary.

"We're happy to be here, Mahiro. This is Koyomi the ninja," she said, pushing Koyomi forward. "She's older than me, so she'll be a big help to you."

It wasn't a lie. Nayuta, at the very least, thought of Koyomi as reliable help.

Mahiro was dressed in a *hakama* underneath, with a samurai torso and breastplate, gauntlets on her hands, and an *uchigatana* sword on her back. Because of her short height, it made the sword look quite long, but it was actually about average for a weapon of its type.

Unlike the demon puppet Onihime, her hair was black and her eyebrows were slender, but her facial features were very similar. Maybe not to the point of being identical twins, but certainly sisters or cousins.

Koyomi bounded over to Mahiro and hugged her by the shoulder. "Nice to meet you! So are you a samurai?"

"No, I play as a tactician. I just look like a samurai because of the armor..."

A tactician was a job with a wider variety of skills than a samurai, but with trickier prerequisites to use those skills and complex added damage conditions. It was considered a difficult job that required a more technical approach.

It was possible to do more damage in spurts than a samurai, but if any of the requirements to unlock that power weren't met, your performance could easily fall short of even the starter jobs, so it was considered a fickle but aspirational job that demanded considerable experience to play well.

Given Mahiro's equipment, she seemed to primarily function as a tank.

I wonder if she'll form a good combo with Onihime...

Onihime the demon puppet was set to be a support player in the back row. If she teamed up with Mahiro on the front row, they would probably make a well-balanced party.

While Koyomi continued excitedly fawning over Mahiro, the detective whispered in Nayuta's ear, "I want to speak to you later."

She could guess it was about the way she'd turned on her AmuSphere in front of him earlier.

"I'm pretty sure I know what it's about already, but that's your fault to begin with," Nayuta shot back, which elicited a rare look of pure umbrage from him.

"My fault? I have to take issue with that..."

"You keep saying you're afraid of being unjustly accused of

wrongdoing or being framed, or that teenage girls frighten you— all of which tells me you have no trust in me. Unless I make it very clear by my attitude that I trust you, I don't think you're going to fix your attitude—so consider this a kind of shock therapy."

He froze spectacularly.

"...You're right. It's my fault."

One of the tragic parts of his character was that his senses of logic and reasoning were so strong, he had no defense against a sensible argument.

"...But...but still, that doesn't mean you should..."

"We can keep discussing this if you want, but Koyomi will hear," she murmured back. The detective's mouth clamped shut. He wasn't in the habit of barbecuing over an open grill next to a pile of explosives.

At that very moment, Koyomi turned to them. "Nayu, Nayu! Why don't we show Onihime to her? She might be a bit shocked if the first time she sees her is in the middle of a battle!"

Nayuta agreed. She selected the demon puppet from her item list. Onihime appeared next to Nayuta in an aura of light. Mahiro's eyes went wide.

"...You're right...she does look just like me..."

Tactician and *onmyoji*—their jobs and positions in battle were polar opposites—but standing side by side, the resemblance was undeniable.

The puppet stared into nothingness and did not budge. Mahiro, meanwhile, was so intimidated that she froze up, which made her look like a puppet in her own right.

Eventually she mumbled, "I think...Daddy built this puppet." Her voice was even a little mirthful. "A long time ago, Daddy asked me if I wanted anything, and I told him, 'I want a little sister I can play games with.' I just didn't expect it would happen like this... Ha-ha... If they really put this into the game, I'll have to put in the work to get one, too."

"I see...," Nayuta murmured, smiling.

As someone who created a false version of her own family in order to live off it and her memories, this was a topic Nayuta had many thoughts about. She wouldn't deny this girl her desire out of hand, but she wouldn't recommend it without reservation, either.

In Mahiro's case, her circumstances were wildly different from Nayuta's, and while you could take her statement as a simple recollection of the past and nothing deeper, the young girl's desire to see her father was clearly real.

Apparently, the preliminary investigation the detective did on her father, Munemitsu Yamashiro, wasn't looking very good. The company also wasn't sure about the whereabouts of Endou, the programmer who'd recently quit.

The rental unit he'd been living in before his disappearance was all paid off, and no one knew where he'd moved. No one even knew the name of the company that had hired him away. The most reliable information they had was just a secondhand report about what he had told others. At this point, it was doubtful whether he had even really taken a new job or not.

In short, they had learned two or three days of investigation weren't going to turn up the truth. Ever since hearing this, Nayuta had prepared herself for the worst.

Mahiro's father, Munemitsu Yamashiro, had assumed the identity of Tooru Endou, a programmer, and joined the development team of *Asuka Empire*.

They didn't know the reason for this disappearance, but it was clear something had gone wrong with him. While Klever and Nayuta had nothing more substantial than a hunch, Mahiro seemed to sense something was wrong, too, and it was showing on her face.

After setting up their in-game party, the group left the office.

They were heading for the sixth story of the Thirteen-Floor Underground Labyrinth, where they were likely to find...*something*.

As they took their first determined steps toward their goal, Nayuta reached down and squeezed the girl's little fist.

A Companion for Your Dares—Demon Puppet 1

The "demon puppet" feature overcame the criticism that it contained the radical for "rice paddy" too many times (five in four kanji!) and made it into the game as a major feature, with great hopes for both players and developers.

The dare-type quests in the 108 Apparitions event require solo play, meaning that the difficulty level could fluctuate wildly from player to player, depending on which job they undertake. The team felt they had no choice but to make the enemies easier and lower the level of difficulty across the board to ensure everyone could finish them.

But by introducing these fighting puppets, players can now bring a companion to fight on either the front or rear line, making up for their personal weakness and allowing for a greater level of strategy.

Demon puppet stats are placed roughly five levels below that of their owner, and will increase along with yours. However, the benefit of equipment in *Asuka Empire* is fairly massive, and this holds true for puppets, too.

In other words, if you found some excellent gear that wasn't for your job, and was sitting around gathering dust in your inventory, you can now give it to your puppet.

The base models come in several forms, such as human, animal, and *yokai*, but it's clear that the most popular are those with a pleasing appearance, such as the active beauty Raika, the cool and low-key young Onihime, and the adorable little boy Ginya. As in life, a doll's looks are its soul.

Chapter 4

The Book of Onihime, Part Two

Munemitsu Yamashiro, the programmer, once had a wife and family.

Now they were divorced and lived apart.

There were multiple reasons for the divorce, but the clincher was a request from the wife for him to stop involving them in danger.

Yamashiro accepted her request, and his wife and daughter returned to her family name. Not much time had passed since the divorce when his now ex-wife's concerns abruptly proved themselves prescient.

"...You're in trouble, man. The Tonami guys think you ran off with the investment deposit. That idiot Asanuma lied that you were the ringleader before they could dump him into the harbor," warned an older coworker over the phone. It was a death notice. His mind went blank.

If he'd been driving at the time, he would have crashed his car at once. Sadly, he was stationary. A thought passed through his mind: how much easier it would've been to just die without warning, without time to worry about anything.

"But...but I'm just a systems guy! I never took anything more than my salary...!"

"They don't see it that way. You were the computer guy, so they don't know your face, which only makes you more suspicious to them. They're not going to listen to reason from you, so you need to go into hiding. Got any places where you can hole up?"

Yamashiro shook his head. His voice trembled. "Of course I don't have anything like that!"

He certainly couldn't go back to his ex-wife and daughter. He'd cut off ties with every other relative and friend.

The older coworker clicked his tongue at the sound of fear in Yamashiro's voice. "Look, sheltering you will mean putting myself in danger. You gotta figure this one out on your own. Later."

"Huh?! H-hey, wait!"

The other man hung up.

Yamashiro tried to call back in a panic, but his coworker wasn't answering.

He ran his hands through his short blue hair in shock. Before the divorce, he had gone with his natural black hair to emphasize his diligence and professionalism, but because his looks were exceedingly plain, having a boring hairstyle as well tended to single him out as an easy mark to others in the group.

But no matter what he did to his hair and clothes, he could not deny to himself that he was just an idiot and a coward.

"...Goddammit...I just can't...like, what? Where am I supposed to run and hide...?"

He couldn't formulate a single useful thought.

If he sought the protection of the police, they might take him into custody on a minor charge, but once he was released, they'd just kill him anyway. There was no way for a common, jumped-up thug to find safety and solace.

Could he just pick someone on the street at random to slaughter and get a longer sentence in a proper prison? No, he didn't have the guts for that. And it would only ruin the lives of his ex-wife and daughter.

He combed through the contacts on his phone, desperate for anyone who might be able to help. All of a sudden, the phone began to ring in his hands.

"...Aieee...!"

Someone was calling him. The number was unlisted.

"H...hello...?" he asked, wiping a cold sweat from his brow.

A muffled voice replied, "Mr. Yamashiro...? It's me, Kurage... Seems like raw shit is going down."

Kurage was a former coworker from the company. It wasn't really a "company" so much as a malicious investment fraud scheme that went through repeated bankruptcies and fresh starts, where Yamashiro developed the system and performed maintenance.

He and Kurage had only worked together for a short time. He remembered him as a gloomy and tedious young man.

In short, the same as me.

"Oh...it's you... I'm going through hell, man... I knew I shoulda gotten out of this business last year. Take a lesson from me and get out while the going's good."

"You're a good programmer, Mr. Yamashiro, but you don't know much about how the world works. Not that I'm much smarter, but at least I know when to pick my battles..."

"Fine, fine...so what's this about? Are you helping me or what?" Yamashiro grunted sardonically. He wasn't expecting the answer he got.

"That was my plan. I don't know how to make a living for myself, so having you around helps me, I guess... Are you in your car? Can you get to the Jukai area?" he asked, as casually as an invitation to go out to karaoke.

"...What? But...Jukai is..."

The "Sea of Trees," Aokigahara, a place famed for its seclusion and thick forest—a place where people often disappeared.

"I'm gonna drive over there now, so let's meet up there. Then you can get into my car and leave the company car there with your phone inside. That way you'll go down as missing in the forest. The Tonami folks will probably find it before the police, so it won't even go in the government record. They won't believe you committed suicide, I'm sure, but it buys you time and throws them off your trail... We can discuss the rest once we meet up."

Yamashiro was even more confused now.

"But...you know what I'm dealing with now, right?! I'm in deep shit! If you help shelter me, you're gonna be treated as an accomplice..."

"If things really start looking bad, I'll say you came seeking me, and I didn't know anything about what was going on, and I'll run away. I'm sure it won't come to that, though... What do you say?"

We picked the wrong party to fool this time. And the attempt to put out the fire afterward was a disaster.

Yamashiro didn't know who had taken the money and run with it, but it was obvious he had been made the scapegoat to throw the mob off his trail.

If they caught him, they'd kill him to serve as an example.

If he knew where the money was, he could at least tell them, but he didn't even know that.

It was an odd and somewhat suspicious offer of help at a time when he desperately needed it. Munemitsu Yamashiro didn't think he had much of a choice.

"...Thanks. I need help," he rasped.

"No prob. We'll talk about details when we meet up. Here's the location..."

At the end of the phone call, Yamashiro woke up from a sweaty, unpleasant slumber. He didn't feel like he'd slept at all.

"...That dream again..."

It hadn't been that long ago, but it was hard for him to tell if his situation had improved or gotten worse since then.

The senior coworker who'd hung up on him was dead now, apparently. Probably murdered.

Kurage was dead, too. He'd died of illness while bathing. Yamashiro didn't know what to do with the body. As it happened, someone came along and took it away before he did anything.

Yamashiro did not really know anything about the identity of this "someone."

They were the ones who hired Kurage. They were quiet, blunt, and always in a hurry.

After Kurage's death came to light, they swept in to inspect the place, stepped aside to confer on the matter, then said to Yamashiro, "We want you to continue performing Kurage's job."

Sensing that refusing this request would lead to him being permanently silenced, Yamashiro wisely accepted. But it meant he would be unable to perform any public jobs.

After a bit of time off, the game programmer known as Tooru Endou vanished with a hint of a job relocation, while Munemitsu Yamashiro, who was staying hidden on the run, cut off all contact with his daughter, Mahiro Kirihara.

He abandoned his family, lost a friend to death, and cut loose his own past. He didn't have his own name anymore.

He was all alone in the world.

§

It was the 108 Apparitions, a year-long ongoing event in *Asuka Empire*.

The thirteenth quest associated with the event was called the Thirteen-Floor Underground Labyrinth, and was a dramatic escape from a very mysterious prison.

It started in a detainment area underground.

Concrete walls hemmed them in on three sides, while the fourth wall was blocked by iron bars. There was no window in the cramped room.

The portal gate Nayuta had traveled through disappeared behind her, leaving her trapped in the cell alone. There was a simple wooden bench meant to serve as a crude bed—and nothing else.

A few seconds later, a high-pitched and familiar voice came from the adjoining cell on the other side of the wall.

"Whaaaa…? I'm alone all of a sudden?! This sucks! Where's Nayu?!"

"Calm down, Koyomi," Nayuta replied. "I'm right next door."

The change in attitude was palpable. "Oh! Thank goodness! I was afraid it was like Ghostly Orchestra, and we were going to have to find each other. So, um…can I just bust this wall down to reach you?"

"It's very reassuring to know you have such a powerful impulse for destruction, but I doubt that's an option."

Whether it was possible or not, Koyomi was surely serious about trying. She could turn into a true demon if it helped distract her from her fear.

"According to the strategy site, once all the party members are inside the quest, the metal bars automatically open up and release us. Just be patient."

Since it was one of the earlier quests in the event, there were already guides all over the net. It was a long quest, and she couldn't mentally keep track of every detail, but Nayuta at least understood the general route to the sixth basement level, where Munemitsu Yamashiro, Mahiro's father, had supposedly left something.

"Detective, Mahiro, are you here yet?" Nayuta called out to the other cells. They had just passed through the portal; she heard footsteps and voices.

"Yes, I believe I'm just on your left," the detective said.

"And I think I'm on his other side," Mahiro added.

Now that the party was all together, an unbearably cheery and raspy announcement came from nowhere and everywhere at once.

"Death row prisoners, welcome to the prison of the dead! To accommodate your wishes for a better execution, all our capital punishments at this facility are available for self-service. When you wish to die, simply leave your cell and proceed downstairs. There will be no rationing of food, so if you'd prefer to avoid the hassle of moving around, you can remain in your cell until starvation takes you. Unhappy Execution!"

A deep, sonorous bell sounded, marking the start of the 108 Apparitions quest, and the doors to each of the cells clanked open.

From now on, they could be attacked by enemies at any time. Nayuta proceeded carefully out of her cell and saw Koyomi, whose face looked gaunt.

"That was the most *tasteless* public service announcement I've ever heard…"

Nayuta would have to agree, but when the detective emerged from his cell, he was faintly amused.

"Seems rather moot to complain about horror being tasteless. I believe this quest was submitted by a club of students at a specialty school. Their other quests are similar in style, and from what I hear, they've got more than a few fans."

"Oh, I have a couple of that club's games," said Mahiro at once. "Though lots of them are really messed up, like *The Village in Question* and *A Bookmark of Hair*."

"…Hmm? Mahiro, do you…*like* the horror genre?" asked Koyomi, who was barely any taller than the girl. She got right up in her face.

Mahiro smiled a bit awkwardly. "Yes, I love horror. Spooky stuff, articles about ghostly phenomena… Daddy hated that kind of stuff, though," she said, dressed in her bold samurai armor with a katana on her back. For one so young, she sounded brave. Combined with her dignified facial features, she really did seem like a samurai heading off to vanquish an evil spirit.

The only thing that ran counter to this impression was the word "daddy" that came out of her mouth, which only underlined the tragic circumstances behind the situation.

Mahiro Kirihara's father, Munemitsu Yamashiro, was working on the *Asuka Empire* development team using the identity of a total stranger, Tooru Endou—that much was fairly certain at this point.

Nayuta and the detective had narrowed down their points of interest to three questions.

Why did he use someone else's identity to hide his background?

Why did he disappear?

And was he safe and sound somewhere?

Depending on the answers to these, they might need to uncover the identity of the man named Tooru Endou, whose name he was using, but given that this all started from Mahiro's search request, it was a lower priority on the list.

In his last text message to his daughter, Mahiro's father left a code.

13, B6P, Munemitsu.

Klever suggested this referred to the thirteenth quest of the 108 Apparitions, Thirteen-Floor Underground Labyrinth, in sector P on the sixth floor. Perhaps they would find somewhere there what Munemitsu Yamashiro had left behind for his daughter.

Whether it was a hint to his current location, an explanation for why he vanished, or something else entirely, they wouldn't know until they found it. But Klever already had a hunch about what they'd find.

He had spoken to Nayuta earlier, while they were preparing their dinner.

"Remember what Mr. Torao said about the whole Onihime situation. Endou had been furious at their treatment and scrapped their work history before taking a new job. It just doesn't add up for me. I didn't know him very well, but the impression I got was not of someone who would pull a nasty, vengeful prank before leaving. I think it's more likely that he didn't want someone else seeing the work history…and that creates the possibility that his anger over poor treatment was just an act that gave him an excuse to delete the work history and abandon his job in a way that wouldn't arouse suspicion."

If this logic was correct, then in that deleted work history would have been traces of some private actions he took to leave his daughter something.

Freed from their prison cells, the foursome carefully made their way forward. At the end of the hallway lined with cells was a door made of steel. There wasn't even a window to be found anywhere.

Because the passage was cramped, they were naturally compelled to make a two-by-two formation.

"Koyomi and I will go in front. Mahiro, you act as a shield for the detective. Detective...just do whatever."

Due to his stats, there wasn't really anything he *could* do. Because of his luck stat, he was good for unlocking treasure chests, but Koyomi the ninja was good at that, too.

Mahiro looked up at him with surprise. "Are you bad at games, Detective?"

"I like puzzle and strategy games. I'm just not very good at fighting," he said breezily.

Koyomi fixed him with a look and muttered, "I've been noticing recently...when you don't want to bother with playing the game, you usually get knocked out on purpose and use the login delay penalty to avoid playing more, don't you...? How many times did you get knocked out during the Twelve Capybara Generals?"

"I don't have any idea what you're talking about," Klever said coolly. Nayuta had noticed this long ago, but she'd chosen not to bring it up out of consideration for his mental state. Koyomi did not share that same consideration.

She hugged Nayuta's arm and glanced over her shoulder at Mahiro.

"You know, this guy put all his stat points into luck, so even wimpy enemies will take him out in one hit... He can run away really fast, so he's surprisingly tough to kill, but if he takes his eye off the fight for a second, he'll easily get knocked out. If you feel like it, keep him safe. Especially from back atta...aah...*aaaaaah!!*"

The scream drew Nayuta's attention to the rear. From behind them—which they had assumed was just empty cells—a number of enormous cicadas had flown toward the group.

The very first thing that happens to us is a back attack?!

The cicadas were larger than human heads, and the hideous sound of their wings vibrating raised her hackles. These were weaklings called chirping cicadas, but if they stuck to the wall and started to chirp, the cacophonous sound would bring other enemies closer.

The best thing to do was beat them while they were flying, because their defense was weak, but coming up from behind in this narrow corridor meant the detective and Mahiro were blocking the way to the enemy.

But they wouldn't need to push the slow-reacting detective aside.

"*Seyyy!*"

With a sharp cry, Mahiro drew the sword on her back and swung it as quickly as lightning. It was a modified kind of drawing technique utilizing the sheath on her back, such that the sword was glowing the instant it slid from its scabbard.

The attacking cicada was split in two. Before the halves had even touched the ground, her katana had shot vertically upward. That second slash sliced up through the following cicada, turning the two cicadas into four dead pieces in an instant.

"...*Zzzt! Zzzzzt!*"

"Yeeeep!" squealed Koyomi. As she fled from the bouncing pieces of cicada, she maintained her grip on Nayuta so she swung around in a circle.

A moment later, Mahiro easily sliced through the third flying cicada, and when she was certain that no others were joining the fight, she returned her weapon to its sheath.

The detective clapped his hands, impressed by her very flashy handling of an attack they hadn't seen coming.

"Well done. An overhead chop to an upward slice."

"Yes," Mahiro replied. "It's a combo skill called Fan Drop. Low on power, but it's a drawing skill, so it's very quick to activate. Also, the follow-up slice has a higher accuracy boost than the first one, so..."

"Nyaaa! Nyaaaa!"

"...There's a very annoying cat around here."

Though she wasn't trying to ruin their conversation, Koyomi's screams were definitely louder than the cicadas. She was so desperate to avoid their surprisingly bouncy corpses that it made Nayuta feel just a bit sorry for her.

She kicked the skittering cicada pieces away and patted Koyomi on the head to calm her down. "Are you really that afraid of cicadas? You touch crayfish and stag beetles without a problem, don't you?"

Koyomi maintained a death grip on her friend and stammered, "B-b-but they're too big! A-also, there was another quest...where those huge cicadas were using their straw-like mouths to slurp up all the guts from these decomposing bodies and it was *sooo* disgusting... Ever since, I feel traumatized whenever I see them..."

"Oh, are you talking about The Carnival of the Venomous Larvae?" asked Mahiro, latching on. "I wanted to see that one, but because of the age ratings, the dead bodies were turned into a puddle of water... I heard that scene got so many complaints, they had to completely switch it for something else. You got to see it before they censored it, Koyomi? I'm so jealous..."

She sounded truly awed by the idea of such a grotesque vision. Koyomi looked queasy.

"M-Mahiro, are you even darker at your core than Nayu...?!

What happened to you?! You're too young to be into this stuff! Is there anything I can do to help?!"

Koyomi started to reach for Mahiro, intending to give her a comforting hug, but Nayuta grabbed her by the back of the collar and snapped, "Calm down, Koyomi. Having an interest in horror does not make her dark by nature. Horror fans might be a minority, but when it comes to those who are actively playing the 108 Apparitions event, pretty much everyone is a fan of horror or at least has a natural resistance to it."

"That's a lie! I can't stand horror!" raged Koyomi.

The detective pressed his fingers to his forehead, like he was dealing with a headache.

"It's one thing for people like me to be playing it for work. But despite your claims that you can't stand horror, you're clearly enjoying the experience. I think the lady doth protest too much..."

"Well...there are very few events where you can naturally grab onto a teenage girl and not get yelled at," Koyomi said. Now it was Nayuta's turn to deal with a headache. She knew it was a joke, but she couldn't help but feel that some of that was an honest opinion, too.

"You would be grabbing onto me even if there wasn't any horror involved. Why don't you try clinging to the detective for once instead?" she suggested, which earned her quite a distasteful look.

"Ewww... He's just not the same... I think he has a handsome face, but he's not really the kind of person I want to hug... Either he's just not lovable enough, or he doesn't set me at ease the way you do... I sense a kind of darkness inside him, like if he saw me frightened, he would smile and kick me over the cliff into Hell..."

"I see. Quite a character assassination," he muttered, although he made his voice sound insincerely cheerful.

"I thought Mr. Kurei seemed nice," Mahiro said hesitantly. "When I met him in person, he seemed like a very kind and helpful man. I also thought Miss Nayuta was very pretty..."

It was at this exact point that Nayuta had a very grave realization.

Oops...we didn't get our story straight with Mahiro.

She hadn't told Koyomi they'd met with Mahiro and her handler at Klever's house. Instead, she gave her a rather weak story that she had coincidentally happened across the detective and Mahiro meeting at the station.

If it got out that she was having meals at Klever's apartment, it was going to deal a major blow to his social standing. Even if she didn't tell the police about it, Koyomi could easily lambaste him with enough scorn that Klever got paranoid and ultimately refused to allow her into his home.

And that was an outcome she wanted to avoid.

His kitchen is bigger and easier to use than mine, plus he pays for the groceries I cook, and he can get ingredients like wine that are difficult for a minor to buy, and when he has time, he helps me with my studies...

For now, there were nothing but upsides to this arrangement.

And most importantly...it was lonely eating by herself.

Hoping to derail the topic of conversation, Nayuta interjected, "Mahiro, may I have a minute? I want to go over the route to the sixth story, just in case we get separated..."

"Ah, of course. All those staircases are rather complicated, aren't they? The fifth-story sector M is the relay point, which is easy enough to find, so if we get split up, that's where we should find each other."

Each story was arranged in a five-by-five grid with each sector being labeled by letter, and a hidden sector Z for the boss of every floor. The top-left corner of the map was sector A, with B, C, and D following it to the right, until sector E in the top-right corner. Then the second row was F on the left, followed by G, H, and so on.

There were warps and shortcuts that took you to nonadjacent sectors, too, making the whole map extremely twisted and enigmatic, but once you reached a save point, you could travel between them freely.

Ordinarily, this process would involve painstakingly combing through the dungeon for a week or more, but if they were just heading for a single sector in the middle of the dungeon and skipping any and all side events, it shouldn't take even two hours.

Koyomi tugged on Nayuta's arm and wondered, "So what's in sector P on the sixth floor? I mean, not the message waiting for Mahiro, but what would an ordinary player find there if they passed through...?"

As breezily as she could, Nayuta said, "Each story of this quest has a different style to it. The first basement floor here is a prison, the second is an office, the third is a school, the fourth is a sewer, the fifth is a natural cave...and the sixth basement story is a research laboratory. The P sector there is an isolated area for test animals."

Koyomi blinked rapidly.

"...Question, Miss Nayuta..."

"Yes...? What is it, Koyomi?"

Her eyes wandered aimlessly and her body shivered.

"Well, Koyomi was looking around the internet recently and spotted an article called 'Top 10 Most Traumatic Scenes of the First Half of the 108 Apparitions'...and number three on that list was 'Undying Death Row Prisoners in the Horrifying Human Experimentation Lab'...and it sounded so scary that I just skipped right past it without reading. You don't think...that's referring to..."

"That's the one," Nayuta admitted gravely. "But we'll be all right. We have Mahiro with us today," she said, putting a hand on Mahiro's shoulder.

Mahiro smiled uncomfortably, but Koyomi didn't understand why. She was still terrified.

"Huh...why...what do you mean...?"

"It's because of the rating system," Mahiro said, sounding much more mature than Koyomi. "If any player in a party is under the age of fifteen, the entire party is placed under an age-restricted setting. In other words, as long as you're with me, you won't see any realistic dead bodies or grotesque, violent imagery. The worst you'll get is probably enemy zombies and those cicadas just now."

After a few moments to take that in, Koyomi pulled up her game menu. "Mahiro...can we also be in-game friends, not just party members today? Will you chat with me even after we're done with this? In fact, can we play together forever? We can name our guild, uh...ah! We'll take the first character of each our names—Nayuta, Mahiro, Koyomi—and call ourselves the Namako Gang...after the noble sea cucumber."

"I'm happy to keep playing with you," Nayuta pointed out, "but absolutely not with that guild name."

Between her practice of raising brine shrimp and catching crawfish as a high schooler, Koyomi seemed to have a strange connection to marine animals like these.

Mahiro covered her mouth with her hand. Her shoulders shook. "N-Namako...*pfft-ha-ha*...!"

"What...? Wow, your sense of humor is so weird, Mahiro," remarked Koyomi, who seemed concerned about how hard Mahiro was laughing.

They flanked her to offer protection while she was distracted, and made their way out of the prison area. It was sector A of the first basement floor of thirteen. There were no windows—only a few fluorescent lights that bathed the dingy concrete walls in a pale glow.

The passageway was wide enough for three adults to walk shoulder to shoulder, which was enough for travel but rather cramped for battle. It made it harder to run from or burst past enemies, and therefore required you to beat all of them in order.

Klever went into his inventory and retrieved a censer the size of his palm.

"Let's use some white lotus incense, just in case. That will lower our enemy encounter rate somewhat, though it won't help with any fixed encounters…"

"That's not a problem. We have Onihime if we need extra help," said Mahiro.

Based on the fight with the cicadas, Mahiro was a better fighter than they expected, too. Unlike Nayuta and Koyomi, who were spec'd out for speed, she had an ideal build focused on building up attack and defense. And of course, she was light-years beyond the detective, who only had his luck to rely upon.

"I just had a sudden realization," Koyomi said, the light quickly vanishing from her eyes. "In terms of makeup, the detective is totally like the protagonist of your average mobile game these days… He has a bunch of cute girls doing the fighting for him while he takes command in the back, just like all the hit gacha games. He's got an ultra-rare Nayu and a super-special-rare Koyomi…"

You would think the generation gap would mean Mahiro didn't understand this, but she just nodded sagely.

"Oh, like whenever there's an event and they put out new versions, like a Valentine's Day bridal dress edition, swimsuits, or Sports Day cosplay. And the detective playing the main character would pay microtransactions for the chance to win them…"

"Ooh, you get me, Mahiro. He's going to keep buying ten-packs of rolls, hoping for that 0.03 percent chance of winning an ultra-rare cheerleader Nayu flashing underboob, and the next thing he knows, he's sitting on a useless pile of rare capybara Koyomis… Poor, poor, detective…," Koyomi joked, pitying him.

The detective exhaled loudly. "That's not funny. Narafushi fell into that trap when he was in high school. Thankfully, he learned from the experience and stopped playing games entirely. It's how he managed to avoid the whole SAO disaster, so in a sense, he was lucky…"

"Hmm? Who's Narafushi? A friend of yours?" Koyomi asked. Of course she didn't know who Narafushi was.

"That's Mahiro's manager, the one I was telling you about," Nayuta whispered. "It was thanks to him that this job came to us…"

"Ohhh, the guy you mentioned at Nyanko Soba. The one who tried to scout you for the talent agency?"

Mahiro nodded. "I can see why. He was very disappointed about that all day. If you tried, it might be much easier than going to the detective's house every—"

"Koyomi, enemies!"

With perfect timing, some monsters came around the corner ahead, just when Nayuta needed any excuse possible to stop Mahiro from talking. She readied herself for battle, thankful to fight for once in her life.

First, there were three zombies dressed in prison uniforms.

Behind them, two wolf-men wearing guard outfits and holding whips.

The prisoner zombies were weak, but the wolf-men were a fair bit tougher. These five together weren't a problem at all, but farther behind them was something much worse.

It was a half-man, half-horse armored samurai carrying an enormous golden beheading ax.

Its entire body from hoof to helm blazed with gold, making it obvious at a glance that it was not like your usual scrub enemies.

Nayuta's eyes widened with amazement.

"A golden executioner…?!"

"Whoa! I've never actually seen one before!" exclaimed Koyomi. It was hard to tell if she was excited or horrified.

Golden executioners were a rather infamous rare enemy that appeared in a number of quests. They were said to appear only once in at least a thousand times, but they were not the sort of thing one was glad to stumble across.

To be sure, their loot could be sold for a lot of money.

They gave out plenty of experience points.

But they didn't drop any powerful gear, were powerful enough to wipe out even veteran parties, and moved quickly and without tiring, meaning that escape was impossible.

In other words, they were annoying game-obstructing enemies, a classic example of a high-risk, low-reward combat scenario.

Koyomi spun around and glared balefully at the detective. "Um, would this have anything to do with your luck stat...?"

"Ah, is this your first time seeing one? This is my fifth encounter. They seem to have a knack for finding me."

The lucky detective, who had drawn this very unlucky card for them, smiled and stepped backward.

"The other four times, I was forced to log out to escape them, but since I have three experienced fighters with me today, I have high hopes for our success. Good luck with the rest."

"What?! Hey, get back here, dammit!" Koyomi roared. The detective was already preparing to be a passive observer. Clearly he wasn't going to be any help anyway, but it was still infuriating.

"Argh...Onihime! Battle readiness!" Nayuta said, selecting the demon puppet from her item list. She could already tell this was going to be a bad one.

The *onmyoji* puppet gazed upon the enemy with a cool stare that was very reminiscent of Mahiro's.

"Mahiro and Onihime, protect the detective! Koyomi and I will take out the executioner!"

"Okay! We'll handle it!" Mahiro said.

"...You'll pay for this later, Detective!"

It was the start of a desperate battle in narrow quarters, with no possible escape.

What they did not know yet was that in the Thirteen-Floor Underground Labyrinth, all fixed encounters were affected by luck at a much higher rate than in the average dungeon. A luckier player would come across rarer enemies more often, and unluckier players would only ever see the most typical weaklings.

Meanwhile, the rare monsters appearing there, much like the

golden executioner, were much stronger and yet had very little reward to show for it.

Their tragic—some might say desperately vengeful—cries echoed throughout the labyrinth for even longer than the battle lasted.

§

They were in sector Q of the sixth level of the Thirteen-Floor Underground Labyrinth.

It was a white and clean interior space meant to look like a modern research facility. It was a bit unnerving that it was so bright despite the lack of windows, but after the gloomy cavern that was the floor above them, it was nice just to have flat, level ground to walk on.

The party had reached the sector adjacent to their destination. All of them except for the detective were exhausted and frazzled.

They had been through over twenty encounters on the way there. That was over a hundred enemies defeated, with twelve of them classified as rare. For some reason, they ran into *three* golden executioners, who were only supposed to appear less than one in a thousand times.

Over three hours after logging in, it was practically a miracle that they'd gotten this far without losing anyone.

Nayuta felt the exhaustion in her virtual bones. If not for Onihime playing a valuable support role from the back row, she would have perished along the way, and if not for the addition of Mahiro, Klever would have been the first one to go.

Not only did he hold them back, he was the very cause of their anguish, and now he leaned back against the white reinforced resin and leisurely opened his map to peruse.

"Ah, we're nearly there. It certainly took longer than I expected, though."

"...And whose fault was that...?" Koyomi asked.

"Koyomi, I understand how you feel, but…actually, yes. I completely agree," Nayuta said, changing her mind.

Setting aside the detective and his casual spectating of all the combat, the three actual fighters weren't in the mood to speak much. Even Koyomi, who initially raised hell about each new party of enemies, eventually lost the spark of emotion in her eyes and transformed into a killing machine who sliced and diced her foes.

Mahiro sat down while they checked their maps and hung her head.

"…Now I understand why the detective is at such a high level. He lets the other members do all the fighting, but with the number of rare enemies he encounters, his level is bound to shoot upward."

"Actually, it's not usually this bad," he said, shrugging. "It seems the rare encounter rate in this dungeon is higher than usual. Or maybe it's designed to have the luck stat play a larger role… In any case, our destination is just ahead of us. Let's be on our guard."

Klever walked off breezily, but the others were more sluggish in joining him.

"Nayu…the next time we encounter a rare enemy, you want to offer him up as a sacrifice?" Koyomi asked.

"Since we've brought them this far, let's hold out a little bit longer, for Mahiro's sake. Once this is all settled, *then* you can be a little bit cruel to him."

He spun around with a frosty smile. "No, you can't. And if you're going to hold such ghastly conversations about me, at least show me the respect of conducting them out of earshot."

"If we didn't do them where you can hear, they wouldn't serve as much of a threat," Nayuta shot back at once. She straightened up. "Now, what are we supposed to be searching for in this sector P? If there's a message to Mahiro from this Yamashiro person, I would assume he hid it in a way that other players wouldn't understand…"

The detective winked. "I can't say anything without seeing it for myself, but it shouldn't be anything that tricky. It's pointless if Mahiro can't figure it out, of course, so I would expect she'll know what to do as soon as she sees it. The only concern left is time... Are you all right in that regard, Mahiro?"

It was already after ten o'clock at night. That was quite late for a primary school student to be awake playing games.

"I'm fine," she said. "My mother gets home from work late, so she'll expect me to be asleep already. If she opens the door to look inside, she'll realize I'm playing a game...but that's typical, so I'm sure she'll overlook it."

"That's a relief to hear. Now—here we are."

The corridor ahead of them was blocked by both metal bars and shutters. Beyond them was the goal of the day: floor six, sector P.

On the wall nearby was a security control panel. It should open the shutter for them if they put in an entry request. Nayuta breathed deeply, steeling herself for what would come next, and clenched her fists.

"We don't need a key to get in here, do we?"

"Not to get in. But once we're inside, we won't be able to escape without finding the key to get out. It's a kind of trap where part of the process of searching for the key involves watching vivisection and torture experiments on the undying prisoners," said Klever.

Koyomi shivered viscerally and wound her arm around Mahiro's.

"I'm counting on you, kid!" she said.

Mahiro just gave her an awkward, confused smile. "Umm...it just means that nothing will happen for a while. I don't see why you'd be counting on me for that..."

"That's just it! 'Nothing happening' is extremely important! Peace and tranquility is what's best in life! Remember, *Asuka Empire* is designed for you take naps while buried under capybaras!"

"That's not correct. Although I agree with you that peace and tranquility is best," Nayuta said, pressing the OPEN button on the control panel. In the next set of options, URGENT was a trap that would sound an alarm and call down enemies upon them, and EXTENSION would play a recorded hint. There was also a button for CLOSE, but of course, they couldn't select that now.

While the shutter and bars slowly opened, Nayuta whispered to the detective, "Should I press the extension button, too?"

"Go ahead. From what I hear, it won't flip any story switches, but it's not a big enough deal to fret over."

She pressed the button and a static-y, distorted voice began playing from the speakers near the ceiling.

"The sector is currently off-limits due to a system rampage. All prisoners should be careful, as you cannot die within this space."

In the sector ahead, they wouldn't be able to die even if they wanted to.

The detective grunted to himself. "I think I see the point of this quest. This isn't reality. I mean…of course not—it's a VR game—but even within the game's setting, this is another layer of virtual reality. There are fatal traps and nonfatal traps, giving us Death Row prisoners a chance to choose how we would prefer to die—but there is also a nightmare scenario where we cannot die even if we want to do so. I wonder why Mr. Yamashiro chose this quest to hide his message."

Whatever his intent, it didn't sound like the sort of thing you'd want Mahiro to hear. Her eyes clouded over a little, in fact.

"The team that produced this quest left some commentary about it on their blog. 'From the moment we're born, we are all destined to die.' 'This world is a prison, and we're just serving our life sentences until we reach the end.' 'So you might as well be a model prisoner, so you can die peacefully.' I thought that was a very pretentious and childish attitude, but I also see how that mindset is reflected in the quest," said Nayuta.

"I see. It's quite twisted, really," Klever chuckled. "But while Death Row prisoners cannot choose life or death for themselves, we can choose our own lives and reach death as a result of the lives we've lived. Some deaths are unavoidable due to unexpected accidents or disease, but at least we have the option of choosing how to spend our days until that moment comes. This makes us quite different from prisoners awaiting a death sentence."

He gave Mahiro's head a gentle pat.

"...Of course, there's a wide variety of options depending on your personal circumstances and how lucky or unlucky you are. But I feel certain you'll have a better chance at a better death if you live your life with optimism, rather than thinking of the world like a prison whose sentence you must drearily live out. At least, that's my view of it."

Nayuta reached forward and hugged Mahiro around the shoulders. Everyone's life ended with death. That was an undeniable truth of the world, but it didn't mean everyone's life was the same.

To live your life like it was only ever a prison was a miserable path to choose for yourself. Mahiro hung her head, deep in thought.

"I understand how the creator feels, however," he said gently. "Is life just a prison until you reach your execution or not? A sneaky cheat of an adult might try to escape giving a real answer by saying, 'It's up to you to decide that or not.' But the truth is that in your life, there are only a few precious times where you'll feel like you're truly free. While you're a student, your time is very limited, and you don't have the income to hang out and have fun. Once you're an adult with a job, then you have to work to live. If you get sick of any of this and try to escape it, you'll be dropping out of life with very few doors open to you in the future. Calling us Death Row prisoners might be a bit edgy, but there's no denying that the world gives us very little freedom. But even still, compared with ancient history and the Middle Ages, where even getting enough food was a major challenge, the progress of the last few centuries is really remarkable."

They started to walk through the open shutter into the new sector. Koyomi was still arm in arm with Mahiro.

"Umm, I'm not sure if I have this right," she said in a daze. "Are you saying if you already know you're going to be put to death, the possibility is high that you would make a move on Nayu, drop out of life due to a burst of momentary lust, and end up suffering a fate worse than death?"

All he could do was press his fingers to his temples.

"I realize the story I just told you was a bit of a detour, but it sounds like you interpreted it by hearing all the worst words and simply changing the order in the most malicious possible way..."

"You take too long to get to your point, that's why," Nayuta said. "Koyomi, he's just saying she should follow *your* example of how to live life."

"Whaaat...?" she exclaimed. "Is that what you were saying, Detective? No joke?"

"Unfortunately, I must admit she's not far off. I think your way of life is mostly correct."

It would seem Koyomi had mastered the act of enjoying a life that was not that long in the big scheme of things, lasting less than a century. As the saying "fortune comes to a happy home" would suggest, her lovable personality endeared her to those around her in life.

In the picture of Mr. Yamashiro, Mahiro's father, he looked... kind of weak-willed, Nayuta thought. He had seemed nice, but also kind of unreliable.

Of course, there was no way to judge him from a picture alone. Plenty of people looked like saints but were diabolical in person and vice versa. Klever looked like quite a creep, but he was actually a very reasonable person who cowered away from teenage girls. Koyomi looked like a little girl, but was an adult who worked an office job. Mahiro looked like a serious and mature child actor, but was just a normal girl who got giggle attacks and felt lonely when she didn't get enough interaction.

Dying your hair, growing out a beard, or even just holding a different expression would lead to a very different impression on strangers. If Nayuta bleached her hair and got a dark tan, people were bound to treat her differently, even if the person on the inside was exactly the same.

So what did this mean for the programmer named Munemitsu Yamashiro?

Given that he was falsely using the identity of Tooru Endou, his faithfulness to the law was already suspect. On the other hand, he had chosen the option to work diligently at a real job recently, at least until April.

They still didn't know what he was dealing with privately.

But now they were there: floor six, sector P.

At last, after hours of fighting off rare and deadly enemies, they reached the research lab that was their goal—and it was so quiet, they thought their ears might have gone numb.

§

"Yikes. There's really nothing here…"

Koyomi was crestfallen. She looked around the carefully partitioned research sector without much luck.

The walls were spotless and white. There were no people on or around the surgery tables, and all the cages and binding implements were empty of subjects.

It made this modern—even futuristic—lab seem lonely, to be sure, but nothing about it was at the level of being scary. Just in case, Nayuta went through all the storage spaces along the walls, just in case there were enemies waiting to jump out at them.

"Normally there's supposed to be blood splattered all over the place, with people screaming and crying. It's like a glimpse into Hell. Good thing we don't have to get traumatized like that."

The storage spaces were virtually empty. There was hardly a

thing to be found in them—not even a creepy blob of quivering, undying flesh or anything.

"Yeah, you said it," Koyomi said. "It would be so much easier on my mind if all the quests were like this...In fact, this is the normal way of things! I keep forgetting ever since the 108 Apparitions started, but *Asuka Empire* isn't a horror game!"

"That's true," murmured the detective, whose eyes narrowed. "There were lots of *yokai*-hunting and ghost-busting quests at the start of the game, so this seems to fit in with that, but I do understand where you're coming from. While there are normal quests unrelated to the 108 Apparitions going live, too, the pace has noticeably slowed, because they don't have enough development resources to do everything. It sounds like Mr. Yamashiro was working an extreme schedule, too..."

"If they're that busy, it seems strange that they had time to create experiments like the ghost cat hotel and the night express train, doesn't it?" Nayuta wondered.

"Well, not every department is perpetually slammed. There might be times where they're waiting for certain design decisions to come down...but once there's a major issue, they're pretty much pulling all-nighters to solve them. Mr. Torao's department really has nothing to do when the going is smooth, but when they get busy, I won't hear from him for an entire week at a time."

"Daddy said that, too," noted Mahiro, who was on the lookout for danger. "He didn't tell me where he was working, but he mentioned that sometimes he was very busy, and sometimes he suddenly had nothing to do. It was hard for him to put together plans."

Klever nodded. "Mm-hmm. And was there anything else in your conversations with your father that sticks out to you? I think you should already have the right hint to know what he hid here and how."

But she just looked confused. "I'm sorry, I don't know... It was usually about my acting career and school. We almost always talked about me, because Daddy didn't really talk about himself. If I ever asked, he would usually avoid answering the question."

"I see. In that case, the only real hint you would have is in that final message, I suppose. 13, B6P, Munemitsu...I would assume the place is right in this vicinity."

"Remember, sector P on its own is pretty spacious. If we have to cover every square inch looking for clues, it's going to be very inefficient."

There were few branching routes in this sector, but there were many, many small rooms to check.

Nayuta stopped rifling through storage cabinets for a moment to think it over. Meanwhile, Koyomi began grumbling to herself.

"I have a lot of trust in the detective's logic, but maybe he's just wrong this time. It was really hard just to get here on the sixth floor. It probably would've been impossible for Mahiro on her own, and would he really hide a message for his daughter in such an annoying and obscure way? He could've left it on the first floor..."

A smirk crossed Klever's face; he had realized something.

"Koyomi...you have a very keen eye, indeed. Why *must* the hiding spot be here on the sixth story, indeed? The difficulty factor can be dealt with. Miss Mahiro has friends of her own, and our difficulty in this case was affected by my unique luck and not a typical experience. But you're right that if he only wanted to leave a message for her, a higher floor would've been fine—but I think I'm starting to see why he chose this sector."

He called off the search and pointed toward the end of the hallway.

"If my suspicions are correct, there's nothing around this area. But there is a communications room at the end, so let's head there. I'll explain as we walk."

He strode forward with purpose in his step. Nayuta hurried to catch up to him.

"Please don't rush ahead of us, it's dangerous," she warned. "If you die in a single hit from a sneak attack after all this trouble, it won't be funny. Anyway…what did you pick up on?"

He winked at her. "Basically, it's a rating issue. This area, sector P on the sixth floor, is high on the list of the most grotesque locations in the game. But when it's placed under an all-ages rating, virtually all the events that occur here don't unlock. However, the one thing they cannot remove is the switch that allows the player to escape this sector."

Nayuta gasped softly.

He continued walking. "This is the normal escape method: You defeat the researchers and prisoners that attack, and use the communications room to interact with the security system. This requires a lot of searching around for the key to the communications room, passwords, and various hints. But if the player is a child, basically all the gory images get cut out of this sequence, and the search itself is greatly simplified. However, the part where you place a request with the security system from the communications room is required to escape, so it's still present. If he's set up a trick to uncover, it's going to be *there*."

She mulled over the detective's explanation. It reminded her of what Torao had said when they found Onihime the demon puppet: "Where better to hide a tree than in the forest?" If you were to add an event in a place that was already relatively featureless, the difference from before would be noticeable. But if you added one to a place already packed with features, the difference was likely to go unnoticed by those you wanted to see it.

So where was an ideal place where the development team was unlikely to spot a difference, but it would be easy for his young daughter to notice?

This was it.

"So it's a hidden message taking advantage of the game's rating system…," said Nayuta.

"There are other reasons he would have chosen this quest. Thanks to the map construction, it would be easy to place a short code at the end of his message to indicate a location, and because it was early in the event, this quest would have already been patched and adjusted for errors. It's quite unlikely that the team would go back to change an early quest like this one, and they wouldn't easily notice a difference in the content. Considering that he made a show of being angry and deleted his work history, it's quite a thorough plan altogether."

They arrived at the heavily locked communications room, where the detective examined a control panel on the wall.

"As I thought, it's made to open up with a control panel in our case. Ordinarily, you're supposed to go through a lot more to get to this point."

The lock clicked loudly and the heavy metal door swung open.

Beyond it was a small room filled with security monitors and communications devices. On a pedestal in the center, practically begging for attention, was a phone receiver labeled EMERGENCY LINE.

At the detective's urging, Mahiro picked it up.

"…Um, hello…?"

"Please provide the password to access the security system," said a robotic voice. Mahiro gave Klever a worried look.

"Normally we would have to search around to find it…but that won't be necessary here. It's your father's name."

He had included it, unnaturally, at the end of his text message.

Through trembling lips, Mahiro said it into the phone.

"…Mune…mitsu…?"

"Please wait on the line."

The robotic voice ended, leaving high-pitched music box tones coming through the receiver.

Koyomi swung her finger back and forth like a conductor. "Ohhh, I recognize this song. What's it called?"

"Pachelbel's 'Canon in D'. The one you hear all the time when you get put on hold."

The graceful, memorable, looping melody came trickling out

of the phone in a plinking, delicate music box style. Mahiro murmured, "This song is the ringtone on Daddy's phone."

"I see," Klever said, his eyes narrowing. "Nayuta, Koyomi, don't say anything until I give you the go-ahead. Mahiro, just talk on the phone as though we're not here. If you get asked about any companions, say your friends are with you, but searching in other rooms at the moment. Assuming anyone answers at all, I think this phone is likely to connect you right to him."

Mahiro's skinny limbs tensed up. In order to prevent anyone else from finding and accessing it, Munemitsu Yamashiro didn't leave a text message here, but set up a hotline to connect to himself using the keyword "Munemitsu."

It was probably going to end up being one of those computer-generated voice chat bots, but if anyone else actually managed to find this device, it was going to be a wrong-number dead end. Also, by trading words directly with Mahiro, he would be able to hear out her questions.

One minute passed. Then another.

After quite a lot of time and a number of cycles of the ringtone, the call finally went through.

"…Hello?" said a man's voice. It sounded tremulous.

Mahiro lifted her other hand to cradle the phone in both.

"Daddy?! Are you all right?! Where are you?!"

"…Mahiro? Ha-ha… You really figured out that code… So… did something happen?" he asked. His voice was hoarse with uncertainty.

Mahiro was normally very calm and collected, but now she shouted into the phone. "You're the one something happened to! Do you have any idea how worried I've been?!"

She couldn't see him, but the sound of clothing rustling made it clear that he was feeling hesitant.

"S-sorry! Are…are you alone right now?" he asked.

Klever promptly lifted a finger to his lips. Just in case, Nayuta put her hand over Koyomi's mouth.

Without any change in her voice or attitude, Mahiro replied, "Yeah, it's just me. I was getting help from some friends along the way here, but we split up, and they're in other rooms right now."

Her experience as a child actor came in handy when throwing in a casual lie or two.

"O-oh...that's good. Well, I wanted to tell you that in a hidden locker straight ahead from where you leave the room, there's an Onihime demon puppet that..."

"Don't change the topic, Daddy. Where are you now? What happened? Why did you disappear? I'm not going to back down until I get honest answers for all of these."

On the other end of the phone, Yamashiro gave a pathetic little whimper. "I'm sorry...I can't tell you anything," he said. "But I'm all right here. Just forget about me, Mahiro, and live a good and honest life with your mother—"

"Wait! If you can't tell me, then you don't have to. But you can at least meet with me!"

"...I don't want to put you two in a bad situation. You're still working hard at acting, right? With me around, you might actually end up endangered at some point. So just—"

"Aha! I knew you were lying when you said you were all right!" Mahiro shouted. "You can't cause me to worry myself sick and then say, 'Don't worry about me.' It doesn't work that way! I just don't understand... All I want is to see my daddy..."

Unlike when she talked with Nayuta and the other adults, Mahiro's voice was now properly childlike, reflecting her real age. This couldn't be an act.

Poor Mahiro... She really is putting on a brave face all the time...

Living alone with a busy mother and performing at acting jobs to support the family finances, there was probably only a single person in the world she felt safe confiding her secrets with: her father.

Nayuta quietly grabbed the detective's arm and gave him a

look. It was her way of asking, "May I ask him a question, too?" But the detective shook his head and leaned over to her ear so his voice wouldn't get picked up by the phone.

"Hold it in for now. There's a chance someone else is there with him. If they were to find out about us, he could be in danger."

She clamped her mouth shut. Klever had calculated the risks far more comprehensively than she had, and was looking for the safest way out. Nayuta wasn't stupid enough to sabotage his attempt over a temporary emotion.

"I'm sorry, Mahiro...I can't talk for very long. If anything happens, I'll try to keep this phone number up and available... Of course, if the team doesn't find out about it first, I might think of more. For now, just forget about seeing me. This is all for your own safety..."

His pained, desperate voice did not sound like it was lying. At the very least, he wasn't trying to tell her, *I have a new family now, so I've chosen to cut out the old family.*

"Daddy, wait! If you can't explain anything, at least tell me what I can do..."

"......Don't try to search for me. It's really dangerous. The reason I was meeting you in the game is because I was desperate to see you, and I was naive about the danger. But now the situation has changed. From this point on...I don't think we should meet even in VR. I want to avoid using the headset."

A furrow appeared in Klever's brow.

"No...," Mahiro mumbled. Nayuta reached out and placed a hand on her shoulder.

"I'm sorry, I've got to hang up. The point is, I'm just fine... I want you to believe me on that one. Please, Mahiro, find a way to manage on your own."

"...I will."

He ended the call, desperate to escape.

The girl's shoulders drooped in powerless sorrow. Nayuta hugged Mahiro to her chest.

"Nayuta...I..."

"...Isn't that nice, Mahiro? Your father's still alive," she whispered. Mahiro's shoulders shivered.

"Oh...y-yes! You're right...he *is* all right..."

Mahiro was conflicted, unsure if she should be relieved he was safe, or sad he was cutting her off. She buried her face in Nayuta's chest and began to sob. Nayuta rubbed her back gently and gave a look to Klever.

The detective winked. "Thank you, Mahiro. That conversation taught me what I needed to know about his situation. The rest of this is for a grown-up to take care of. I'm going to log off and get to it."

This was a surprise to Nayuta. "Detective, what did you figure out? I didn't think there was any real hint in that conversation," she said.

Yamashiro, Mahiro's father, did indeed act shifty, and what he said was mostly nonsensical. There was very little actual information. He basically said he couldn't say anything and hung up on her.

"On the contrary," he said, pulling his deerstalker cap low over his brow. "It was a treasure trove of information. He's undoubtedly involved in criminal acts. There are multiple other people, and the kind who are dangerous enough that they represent potential harm to his family. But Yamashiro's being kept alive because he represents value to them. That's enough intelligence to give us a direction to investigate."

He crouched down so Mahiro could see him at eye level through her tears.

"Mahiro, first I want you to wait out an entire week without doing anything. Do not attempt to look for him at all. If they figure out what we're doing, it will put your father in danger. Don't call him here, either, until I let you know. Can you promise me that?"

She nodded, and he gave her a reassuring smile.

"Good. Then I'll be going now. Nayuta, Koyomi, take care of Mahiro. You can go to the save point and exit from there."

The detective left the mission, leaving the three girls behind. Because he was leaving partway, the experience and items he gained from the start of the dungeon would disappear. If he logged out from a save point, they would be saved, along with his quest progress, but he seemed to be too busy to care about those things.

"Man, what a waste! After all those rare enemies we came across... And as long as we don't run into any more, it's only ten minutes to reach the save point, isn't it?" Koyomi said, mystified, as she patted Mahiro on the head.

"That's true... As confident as he always acts, that was a rare show of haste," Nayuta noted. She could feel Mahiro stiffening up in her arms and regretted that she'd caused the poor girl to worry by saying that, so she smiled and said, "Oh, it's fine, Mahiro. Despite his stats, the detective really doesn't care much about in-game experience or items at all. Anyway, shall we find that present your father left for you?"

At the hidden locker right across from the room's exit was an Onihime demon puppet, according to Yamashiro. It was presumably the same model as the one Nayuta found.

The demon puppets had a variety of designs, with plenty of other human types aside from Onihime: holy beast types like dragons and *koma-inu* lion dogs, even creepy *yokai* types like the ghostly *yuki-onna* and spidery *jorogumo*.

They could be customized and altered for a fee, but it seemed her father wanted to give her the gift of a little sister. Of course, gifting a rare item to his daughter was a flagrant ethical violation, but at this point, it had already been decided that the demon puppets would not be sold in the game store but provided as a reward for clearing the special Path of Encapyment quest. After Nayuta and Koyomi's playtest, the quest was going to have a sliding difficulty scale adjusting to the player's level, and as soon as next week, anyone would be able to get their own puppet. At that point, it could no longer be called a "rare" item.

Koyomi stared down the hallway and wondered, "Hidden

locker across from the room entrance...? There's just a wall. I suppose there's a switch somewhere. Nayu, you watch Mahiro! I'm going to take a look around."

"Of course. Be careful," Nayuta said, comforting the silent, crying Mahiro.

A few moments later, Koyomi's voice came down the corridor.

"Nayu, Mahiro! I found an Onihime! But...hmm? It looks... different, somehow."

They left the room and noticed a locker-size depression in a nook of the white wall. Indeed, there was an Onihime there.

But the clothing and coloring were different from the one Nayuta found.

Nayuta's Onihime had silver hair and a white *kariginu* robe. But the new Onihime here featured black hair and shrine maiden clothing, with a *chihaya* overcoat and an elegant red cord tied over her chest.

Koyomi examined it closely, then nodded with satisfaction.

"In terms of playable jobs, this one looks like a dance miko, doesn't it? That means Nayu's Onihime is an *onmyoji* type that specializes in support, while this one is a dance miko type that offers healing. Seems like a very good match for Mahiro the tactician."

After a brief moment of indecision, Mahiro reached out and clasped the hand of the puppet that resembled her so much.

The Onihime puppet was expressionless, and though she had just been crying, Mahiro's face was flat as well.

They looked just like twin puppets. Nayuta felt something clench around her heart.

§

Nayuta parted ways with Koyomi and Mahiro, and logged out from *Asuka Empire* to return to the real world.

She was not in her usual bedroom, but Klever's office and

residence. She took off the AmuSphere and sat up on the sofa, finding that a thin blanket had been placed over her.

The room was dark, but there was some indirect lighting in the corner that kept it from being pitch-black. Klever was not around, but there was a note on the table, along with a 10,000-yen bill.

I'm performing some investigation in VR. It's already quite late, so call a taxi to take you back home.

He was in his bedroom, then. There was even the number to a taxi hotline on the note.

She couldn't take the money, of course, but Nayuta considered the situation. It was after eleven o'clock. She could still make the last train of the night, but it wasn't the hour for an underage girl to be walking around alone.

Still, she didn't feel like going to the trouble of calling a taxi.

For one thing, she was feeling rather sleepy right then. It was a Wednesday, and the next day was an ordinary school day.

I suppose I could pretend I didn't see the note, and just go to sleep right here...

Nayuta's home was only five minutes away from her school. Klever wouldn't approve of it, but she could return early in the morning, get changed, and still have plenty of time to get to school.

Having decided on her course of action, Nayuta had just returned to the sofa, still warm from her body, when the bedroom door opened.

Klever sighed and murmured to himself, "She still hasn't logged out?"

"No. I just turned it off now," Nayuta replied coolly. She could have feigned sleep and ignored him, but as soon as he noticed her AmuSphere was off, he would wake her up anyway. She wasn't going to fight it anymore.

He turned up the lights. "Ah, good timing. You should get going now. I'll give you some money for a taxi."

She sat up and rubbed the sleep from her eyes. "I can't take your money. I'm so tired, and it's such a pain to get home that I was thinking of just falling asleep here—but if you truly insist, I'll take the train."

"Just because I'm a coward who's afraid of being unjustly accused of bad behavior doesn't mean you should take advantage of it," he grumbled. "But I'll admit some of this is my fault, too. I lacked trust and respect for you as a person. I had absolutely no intention of viewing you with the same lens as people who would tar and feather a person with scandal for no good reason, but I can't blame you for thinking that's what I was doing. I vow to do better in the future."

She accepted his long-winded and stuffy apology with a generous and understanding nod.

"I'm glad to hear that you understand. I think that upright part of your character is very laudable."

"...Thank you. Now, in exchange for my attempt to be better, I hope you will practice a bit more caution and self-preservation. My own individual circumstances aside, I hope you will abstain from any public actions society at large might misconstrue within the context of you and any adult man such as myself. In short...I would beg you to keep in mind the danger and power of the eyes and opinions of society," he requested—practically pleaded, in fact.

"I understand. As long as you do not treat me like some kind of tumor any more than is necessary, I will behave myself in the ways that I should. Is that acceptable?"

Klever's shoulders sagged with relief. "I'm glad you see things my way. I'll drive you tonight. If you won't take a taxi, I certainly can't send you out on the streets at this late hour."

She rose to her feet and sighed, "And just like that, I can't help but feel like I'm being treated as a tumor again."

"This is just commonsense helpfulness. If anything happened to you because I made a careless mistake, Daichi would never forgive me. Plus, I'm actually about to go and see Torao. I'm going to perform a number of clerical tasks in a way that doesn't leave an access trail behind. After all, when you do this sort of thing online, there are always logs that can be followed."

As she headed to the door, Nayuta remarked, "Mr. Torao's working this late at night?"

The detective winked. "They trade off maintenance night shifts. As the chief, Torao isn't part of the rotation, but he'll go in when one of his employees can't make it or there's an emergency. Today, I actually asked him to wait for me about this Yamashiro business. He's concerned about his former coworker Tooru Endou, you see. So I asked him to monitor and analyze the quest log, just in case."

"Really...? Then I wish he would have lowered our enemy encounter rate," she grumbled. Nayuta's exhaustion was due to the adventure being much longer and more grueling than she anticipated. By that point, Koyomi was probably fast asleep.

Klever chuckled as they took the apartment elevator down to the garage. "I understand what you mean, but that kind of adjustment is very tricky to do. It's one thing if you're on a test server with no other players around, but making adjustments on the fly to a public map with other people around will have repercussions all over the quest. And there's a record of your edits, so you'll have some very awkward excuses to make if anyone asks you about it. Just because you're on the development team doesn't mean you can just do anything you want."

Nayuta didn't work in a place like this, but she felt she could imagine vaguely what he was talking about.

They were in the parking garage now. Klever murmured, "Of course, if he just temporarily lowered my luck stat, it wouldn't have affected the quest itself and would've made it easier for us to finish our work..."

"Oh."

It all seemed so obvious when he put it that way. Nayuta gave him a searching gaze. He stuck his tongue out playfully as he opened the passenger door for her.

"But if we're not doing a playtest, Torao's not going to do anything like that. If anything, he's only helping us to hopefully make clear the missing Tooru Endou had engaged in illicit behavior. However, if the developers patch out that phone hotline, Endou might pick up on what we're doing. I need to get a brief reprieve for investigative purposes before we act."

He buckled himself in, started the car, and began to drive out of the spot. Nayuta leaned back against the seat and struggled not to yawn.

"By the way, Detective...didn't you say something about not doing any real-world investigate work?"

"And it was truthful, of course. It's dangerous. Amateurs shouldn't be playing detective."

She giggled. "But this doesn't count?"

"Little Miss Mahiro contracted me to accompany her on the quest tonight, and that's been successfully completed. My guide fee was a bit higher than usual, around 20,000 yen—which I'll collect from Narafushi—so what I do from this point onward is simply helping out an old friend who asked me for an annoying favor. It's nothing as fancy as an investigation, and if it turns dangerous, I'll pull out at once, with all apologies to Mahiro. I haven't taken any money for this, so I'm under no obligation to place myself at risk."

Despite the passivity of his statements, Klever's profile was cold and sharp as he watched the road. Having spent a fair amount of time with him by now, Nayuta could interpret the meaning behind his words.

"You're missing the subject of 'if it turns dangerous.' I think you mean to say, 'if it turns dangerous for Mahiro,' correct?"

He pursed his lips. The car obeyed the speed limit, coasting slowly along the road.

"You think too highly of me. If you gaze too long into an abyss, the abyss gazes also into you—if you don't know when to pull back, you'll easily get pulled down. In the past, my status as a police officer was my lifeline, but now that I'm just a civilian, I don't have the same protection. While not having a lifeline means I have the most freedom, it's also easy to wind up traipsing into a pit of quicksand. And you can guess this is exactly what's happened to Yamashiro. Either he missed his chance to get out or he jumped without a lifeline into a world he was never meant to inhabit. I won't know if he can be pulled back out without a proper investigation, but if it seems beyond my means, I'm going to give Miss Mahiro a false report. I'm a sneaky cheat of an adult, after all."

Nayuta nodded along in silence. Yamashiro himself probably believed he had hidden himself for the purpose of keeping his daughter safe. Fortunately, he didn't have the guts to simply kill himself, but he'd certainly considered it. The amount of fatigue in his voice over the phone earlier would suggest as much.

The street lights passed overhead, one by one. Nayuta breathed deeply. She didn't smell the usual kind of unpleasant car odors. The only thing she noticed was the scent of Klever's cologne.

The now-familiar citrus smell caused the fatigue to engulf her mind. She started nodding off and was only awakened by the sound of Klever's chuckling.

"Well, your sleeping face still betrays your age," he said.

She didn't have the energy to retort, but in her drowsiness, she said something that she shouldn't have said.

"...Since my parents died, I try not to take any taxis. I'm afraid to remember...but since I got to know you, I've felt better and better about it..."

Her parents died in a car accident. Because her memory of it was so fuzzy, she didn't think she was suffering from the kind of trauma that would keep her from ever getting into a car again. But once she was in one, she couldn't help but remember. The wounds of the heart didn't heal very easily.

She was practically dreaming already when she said it, but it was enough to silence Klever.

She took advantage of the quiet to fall right asleep.

This time, she didn't have any nightmares.

§

Munemitsu Yamashiro awoke from yet another bad dream to greet the nightmare that was his waking reality.

Just a few days ago, he'd had a dream that his daughter Mahiro had called him.

It must have been a hallucination, a vision born of his frail hopes.

After a tasteless breakfast of white bread, he sat down at his computer once again with dead fish eyes. A number of hand-written notes were stuck to the edges of his monitor. These work instructions came now and then in the post with money for his living expenses.

The instructions were for things like stealing personal information from poorly-secured online retail sites, hacking databases with the help of moles in government agencies, building websites for collecting personal info to use in fraud, and so on. He was quite busy.

Addresses, legal names, ages, personal identification numbers, licenses, insurance forms, credit card information—once he had all of these things assembled, he got a fairly decent reward for his hard work.

His predecessor, Kurage, had built a system for transactions of personal info mocked up to look like an unsuccessful online shop, where people wracked with debt could sell their own information or that of people they knew.

The identity that Yamashiro had used as a game programmer, "Tooru Endou," had apparently come from that site. This alone did not earn him all that much, so being a freeloader of sorts,

Yamashiro used this identity to worm his way into the *Asuka Empire* team and make some real money.

He had no idea where the real Tooru Endou was or what he was doing.

He didn't want to know.

Was he an unidentified body somewhere? Did he turn into a *hikikomori* and shut himself off from society? Or did he end up selling his organs to pay off debt?

The chance that he was just working a regular job somewhere was very small. If so, he ran the risk of getting in trouble based on having multiple income and municipal tax records. It was hard to imagine Kurage would have chosen such an identity to give him. When he offered it to Yamashiro, he had said, "This one's special, just for you," and smirked about it.

People without any immediate family or blood relatives weren't all that rare these days. But if such a person was already dead, and no body had ever been discovered, then their identity on paper was malleable and valuable to those who had a use for it.

And people who wanted to use that information for wicked purposes had even more reasons to want it, a fact he now understood to a painful degree.

The people who had hired Kurage were undoubtedly the kind who were up to dirty business.

Who had hired Kurage? And who was using Yamashiro, now that he had taken over Kurage's role?

He had absolutely no idea.

Maybe he was curious, but it also felt like the kind of information he shouldn't know.

To them, Yamashiro was nothing more than a convenient person they could plug into a gap created after Kurage's untimely death, but to Yamashiro, who was on the run, their existence was a lifeline whose good favor he could not afford to lose.

After the removal of Kurage's body and a move to a new

location, he received a new identity to replace his old alias of Tooru Endou, the game programmer. This would enable him to hide for a while longer.

Someone called him by that new name at the front door.

"Delivery for Anzai!"

He received many things in the mail. There weren't many stores around his new residence, so he got plenty of his necessities sent to his home. He wasn't in the mood to walk around outside anyway.

"Thank you…"

He opened the door and saw a young man in a work uniform carrying a cardboard box—and another man, a young fellow in a suit with piercingly slender eyes.

It was strange enough that there were two delivery men, but Yamashiro also recognized the fox-eyed young man.

"Huh…? Are you…?"

"It's been a while, Mr. Endou. I'm sure you don't want to stand around talking outside, so I'll just let myself in."

Before he could say a word, the foxlike man, Kaisei Kurei, marched right into the cheap apartment. The other young man, who was disguised as a delivery boy, followed him in and pushed Yamashiro back inside.

"It's nice to meet you, Mr. Yamashiro. My name is Narafushi, and I'm in charge of managing your daughter's show business career. Don't worry—I don't intend to threaten you in any way— oh, but there are still others waiting outside, so don't try to make a run for it!"

The bespectacled delivery man cackled with delight. And yet, there was a note of something dangerous, perhaps even angry, in his eyes.

"Huh…? Wha…huh?"

Yamashiro's wits were still groggy from just waking up, and he couldn't fight back. It didn't make sense that Klever from the Three-Leaf Detective Agency, his collaborator from *Asuka Empire*, would be here. And of course, he'd never met the other man, who claimed to be his daughter's manager.

"Uh, wait...Mr. Kurei? What's going on here...? I mean, uh, Endou...? My name is Anzai...not Yamashiro..."

Klever helped himself to a seat in a cheap chair and grinned. "You don't need to bother pretending. We have the information. There are some things I wanted to let you know, and so I looked up your location."

"Looked up...? But...but *how?!*" Yamashiro stammered, trembling.

This was not a man who worked in the criminal underground—as far as he knew. But his mind wasn't able to grasp the full picture yet.

"You had a call with Mahiro, didn't you? The Thirteen-Floor Underground Labyrinth, basement level six, sector P. She hired me to help, and I was the one who solved that code. I asked Mr. Torao and his team for help, and they were able to pin down your location from the communication log. After that, I enlisted the help of a private investigator acquaintance to get a list of single adults who had moved to this local area recently... But none of this stuff really matters. What's important to you is the fact that you don't need to run anymore."

"...Huh...?"

Yamashiro's cheek twitched. Even after all of this, he still had no idea what the young man was talking about.

Kurei explained, "The group that was sheltering you noticed the police attention and have already cut and run. You have no idea that you've been abandoned. You won't receive any money or instructions anymore. I don't know who they are, either, but we do know they had a team that acquired stolen personal information and a group that made use of it. You were a low-level mule on the acquisition team. And as for the case of the investment fraud with Tonami Enterprises that caused you to go on the run in the first place... Well, I don't know who the real culprit was, but they've already finished their purge and recovered the funds, minus whatever was already spent. The suspicion on your head is completely gone. They're no longer looking for you; in fact, they've completely forgotten about you by now."

Now Yamashiro simply gaped.

"H-h...how...?! How do you know all of that...?!"

The fox-eyed man gave him a hateably smug smile and shrugged.

"I looked it up. Our employees are excellent at what they do— Oh, but you'd know that from being on the development team, Mr. Endou. They barely listen to a word the company president says, but as soon as little Miss Mahiro entered the picture, they hopped right to work...the sick freaks."

The extra note of distaste in that last comment was not just a figment of Yamashiro's imagination.

He stood there in dumb shock.

"...The suspicion...is lifted...?"

"Yes. The investment fraud's all been cleared up. It didn't even cross the police's path, which is why they had no information about you after you ran off the first time. And it's not the sort of thing that gets bandied about online," Kurei said, getting up from the chair and fixing Yamashiro with a glare. "That's all I wanted to let you know. There's no one out there after your life. But it's also a fact that you've committed a number of crimes. Please turn yourself in. If you don't, I'll report you myself."

Yamashiro cracked. He started to laugh.

"...Ha-ha...ha-ha-ha-ha! What...what was I running from...? What was it all for...? Fraying my nerves to nubs...moving out to the sticks like this...forced to carry out mysterious crimes for these mysterious people... What am I doing with my life...?" he croaked, his voice barely more than a whisper.

Narafushi clicked his tongue and spoke up at last. "I'm the one who's mystified here. You've got such a sweet little daughter, and what the hell are you doing here...? If you've got skill as a programmer, you should be able to live smarter than this. I don't wanna stand around lecturing an older man, but how do you let yourself get swept up in such nasty stuff?"

Yamashiro had no response. He hung his head in shame.

"...You're right. I'll turn myself in, Mr. Kurei. It's not like I was running from the police to begin with. I was only running because I figured that if I got arrested, they'd just release me after a few years, and *then* they'd kill me... And I was terrified that something would happen to Mahiro or my wife...and now, it...it just feels like...none of it matters anymore..."

He slumped to the floor. Maybe this was just a continuation of the nightmare. It could also be a good dream instead, but in either case, after a long period of brutal tension on the run, his sense of reality had simply gone numb and unresponsive.

Kurei and Narafushi reached down to grab an arm each and haul him upward.

"We have a car out front. We'll accompany you to the police station."

"...I'm sorry for what I said earlier. It was over the line."

The young man named Narafushi was brusque, but a goodnatured sort. He wasn't just Mahiro's manager in a professional sense, but seemed to be doing this out of a real concern for her well-being.

With their support, Yamashiro plodded outside. There was a light van parked in front of the apartment. It looked like a transport vehicle for the talent agency. There was a dark tint on the windows.

The door of the van opened.

Out stepped a young girl with her black hair tied into pigtails. Tears filled her eyes, and her frail body was shaking slightly.

Behind her, holding her by the shoulders, was an older girl he didn't recognize.

"Is that him, Mahiro?"

"...Yes...that's my daddy...," the girl said, her voice choked with tears. Step by step, she began to walk forward.

Yamashiro fell to his knees.

In moments, his beloved daughter was in his arms, slightly taller than he remembered, her greater weight an undeniable fact.

He'd met her frequently in VR, but it felt like they had been apart for so, so long.

She clung to him, tears pouring down her cheeks, and as he apologized desperately, doing everything he could to express his contrition—Munemitsu Yamashiro sobbed.

With each fresh tear, the sense of reality that had grown so gray and dull came burning back to life.

A long, long nightmare was over. Now at last, after so much time being someone else's puppet, he was finally about to be in control of his own life again.

A Strange Issue of Likeness Rights — Demon Puppet 2

The long-awaited new feature, demon puppets, had anything but an easy road to implementation in the game.

They were initially envisioned as a brand collaboration, but the business partner pulled out without warning. There were changes in plans, differences of opinion, chaos among the development team—and through all of these hurdles, just as the team was ready to attempt an experimental rollout, strange rumors began sifting through the online community.

"They say that the Onihime demon puppet bears a strong resemblance to a certain child actor..."

When the developers saw the pictures, they went pale. The resemblance was so strong that no one would believe it was a coincidence.

Through the many redesigns and changes of plans, the puppet designs had gone through a number of individual designers, and it was undeniable that the quality assurance part of the process was a bit lax.

After some internal debate, an external collaborator, K, was able to make contact with N, who knew the child actor in question.

After a friendly and constructive exchange of opinions, it was decided that the similarity in appearance was nothing but "a very mysterious coincidence," and that the actor herself was an enthusiastic player of the game and strongly against altering the design. For this reason, the proposed revision was put on hold.

In the near future, if very similar child actors are chosen to appear in the company's commercials and events, that would be a product of sheer coincidence.

Coincidence can be such a scary thing.

Final Chapter

Jellyfish of the Night Sky

The world is boring.

Shockingly boring.

No complaints about unfairness, no whining.

At the end of the day, enjoying things requires the talent to do so.

The talent to frolic at the beach.

The talent to read a book and feel emotional about it.

The talent to have a lively cookout at the riverside.

The talent to watch a comedy show and laugh until your sides hurt.

The talent to find cats and dogs adorable.

The talent to gain pleasure from creating something all on your own.

All of these talents for finding pleasure, sadly, were nowhere to be found with him.

Which is why he found everything so boring.

This is probably what you'd call a pipe dream.

All he did was complain about how nothing was enjoyable to him. So he lamented his own lack of talent and coasted along in a miserable inertia, living like a jellyfish that floated along the sea floor.

There was probably a fair number of people like him in the world.

No real enjoyment, no particular interests, working jobs they weren't interested in just to survive, sleeping like the dead and waking up to shuffle to work like zombies, gaining nothing as they played out the string until the end of their lives…

Such people didn't stand out, but they were surely not uncommon, and he was certain there was no other way he could live his life.

"…You one of those guys whose family wasn't rich when you were a kid, and they never bought you any games or toys or anything? Saying it was 'for your education' or whatever," asked a onetime work senior, Munemitsu Yamashiro.

Kurage, meaning "jellyfish," gave him a weak smile.

"Yep. You got it, sir. How could you tell?"

They stared at separate monitors, working on completely different tasks, trading pointless and miserable words late at night.

"It's a symptom of people who are too used to giving up. You want something but can't get it—so you give up. The more you repeat that cycle, the less you want anything at all. Your brain's reward center has determined that the act of wanting is meaningless, and now your mind is stuck in that rut. Your parents might have thought they were teaching you patience, but the fact is that they just raised you to feel powerless and give up on everything in life… Basically, it's learning the wrong life lessons. Human beings adapt to things; it's what we do. Once you learn to be this way, it's very hard to correct. You'll probably be like that for the rest of your life."

He wasn't joking and laughing about it, nor was he criticizing and scolding. He was just telling the plain truth.

"Of course, not everyone who's forced to deprive themselves turns out that way. Some people grow up and then get completely addicted to pleasure and lose their way in life…but I think it makes perfect sense that if you get raised in a different way from other people, you end up turning into a social outcast who can't see eye-to-eye with the rest of society."

"Yeah, exactly," Kurage agreed. "But it's not like I have no desires of my own. I desire sleep, fresh air, defecation…I have all the wants you need to continue existing."

"…That's just a minimum of physiological needs, man. If you don't have them, you'll just die. I'm talking about the desire for *things*, for sex, for fame and glory."

"Yeah, that's a little more iffy. I guess I give up on those things pretty fast… I mean, if I wanted fame and glory, I wouldn't be here assisting in small-time fraud."

"Of course not," Yamashiro snorted. "But thanks to that, it's a big help to me."

"Listen, you're doing me a huge favor too, Endou. I hate doing all the chores, living alone."

"Honestly, that's about all I'm good for."

At that point in time, Munemitsu Yamashiro was going by the name of Tooru Endou, a temp worker.

This identity had *not* come from Kurage and his personal info collection site. He had skipped over the details and lied to Yamashiro about it, but in fact, the history of this particular name was a bit trickier than that.

He had zero intention of explaining it in detail. It would only earn him a nasty look, and being an illicit identity, now that he was working a job with it, there was no way to change his name.

"I'm surprised that a team like *Asuka*'s would hire on an imitation programmer like me. I heard they had a reputation for crunch, but it's just a lot of work—no physical abuse, no shouting, and they pay well for overtime… I realize they're shorthanded because they're prepping for this big event next year, but I still couldn't believe they'd just hire me on the spot after the first interview," he noted, and not for the first time. Yamashiro had taken home some of his work that wasn't confidential and had diligently made his way through it. He had changed his name and gotten a temp job with the *Asuka Empire* dev team in order to cover his cost of living.

This had been a very good thing for him.

Some game developers were very forward-thinking about setting up experimental VR offices before most other industries had ever considered it. Yamashiro's job only required him in the building a few times a month, while the rest of the time, he could access the workplace from his AmuSphere at home.

Not needing to commute to work everyday was very convenient for someone trying to hide. It greatly lowered the chance that he might run across someone who recognized him.

Because he had a plain face to begin with, and he had changed his hair and clothes and put on glasses to make himself as nondescript as possible, Yamashiro didn't think most people would recognize him, but the basic denominator of reducing as many trips outside as possible was the best strategy of all.

Kurage organized his collection of personal data and chuckled to himself.

"Yeah, 108 Apparitions, right? People online are talking about how desperate their help wanted ads are, trying to be ready in time for this big event. Most people were saying it must be a trainwreck there, but I've played that game, and I think they have a real capable team—which is why I figured you'd hold your own there, Endou."

"...Well, I appreciate that," Yamashiro said, raising an eyebrow, "but why did you give it to me? You could have taken it yourself and freed yourself from this nasty business. Your programming skill is more or less the same as mine."

Kurage rested his heavy body against the chair back. "I find this to be easier. For one thing, I'm terrible at working in a team and being on the clock. Like hell you'll ever get me to participate in crunch. Don't expect me to wake up and get to work on time. It's not gonna happen."

"What?" Yamashiro said. "Your last job was a regular one, and you went to that just fine. I thought you were a valued member of the team."

"Yeah, because they were super flexible. As long as you did the work they needed you to do, they didn't care if you showed up late or took naps or played games. The only one who worked the proper hours there was you, Yam...Endou," Kurage said, correcting himself before he used the old name.

Maybe working harder than anyone else there was the reason Yamashiro had been confused for the culprit of the investment fraud. He hadn't thought of it that way, but now it made sense.

"Now that you mention it, I don't remember anyone else following the proper work hours there. Some folks practically lived out of the office, though."

"Yeah, that's why the president couldn't let you go, Endou. But me? When someone he knew asked for a piece-of-shit engineer, he said, 'I've got just the guy' and sold me off to him. Then I got transferred from job to job until I wound up here."

"It's ironic that it turned out better for you this way... If they'd caught me, I wouldn't even be alive right now," said Yamashiro. His misery was significantly lessened compared with when he first showed up there, but the exhaustion was still evident in his voice.

"Hey, it's only temporary," Kurage grinned. "Those folks who live on the edge end up dying young or getting arrested on other charges. It's a messy life...but if you keep living this life as Tooru Endou, get middle-aged and fat, lose your hair and start dealing with back pain, they'll have forgotten all about you by then."

"...Over ten years of this, huh...? Well, I guess I should expect that much at a minimum, knowing how persistent they can be," he lamented, finishing his coffee and powering down the computer. "I'm going to take a bath."

"You got it. Gonna visit your daughter in *Asuka* when you get out again?"

Yamashiro grunted. "That's the problem," he said, his voice darker than before. "You really think I can keep meeting her like this?"

Kurage's eyes narrowed. "Huh? What are you talking about?"

"I mean…if they somehow find out I've been meeting my daughter regularly, even in VR…it's going to mean danger for them, even after going to the trouble of divorcing and living apart…," Yamashiro fretted, much to Kurage's annoyance.

The units on either side of them were empty—because Kurage's employer had rented out the entire apartment building to treat as employee housing, they didn't have to worry about neighbors over-hearing them. Even still, it wasn't the sort of topic to shout about.

Kurage leaned closer to Yamashiro's face and practically whis-pered, "You did tell your daughter not to talk, right? For one thing, the Tonami don't even know about your marriage in the first place, much less the details of your divorce. You went as a bachelor the entire time you worked there. You kept it completely under wraps."

"Yeah, that's true, but…you never know…"

Kurage was aghast. Yamashiro was a decently clever man, but when it came to himself and his family, he completely lost all objectivity. If she wasn't able to reach him, the daughter might get suspicious and start looking for her father. If she made a big mistake and Yamashiro's name popped up online as a man whose family was searching for him, it would lead to chaos.

"You're the kind of guy who always assumes the worst and leads to his own downfall, aren't you, Endou? It's like you don't know how to sit still and behave. Just go ahead and meet with your daughter in VR. It's way safer than doing it in reality. Wor-rying about the risks of VR is like worrying that taking a breath might make your heart stop, so you try to hold it forever."

That was a dramatic way of putting it, but Kurage truly did see the current danger to Yamashiro's family as close to nothing.

Time had passed since the divorce, so it wouldn't be easy for them to even detect that such a family existed. And on the off chance that they did, it would take a very talented investigator—who would certainly be able to look at the mother and daughter, realize they had no money, and in the absence of any red flags, assume that the two of them knew nothing.

If anything, it was far, far more likely they would realize he was hiding out with Kurage. If Yamashiro should be wary of anything, it was his own circumstances, not those of his family.

But warning him about that would only cause him to worry more and increase the chances he made a mistake, so Kurage chose to just let that topic slide.

For one thing, he hadn't "saved" Munemitsu Yamashiro.

The end result might have benefited Yamashiro, but Kurage's real purpose was something much more immature; even he sometimes doubted his own good sense.

Kurage carried out a strange shared living situation with Yamashiro, never revealing his real reason for it.

While Yamashiro bathed, Kurage wrapped up his work and logged in to *Asuka Empire*. He didn't have anything in particular to do; he just wanted to check his in-game messages.

There was one new arrival, sent the previous day.

Thank you for your advice, Kurage. I'll be seeing Daddy tomorrow, so I'll tell him I was scouted by a talent agency. I'm sure he'll be against me working in show business, but the agency doesn't look shady at all. Your advice helped me make up my mind. I hope we get to try some more quests together!

Inside the game, Kurage sent a generic response to his friend's message and grinned to himself. His unfortunate facial features and inability to smile like a normal person made it look creepy, but he didn't have anything wicked on his mind.

He had met her in the game during a scavenger hunt for rare items in a particular quest. Kurage happened across a player duel taking place and, on a random whim, decided to help the girl who was losing. They both lost badly as a result, but the day after, they met up again and added each other as a friend.

It wasn't until later that he realized who she actually was. For as vast as it could seem, the VR world was actually quite small.

After the trading of messages, Kurage logged out at once and returned to reality. Yamashiro had finished with his bath and was sipping barley tea at his computer.

"What's up? You look positively radiant. Something good happen?"

"No, nothing," Kurage lied. "Whenever you have a meeting, you dip in and out of that bath in no time, huh?"

"I don't want to show up late and make her worry. Unlike her father, she's quite delicate."

There was still over half an hour before he was scheduled to meet with his daughter. Kurage couldn't bring himself to say she actually *resembled* her father in that way, so he just offered a half-hearted agreement.

Life was mostly boring.

But there were still moments where things seemed to get just the tiniest bit interesting.

The ones who could create such situations on their own were usually the winners of life, who had satisfying stories. Kurage didn't have a shred of their talent, but even he could be the recipient of a little miracle once in a blue moon.

He wasn't particularly fond of her in any way. He felt more protective than anything, like a brother watching over his little sister, but even that wasn't quite the right analogy.

Perhaps the best way to describe her was like a neighborhood child who had taken a liking to him. So he developed a very silly, trifling kind of desire—to look like a cool adult in front of a child.

So Kurage decided to help out Munemitsu Yamashiro with his trouble. In his mind, that would mean she wouldn't need to lose the father she loved so much.

"Well, you enjoy, Mr. Endou. I'm gonna get back to work."

"Sure. I'll be back in two or three hours."

Once Yamashiro had logged in and detached his mind from the material world, Kurage pressed a hand to his heart and muttered, "Ugh...I feel like crap..."

Not because of Yamashiro, but because of his own health. He lived with a heart defect.

It had only arisen in the last few years, but the doctor warned him it could lead to a heart attack at any time. He recommended that Kurage improve his diet and try not to put any undue stress on his heart.

Maybe nothing would ever come of it, or maybe his pulse would simply stop at some unexpected moment.

It was worrisome, but everyone died sooner or later. This wasn't unique to him, and patients with issues like his weren't particularly rare.

Even Yamashiro, whom he'd saved, would eventually grow old, waste away, and die, no matter how much he struggled to stay alive.

Every human being, including himself, would one day die.

You couldn't take anything with you.

Not money, not fame, not even memories. All people were equal in becoming corpses, losing their consciousness, and fading into ash, to be forgotten forever.

But while you couldn't take anything with you, you could leave things behind.

Children, wealth, records of your works and deeds...

In other words, objective proof that you were once alive.

And by his nature, Kurage had almost no experience or connection to such things.

Having become completely accustomed to giving up, he just floated along like the jellyfish of his name.

Scum like me are meant to die a meaningless death...leaving behind nothing. Forgotten by all, he thought earnestly.

§

Several days had passed since Munemitsu Yamashiro, Mahiro's father, turned himself in to the authorities.

Mahiro visited the Three-Leaf Detective Agency in *Asuka Empire* and found herself in a slightly troublesome situation.

On either side of her was an Onihime—one dressed as an *onmyoji* and the other as a dance miko, each attending closely to Mahiro the tactician. It was like seeing three differently dressed versions of Mahiro in a row, or perhaps identical triplets, although the two on the sides did not speak a single word.

Meanwhile, Koyomi held up a camera and shouted out orders.

"Number Eight, rub your cheek up against Mahiro's shoulder! Number Ten, give a little upward gaze! Ooh, yes! That's perfect! Nayu, give us a little more lighting from below!"

Nayuta was in charge of lighting. She adjusted the reflector in accordance with her instructions. Camera lights flashed and shutters clattered in succession.

"That's awesome!" Koyomi shrieked with excitement. "You're so adorable! You look amazing, Mahiro! We could slap this image right onto a poster! I'm gonna send a screenshot to Narafushi! Number Eight, take your right hand and hold Number Ten's left hand! No, not like that! You need to tangle the fingers, like… Mahiro, you show them! The lover's grip!"

"I don't know what that is…"

Expecting a grade schooler to understand these concepts was a bridge too far. Off to the side of the Onihime sisters' photo shoot, the detective at his work desk cleared his throat and sighed, "I'm not going to tell you to go somewhere else. It would be a much bigger problem if you did this outside. But I have to ask…what are you going to do with these photos, Koyomi?"

This question seemed to mystify her.

"Huh? Just sit there and grin at them by myself…or maybe make them my phone background. But then again, I like our pic

together, too, Nayu. Which do I pick? Maybe I can get one with both of you intertwined—"

"Don't say intertwined. C'mon, let's wrap this up. Mahiro must be tired of it by now."

If it were for work, she would be tough and say she was fine, but on this particular day, she was happy to let Nayuta argue for her. After the Thirteen-Floor Underground Labyrinth the other day, she told Koyomi she wanted to thank her for the help, and had promptly been roped into this photo shoot.

It wasn't clear if this was actually counting as her return gift or not at this point, but at the very least, Koyomi seemed to be wholeheartedly enjoying herself.

When Nayuta unilaterally declared the photo shoot to be finished, Koyomi pouted. "Aww, already? Well...I guess that's enough for today. Next time, we'll get Nayu involved, too— wearing a bathing suit!"

"...Make sure you refuse, Mahiro. Koyomi is very serious about this," Nayuta warned, putting the *onmyoji*-style Onihime Number Eight back into her item list.

Mahiro did the same for her dance miko-style Onihime Number Ten and said, "I don't know if I want to wear a swimsuit, either... although I would probably look better if I had a figure like yours."

Koyomi put her camera away and clung to Nayuta. "She's really something, isn't she? There aren't even many pinup models with a body like hers! I totally understand why Narafushi was upset that she turned him down. Oh! But you've got charms of your own, Mahiro! If anything, you've got the potential to be even *better* in the future! Narafushi really values you highly, I can tell!"

"Narafushi...," Klever mumbled, slumping his shoulders. "I really wish he had not met you..."

Mahiro's manager, Narafushi, had not yet met Koyomi in the game. He didn't even have an account, but he'd said he wanted to thank Koyomi for her assistance, too, so Mahiro acted as a go-between on the phone.

For some strange reason, they seemed to share the same wavelength, and bonded over Nayuta's remarkable assets and Mahiro's future potential. Then they moved on to their envy of Klever and the trust he had earned with both girls. It turned into quite an enthusiastic alliance.

Mahiro, who was listening to their conversation nearby, was amazed and alarmed by the speed with which resonance between two highly communicative people could develop and grow.

Both Mahiro and Narafushi were both forbidden to mention a word about how Nayuta was visiting the detective's home. But while Mahiro was obedient, it seemed very likely Narafushi might let it slip in a thoughtless moment of excitement, so Klever was once again dealing with a disastrously explosive situation.

Mahiro couldn't deny she felt some pity for him, but reminded herself to help stick up for him in case the delicate situation came out into the open.

There was a knock at the door of the detective's office, and a man in a Shinto priest robe slipped inside.

"Kurei, do you have a minute—oh?" His eyes flared when he noticed Mahiro. "What's up with you folks? Already customizing your demon puppets? They're all front-row types, so you'd find an *onmyoji* Onihime to be a much bigger help—"

"No, I'm the player," said Mahiro, who was carrying the large sword on her back. The priest stepped backward.

"Oh! So *you're* Endou...I mean, Yamashiro's daughter. My apologies. You look so much like Onihime, I just thought...," he stammered, bowing awkwardly.

His reaction made sense. When Mahiro looked directly at an Onihime, she felt like she was looking at herself in a mirror with a different outfit.

Klever rose from his seat and said, "This is Miss Mahiro,

whom I told you about the other day. What brings you here, Mr. Torao?"

The man in the priest robes was someone on the development team, then. In other words, he was her father's coworker or boss, back when he worked there under a false name.

Torao smacked his head lightly, then sat in an empty chair and accepted a cup of barley tea from the *nekomata* bot.

"Ah, thank you. Well, I was just responding to police questioning about Yamashiro. Sounds like the situation's much more complicated than I realized. I thought I'd tell you about what I learned."

"I'm fairly certain I have the gist of it already," Klever said, mystified.

"Well, I'm guessing you don't know this part: They found Tooru Endou's body."

For a moment, Mahiro wasn't sure what she'd just heard.

Tooru Endou was the false name that her father, Munemitsu Yamashiro, had used.

Torao sipped his tea and hunched over even further. "Of course, I'm not talking about Endou the programmer whom we knew and worked with, but the real Tooru Endou. It was an unidentified body found floating in a river somewhere. The police were suspecting that Yamashiro might have killed the real Endou, but that suspicion's been cleared. The autopsy found he had a weak heart, and it was natural causes. According to Yamashiro, he'd died in the bath, and someone came along and removed the body—presumably, it was done by members of some kind of organization the authorities are tracking. They just dumped the body in the river—real sloppy work—but it's the quickest way to be rid of one. And as long as there are no external wounds, it's easy to assume they just fell in the river and drowned."

As he'd said, it was a rather complicated situation. Mahiro didn't know what to think, and that translated to an uneasy look that Torao noticed.

"Oh, no, no," he said quickly, "this isn't a bad thing for Yamashiro, trust me. It's just kinda baffling. A real strange scenario… After the investment fraud, Yamashiro went on the run, and it was this other Endou who took him in. They'd worked at the same company for a time, apparently… Not real close in age, but they seemed to be friends. The thing is, this other Endou operated under a different false identity, and Yamashiro didn't seem to know he was actually using his friend's true identity. He probably wanted to keep his real name hidden while he was engaged in criminal activity. So he let Yamashiro use it as an alias instead…"

For once, Koyomi absorbed this information gravely. "Meaning…he was making Yamashiro work in his place so he could earn some extra money in his welfare pension for later in life?"

"…That's incredible. I never thought I'd hear you come up with such a rational deduction in such a short period of time," the detective remarked archly. Torao snorted.

"It's quite a long-term fraud plan. That's certainly a possibility here, but I think he was actually thinking it would be advantageous because they would be less likely to slip up with tax forms and other government business. The other part of it is this Endou seemed like he really was trying to get Yamashiro back on his feet in legitimate society. He was maneuvering to keep Yamashiro away from the group that was hiring them."

Only the detective nodded along with Torao's explanation. The other three didn't seem to understand the implications yet.

"What I mean is," Torao said in hushed tones, "if he fed stolen personal information to Yamashiro, that would make a direct connection between Yamashiro and the criminal group. But it's less of a problem if he was giving Yamashiro his *own* identity. That's just a hypothetical, though. Endou ended up dying out of the blue, and in the confusion, Yamashiro abandoned his work on *Asuka Empire*, said good-bye to Mahiro, and vanished. He picked up Endou's work and took it over, it seems."

Narrowing his eyes, Klever asked, "Does that mean he was the one to extend a hand of salvation when Yamashiro was running for his life after the investment fraud? That was something I couldn't quite figure out in my investigation. I was able to find out about the investment fraud that started the whole alias business through someone knowledgeable about that side of things, and I found Yamashiro's location through the communications log in the game—but everything that happened in between those things is vague. Yamashiro and this man must have been pretty close for him to risk his life taking him in."

"Apparently not," Torao said with a shrug. "They weren't enemies by any means, but Yamashiro himself said he didn't know why the guy saved him the way he did. Maybe he just had some reason that only made sense to himself."

Mahiro decided to say a prayer for the soul of Endou, a stranger whose face she would not recognize. If not for him, her father would probably have been caught and killed by this criminal organization. Even if the man was a criminal, too, she owed him for her father's life.

Yamashiro was going to serve a prison sentence, and she didn't know when he'd be out, but at least he was alive. She'd be able to see him in a number of years. Maybe she would be in her rebellious phase then, but there was a world of difference between "I can see him later" and "never again."

At the very least, she didn't need to cry herself to sleep with loneliness and worry anymore.

The creators of the Thirteen-Floor Underground Labyrinth had said, "The world is a prison, and we're just serving our life sentences until we reach the end."

She had partially agreed with that sentiment, but Klever had also taught her that this could change based on one's point of view. If she continued her life looking backward, it *would* be a prison for her, while if she looked forward with optimism, it might not be that bad. It sounded obvious, but for someone like

Mahiro, who had a tendency to overthink things and get lost in her own head, it was much harder than it sounded.

Didn't someone say the same thing to me once…?

"Mahiro, you have a bad habit of always thinking about the worst possible scenario."

It was something a friend she'd made in *Asuka Empire* had once told her with wry amusement.

While she reflected on that memory, Nayuta quietly asked the detective, "How many years do you think Mr. Yamashiro will get?"

He looked at the ceiling. "Depends on what their investigation turns up—but he was a low-level player and turned himself in, plus he never got more than what they paid him for. Assuming the charges are within the parameters I expect, I would guess it'll be between three and five years. We can't hope for a stay of sentence, but there's room for leniency… Mr. Torao, you're going to submit a clemency petition, right?"

Torao stood up. Even standing, he was still stooping over.

"His actions before he left the company weren't exactly good work behavior, but now that I know the circumstances behind them, I can't knock him for that… For being paid such a low salary, he worked his ass off for us, and he helped get us through the busiest section of crunch just before we launched 108 Apparitions. You can argue about compliance and whatnot, but his coworkers thought highly of him. I hope he's able to bounce back, for his daughter's sake. Anyway, I should be going…"

Once he had taken his leave, Koyomi grabbed Mahiro by the hand.

"Okay, Mahiro, let's go shopping for a change of pace! One of the clothing shops in Ayakashi Alley just got some really cool traditional Japanese-themed Gothic Lolita outfits in. I just know you'd be a knockout in one!"

Her usual pushiness felt comfortable this time. It removed Mahiro's opportunity to sit and fret over it.

"Um, all right. Uh, what will you do, Detective?"

"I'll be working. You should go and enjoy yourselves," Klever said, loudly and conspicuously tapping on the keys. He didn't have the willpower to go shopping with three girls, which was no surprise. Mahiro and Nayuta were on the quiet side, but Koyomi would lead the way, and she was a fountain of energy.

Nayuta giggled to herself and put her hands on Mahiro's shoulders.

"Shall we go, Mahiro? After the shopping, we'll continue with the Thirteen-Floor Underground Labyrinth. You want to finish it, don't you?" she said gently. There was a nurturing, enveloping warmth there beyond her years. Mahiro tried to imagine herself being as mature as Nayuta when her father got out of prison, and couldn't do it.

They left the office and headed down the street. Mahiro found herself opening her friends list. Next to each player's name on the list was a rough breakdown of the last time they had logged in.

Within the last few hours, the last three days, the last week—of course, Nayuta and Koyomi were logged in now, but once a player hadn't logged in for a month or more, it was safe to suspect they had moved on to a different game.

Every now and then she pruned her list, removing the players who had simply stopped playing.

It was different if they had special circumstances, like business trips or hospital stays, but when that was the case, you could leave a message about it in your player profile.

Eventually, her gaze fell to the very bottom of the list.

...Kurage hasn't logged in for a long time...

He was the very oldest friend on her list.

The last login was several months ago. If it were anyone else, she would have deleted the entry already, but Mahiro hesitated now.

For some reason, the name was stuck in her brain like a thorn. Another version of herself inside her head was telling her not to erase this player's name.

After a minute of mulling it over, she decided to close the list without doing anything.

Maybe he would wander back and log in again someday.

When he did, she would have a few reasons to express her gratitude to him.

For giving her advice when she was worried.

For cheering her up and giving her courage when her father was acting strange.

For playing with her when her father was too busy to log in.

Just having that name at the very bottom of her friends list made her feel like she was being watched over, for some strange reason.

"What's up, Mahiro? Why you got your list open? Thinkin' of inviting some friends along for the quest?"

"I'd like to have someone to handle the back row. It feels like we're always relying on Onihime now..."

"I'm sorry," she said to Koyomi and Nayuta, "the person I was looking for isn't online now. Let's just go as a trio today."

At that moment, she felt a sensation like passing by a familiar face and turned around to look.

But there was no one there.

Perplexed, she faced forward and resumed walking. Over her head, the moon loomed large and bright, hovering in the sky like a jellyfish bobbing in the sea.

The End

Afterword

Hello again. I'm Soitiro Watase.

This book, the second volume of *Clover's Regret*, consists of a revised and expanded version of four stories from the *Sword Art Online Character Book*, a spin-off publication of *Dengeki Bunko Magazine*.

It starts off with a creepy trip to a bizarre and run-down old hot spring inn, proceeds into a panic-inducing tale of a runaway profusion of giant rats, and ends with a two-parter about a vengeance-swearing doll whose hair grows on its own. An entire book of classic horror tropes—and yet, looking back, it's just not that scary.

Empty hot spring inn? Scary.
Profusion of giant rats? Scary.
Life-size young girl doll? Scary.

It all seems to be rather scary on paper, as it were, so the fact that it doesn't feel scary must mean I've developed a natural resistance to horror, I figured.

So I loaded up some old horror games to play again, and they still scared the heck out of me. That doesn't make sense...

*   *   *

Okay, enough of this nonsense—before the real horror fans get angry. Of course, this collection of short stories is not horror. But the setting of the 108 Apparitions event within *Asuka Empire* is based on horror motifs.

There are many kinds of horror, where the objects striking terror can be ghosts, zombies, the insane, paranormal phenomena, animals, fish, monsters, aliens, serial killers, haunted mansions, automobiles, natural disasters, extreme circumstances, and so on.

What I've personally found rather intriguing lately is the genre of railway horror. Years back, there was a popular online urban legend around Kisaragi Station, a major battle scene set on a train in a certain very popular zombie game franchise, and a scene from a movie version of a horror game set in a subway station—for some reason, I find these all very appealing. In some regions there's even a very fun-looking ghost train event that gets put on.

Enclosed spaces, the perfect setting for horror; other passengers who are total strangers; the anticipation of arriving at some future destination; the feeling of the abnormal in such a normal and familiar setting—I think it comes down to the combination of all of these points. I've always wanted to write my own railroad horror story, so in this case, I turned my desire into virtual reality.

Of course, for space and time reasons, the night express from Ueno Station only appears for a brief moment, but I'm planning to include a longer story in the third volume in which the gang will travel in a deluxe sleeper car. Forgive me for always chasing after my own selfish interests.

And speaking of interests, to continue what I was saying in the previous volume's afterword: I would really, really like some railroad travel or *Galaxy Express*–type VR content right about now. I have my reclining chair ready and waiting for me.

*   *   *

Now, then...

This book only exists because of the support of you, the reader; Kawahara, for supervising these stories; Ginta, the illustrator; Miki, the straight edge; and the help of many, many others.

I feel very badly that my writing speed has been unstable, but with the great amount of help I've received from others, I managed to make it through my serialization in the *Character Book*. Thank you so much for your support.

I pray we meet again in the next volume...

Soitiro Watase—Winter 2017